THE DIGGERS REST HOTEL

Geoffrey McGeachin changed career in 2004, moving from shooting pictures for advertising and feature films to writing. In 2010 he turned to crime with *The Diggers Rest Hotel*, introducing Detective Charlie Berlin and winning the Australian Crime Writers Association's 2011 Ned Kelly Award for best fiction.

Blackwattle Creek, continuing Charlie Berlin's story, won McGeachin his second Ned Kelly Award in 2013. The judges described the book as 'a flawless novel that offers everything one could wish for in crime fiction.'

The third Charlie Berlin novel, *St Kilda Blues*, was published in 2014.

Geoffrey McGeachin is one of Australia's most highly regarded crime novelists. He has written several other novels and lives in Sydney.

geoffreymcgeachin.com

BY GEOFFREY McGEACHIN

Fat, Fifty & F***ed!
D-E-D Dead!
Sensitive New Age Spy
Dead and Kicking

The Charlie Berlin novels
The Diggers Rest Hotel
Blackwattle Creek
St Kilda Blues

GEOFFREY McGEACHIN

A CHARLIE BERLIN NOVEL

THE DIGGERS REST HOTEL

Penguin Books

PENGUIN BOOKS

UK | USA | Canada | Ireland | Australia
India | New Zealand | South Africa | China

Penguin Books is part of the Penguin Random House group of companies
whose addresses can be found at global.penguinrandomhouse.com.

First published by Penguin Group (Australia), 2010
This edition published by Penguin Group (Australia), 2014

Text copyright © Geoffrey McGeachin 2010

The moral right of the author has been asserted

All rights reserved. Without limiting the rights under copyright reserved above,
no part of this publication may be reproduced, stored in or introduced into a retrieval
system, or transmitted, in any form or by any means (electronic, mechanical,
photocopying, recording or otherwise), without the prior written permission
of both the copyright owner and the above publisher of this book.

Cover design by Adam Laszczuk © Penguin Group (Australia)
Text design by John Canty © Penguin Group (Australia)
Cover photography: Pub: Richard Wayman/Alamy; Man: Stephen Carroll/Trevillion Images
Typeset in Adobe Garamond by Pindar NZ
Printed and bound in Australia by Griffin Press, an accredited ISO AS/NZS 14001
Environmental Management Systems printer.

National Library of Australia
Cataloguing-in-Publication data:

McGeachin, Geoffrey.
The Diggers Rest Hotel / Geoffrey McGeachin.
9780143205500 (pbk.)
A823.4

penguin.com.au

*As ever and always,
for Wilma*

23 JANUARY 1945

Near the German–Polish Border

Berlin found the potato the night before the SS officer shot the Jewess. Around five in the afternoon the German guards forced the column of shivering POWs out of the sleet and into the meagre shelter of a wooden barn left shattered by repeated Russian air strikes. If the winter sun was still out there somewhere beyond the leaden clouds the POWs couldn't tell, and they cared even less. The horse-drawn army field kitchen was nowhere to be seen so the starving men knew it would be another night without food.

The potato was hidden under the layers of filthy straw, dirt and human waste that carpeted the floor where three hundred exhausted men, grateful to be out of the snow and wind for the night, would try to sleep.

It reminded Berlin of home, of his grandmother and a time when he was safe and warm, with a full belly. He slipped it into his pocket and held it tightly through the night. Fourteen hours later the SS officer pulled the trigger. The Jewess died and a part of Berlin died with her.

ONE

Berlin joined the afternoon drinkers at the Port Melbourne corner pub which, like many pubs in the docklands, was dedicated to easing the aches and sorrows of the working bloke through the worship of beer. It was also a tribute to the art of the tiler: every surface that could be tiled had been tiled, right up to the ceiling. The tiles might have been white at some stage, but years of neglect and the smoke from thousands of durries and tailor-mades had left them coated with a nasty yellowish brown stain.

The tiling was a masterstroke of functionality. At six o'clock, when the mad rush of the post-work swill was over, the landlord would hose the public bar clean, flushing spilled alcohol, cigarette butts, sometimes blood and more often vomit out the doors and across the footpath to the gutter in a tidal wave of carbolic suds.

Berlin leaned back on the bar and studied the other drinkers through a thick, blue-grey haze of cigarette smoke. There were the blokes who laughed with their mates as they drank – the ones who were lucky to be alive and knew it. These men had seen death but it had passed over them, and they took each new day as a gift and tried to put the horror behind them. But there were also the solitary souls, men with haunted, downcast eyes and shoulders stooped from carrying a great burden. They had advanced once too often at the machine-gun nests or had watched a mate blasted into a quivering, screaming, bleeding mess of shattered bones and torn flesh and would never forget it.

A heavy-set man in his thirties ambled up to Berlin, choosing a spot at the empty bar right next to him. He was wearing a smart grey woollen overcoat. Underneath it Berlin could see a tailored suit and an expensive silk tie.

The man sized Berlin up quickly. Nicely polished shoes – always a good sign – overcoat clean but showing its age around the cuffs, same for the hat. Office clerk, he guessed, skiving off for the afternoon. He didn't look into Berlin's eyes, which was his biggest mistake.

'Whisky, eh?' He indicated the glass of Dimple on the bar at Berlin's elbow.

Berlin ignored him.

In a pub like this, non-beer drinkers were regarded with suspicion. Whisky was for toffs or for toasting the memory of a loved one who had passed away, or a mate crushed on the docks when a sling slipped and a couple of hundredweight of crates fell from a crane. The barman had poured the drink and taken Berlin's five-pound note without comment, but he'd slapped the change down squarely in a puddle of stale beer.

The stranger held up his empty glass. 'Beer's the go with me, cobber.'

'You should buy yourself another, then.'

The man smiled. 'Just trying to be friendly, mate.'

Berlin picked up his glass and emptied it. He put it on the bar and nodded to the barman for a refill. 'I'm not your mate and I've got all the friends I need right now.'

The second part of Berlin's statement wasn't a lie – at this point in his life having no friends at all suited him just fine.

The man studied the plain metal watch on Berlin's wrist. It had been issued when Berlin was demobbed, along with his now shabby dark blue woollen overcoat. The watch had a plain brown leather band and the letters RAAF on its face.

'Air Force, eh?'

Berlin stared past him.

'New Guinea? The islands? I didn't go. Busted an eardrum from standing too close to a shotgun going off.' The man winked. 'Got me a job on the wharves.'

Berlin knew all about ruptured eardrums and jobs on the wharves. 'Bet you do alright for yourself, then.'

'Can't complain.' He ordered himself another beer. 'You a mechanic or something?'

'Pilot.'

'Fighters?'

'Bombers.'

'Up north?'

'Europe.' Berlin turned his back on the stranger.

The man smiled. 'Nice. Three meals a day and a bit of night bombing? And all them grateful Pommy sheilas to come back to every morning. Bloody cushy billet.'

Berlin let that one go. He picked up his glass.

'You boys had it easy.'

Berlin sipped his whisky. 'If you say so.'

'Get any medals?'

He shook his head. Jesus, couldn't this bastard take a hint?

'Bet you gave those Jerries hell, though.'

'They gave me some back. I was a POW.'

The other man was silent for a moment. 'Right.' He took a swig of his beer. 'In Europe, but. I heard the Germans were okay with our boys. Not like the bloody Japs – in Changi or on the

Burma Railway. Bastards.'

It was all relative, Berlin was about to say, but when he thought about some of the shattered men he'd seen during his time in the repat hospital he decided it wasn't relative at all. Emptying his glass in one swallow, he pushed it back across the bar and straightened up to leave.

The man looked Berlin up and down. 'I'm off the wharves now, but I still have . . . connections. I can put my hands on anything a bloke might need at short notice. Like a new overcoat, for instance. Bloody good prices too – mates' rates.'

Berlin studied the worn cuffs on his coat for a moment before he spoke. 'I don't have any coupons.' And even if he had the coupons he knew his lousy pay wouldn't stretch to a new coat till next winter.

The other man finished his beer and licked foam from his lips. 'Bugger the coupons, mate, she'll be right. So, what do you do for a crust?'

Berlin took a pair of black leather gloves from his pocket. 'I'm a policeman.'

Several drinkers turned towards them then quickly went back to studying the racing results in the pink pages of the *Sporting Globe*.

'And right now,' Berlin continued, 'I'm trying to decide if I should run you in for contravention of the clothing rationing regulations or just take you out the back and belt you till you piss blood.'

The man in the smart overcoat looked a little pale.

'You seem to have a lot of opinions, sport,' Berlin said, pulling on his gloves. 'You got an opinion on that?'

TWO

Berlin kept a room in a ramshackle two-storey brick terrace in Drummond Street, Carlton. Mrs Ivy Goodling, who lived three doors down, described it as a boarding house for broken men, and she knew a thing or two on that subject. Her father had arrived home from France in 1919, kissed his wife and three children and then adjourned to the local pub where, over the next seven years in the company of other returned men, he methodically and efficiently drank himself to death.

Berlin's landlord asked only three things of his tenants: that they paid the rent on time, didn't set themselves and the house on fire by smoking in bed, and kept fancy women off the premises. Berlin was the sole resident who managed all three.

There were nine rented rooms and Berlin's was number six, at the top of the stairs. He was between the bathroom, where a leaking tap in the rust-stained bathtub gurgled all night, and number five, where a wild-eyed and lank-haired former Lewis gunner paced and smoked and murmured and swore and wept, crying out in terror in his sleep. The story went that he had lost a dozen mates, shot away beside him on some hellish island, and had once fought from behind a parapet he'd formed out of the piled bodies of fallen Japanese soldiers. Berlin had glanced in through his open door one afternoon to see an unmade bed, overflowing ashtrays and blinds still drawn. His nose had caught the stink of self-abuse and chronic despair.

Berlin's room was neat by comparison: his bed was always made and he kept the window wide open no matter what the weather. He didn't like to feel shut in. The neatness was a result of his air-force training, as was the ten-minute exercise regimen he performed each morning before washing and shaving with cold water at the sink in the corner of his room.

Berlin was twenty-seven, stood five feet eleven in his socks and weighed just over twelve stone. He had the balance, reach and reflexes of a boxer and a broken nose as a souvenir of his last bout at the Police Boys Club. The nose had been broken a second time in an under-seventeens game of Australian Rules football and now it was slightly twisted and flattened, giving him a brooding appearance that women seemed to find attractive.

The police admissions board had liked the look of him, too. They'd decided his build and slightly battered face gave him a look of barely contained violence that suited their purposes exactly. And the fact that he could use his brains as well as his fists and knew when to keep his mouth shut soon had him marked as someone with potential for bigger things in the force. But that was before the war.

After exercising and before washing, Berlin cleaned his shoes. He had two pairs, brown for the weekend and black for work. Both hand-lasted, round-toed lace-ups, they had been made for him by a shoemaker in Richmond, in a small shop that smelled of new leather and boot polish. At the first sign of wear in the heels or soles, Berlin returned to the shop to have them mended.

He took a black-bristled shoe brush from a string-tied cloth bag hanging on the end of his bed. The bag contained several other shoe brushes and two round, flat tins of Nugget shoe polish, in Black and Nigger Brown. There was also an RAF-issue rolled-up calico bag – a 'housewife' – that held needles, thread, spare buttons and other items used by servicemen for making repairs to their uniforms.

Berlin was surprisingly good with a needle. He had been able to slow down the deterioration of his one work suit with running repairs, and alternate day use of the two pairs of trousers. His suit coat, waistcoat, trousers, three ties and three white shirts were all hung neatly with his weekend suit in the gently collapsing plywood wardrobe.

Berlin sat on the bed in his singlet, socks and underpants, rhythmically working the wooden-handled brush over the surface of the black leather and smiling as the shine came back. He had applied polish to the shoes the night before, leaving it to soak in, and now he studied the stitching connecting the uppers and the soles. If he was careful he would get another five years out of these shoes. His grandfather had taught him that shoes were important – they said a lot about a man and they should be treated with respect. In Poland Berlin learned they could save your life.

On every evening of the twenty-seven days the POWs had stumbled through the howling blizzards and along slush-covered roadways, Berlin had methodically wiped his boots clean of the accumulated muck. On the nights there was a fire he dried them gently, careful not to let the leather dry out too much. Early in the march an air-gunner from Athabasca, in the remote north-west of Canada, showed him how to massage his toes to avoid frostbite. This, combined with his good boots, enabled Berlin to stay on his feet until they reached a railhead, where they were jammed into cattle cars and transported to a camp near Hamburg. When the Red Cross weighed him on arrival he was down to six stone, but at least he still had all his toes.

Berlin washed his hands with Solvol in the small sink. The soap's abrasive grit irritated the grazes on his knuckles and he briefly considered putting some Elastoplast on the cuts but decided against it. They would heal faster in the open air. All wounds heal faster out in the open, or so one of the repat psychiatrists had told him. All the other doctors had just urged him to forget the war, put it out of his mind and get on with his life.

Berlin glanced at the overcoat hanging on the back of his bedroom door. He'd given the smart alec at the bar his old coat in exchange for this one, plus a couple of wallops for his trouble. Not textbook police procedure for dealing with black marketeers but he'd made his point. And a couple of grazed knuckles were a small price to pay for staying warm through the coming winter.

THREE

Berlin left before seven most mornings, walking to police headquarters on Russell Street even though there was a tram stop nearby, on Lygon Street. He walked most places. He walked because he could, because no one was there to stop him. There was no barbed wire, and no warning wire before the barbed wire telling him that to take one step more meant a burst of machine-gun fire from the watchtower or a bullet in the chest from the rifle of a perimeter guard.

Even at seven on a weekday morning the streets were crowded. Factory girls and night-shift workers passed each other, the girls often laughing, the men with shoulders hunched and hats and caps pulled down over their eyes. There was the whiff of stale beer from the doorway of the early openers and some days the smell of hops from the CUB brewery hung in the air.

The night-duty sergeant glanced up at Berlin as he walked in. 'Pleasant stroll this morning, DC Berlin? Not too crisp for you?'

Berlin shook his head. 'Keeps the blood pumping.'

'That's a very nice overcoat you've got there, a fine bit of British tailoring if I don't miss my guess.'

'Well spotted, Sarge.'

'You don't often see coats like that these days, what with the rationing. Must have cost a few bob.'

Berlin ran his hand down the grey woollen sleeve. 'Gift from a grateful friend.'

That was better, the sergeant thought to himself. The boy was finally getting back into the swing of things. It made the others uncomfortable when someone played it too straight. It was the sergeant's job to take new recruits out for a beer and a chat and explain the facts of life to them. They usually caught on pretty quick, or they found themselves manning a one-person station somewhere out the back of woop woop, chasing cattle duffers.

Berlin took the stairs to the third floor. The detective squad office was empty. It seemed Melbourne's criminals and their pursuers both kept bankers' hours.

Berlin's desk was behind Chater's. Chater had been in Berlin's training intake at the St Kilda Road police depot. When the war came Berlin joined the RAAF even though the police force was a reserved occupation and members were discouraged from volunteering for military service. Chater had stayed in the job and now the smarmy bastard outranked Berlin and was enjoying every minute of it. Same thing went for Hargraves, who was a brown-nosing shitkicker before the war but now ran the squad. Hitler and Tojo had been good for some people's civilian careers.

Berlin had just taken off his overcoat when Hargraves walked in holding a thick manila folder. 'Nice coat.' He tossed the folder onto Berlin's desk. 'I tried telephoning you at home, but your landlord said you'd already left. Early bird catches the worm, eh?'

Berlin recognised the case by the file number. 'They're back?'

'Looks like it. That top sheet is all we've got at this stage. The loco sheds payroll at Wodonga this time. They tried to slip the cash in a day early but the buggers were waiting. Early bird got that worm, too.'

'Sure it was the same gang?'

Hargraves shrugged. 'Looks like it. Railways payroll, five blokes wearing balaclavas and carrying Tommy guns, riding jungle-green Harley-Davidsons with sidecars. Which is why you are off to lovely Wodonga to get this sorted.'

'Why aren't the Wangaratta police handling this one?'

'The Wangaratta boys have been made to look like fools by these bastards and the press is starting to pick up on the story. The top brass are pretty pissed off and heads are going to roll if something's not sorted quick smart.'

Berlin picked up the folder. 'Shouldn't this be Chater's case?'

'Wedding's on Saturday.'

The father of Chater's seventeen-year-old girlfriend had angrily bailed up the detective outside Russell Street a few weeks back and Chater had glumly announced his upcoming nuptials two days later.

'I'll go home and pack a bag and take the next train from Spencer Street.'

Hargraves shook his head. 'Fraid not, sunshine. The deputy commissioner doesn't want the leads on this one going cold, so you're flying up to Albury. There's a plane leaving Essendon Aerodrome in twenty-five minutes but they'll hold it for you.'

'I don't have any clothes . . . my razor.'

'Buy what you need up there and put in a chit. That shirt looks clean enough, should do you a day or two more.'

'I've only got a few quid on me and my bank won't be open for a couple of hours.'

'This isn't a fucking holiday, Berlin! This is the deputy commissioner saying you get your arse on that plane in twenty bloody minutes! I thought a flyboy like you would jump at the chance to get up in the air again.'

'I'm on my way.' Berlin picked up the file off the desk and reached for his hat and coat, avoiding eye contact. His heart was pounding, his mouth was dry and he didn't want Hargraves to see the fear he knew was in his eyes.

Hargraves called after him. 'Someone will meet you at Albury Aerodrome when you land and run you back over the bridge to Wodonga. Report to the local sergeant when you get there, name's Corrigan. And keep in touch, Berlin. We don't want you disappearing off into the wild blue yonder.'

As he headed down the stairs Berlin held the file in his right hand. His left hand was in his jacket pocket, fingers clenched tightly around the empty Benzedrine inhaler.

FOUR

The police driver dropped Berlin next to a shiny silver twin-engine aircraft parked on the tarmac. The driver had used the siren on the way out, weaving in and out of traffic and cursing other motorists who didn't move out of his way quickly enough. A man in his mid-twenties was leaning on the metal steps by the passenger door at the rear of the aircraft, smoking. He was wearing aviator sunglasses and an American-style zip-up leather flying jacket. When he dropped his half-smoked cigarette on the tarmac Berlin had to resist the ingrained POW urge to pick up and pocket the butt.

'You must be the cop,' the man said.

'I guess the police car was a bit of a giveaway.'

'Nothing gets past me, sport.' He put out his hand and introduced himself. 'I'm Reg. I'm your pilot.'

Berlin shook his hand. 'The name's Charlie.'

'You got any luggage there, Charlie?'

Berlin held up the manila folder.

'In that case we probably should hit the frog and toad.'

Berlin started to walk around the aircraft, checking the tyres and elevators and looking at the tarmac under the engines for any signs of leaking oil.

Reg was watching him. 'I've already done a pre-flight check, mate. All the bits we need are attached, trust me. I'm going to be up there with you, remember.'

Berlin looked up. 'Force of habit, sorry.'

'You a pilot?'

'I used to be. Wellingtons and Lancs. In England.'

'That must have been fun. How many ops?'

'Twenty-nine,' said Berlin, 'and a half.'

'Been up since?'

'Nope.'

Reg studied Berlin's face. He knew that look, he'd seen it in other airmen's eyes – men who were convinced they'd used up all their luck and their next flight would be their last.

'Here's the story, Charlie. I flew cargo and paratroopers in the islands for four years, so believe me, I'm a pretty good pilot and my co-pilot's no slouch either. As to the kite, she's an RAAF surplus Dakota. Daks are easy to fly and tough as buggery.'

'That's what I've heard, Reg.' The skies over England had been filled with Dakotas, the military version of the DC3 used for general transport, assault glider towing, and the dropping of supplies and paratroops.

'Plus we've got a mechanic who doesn't cut corners.'

Berlin studied the lines of the aircraft. 'She looks in good nick.'

'You bet, she's only got a couple of thousand hours on her. Ex-VIP transport plane, which saved me a packet on the fit-out.'

'Let's do it.' Berlin said the words with more confidence than he felt.

Inside, the Dakota was luxury compared with his old Lancaster. The ten passenger seats were thickly padded leather and looked very comfortable. Berlin followed Reg up the narrow sloping aisle.

'Not many passengers this morning, Charlie, so you can have any seat you fancy.'

The only other person in the passenger cabin was a blonde sitting in the rear. She was smoking Craven A cork tips and reading the *Women's Weekly*. Berlin chose the front right seat and carefully did up his seat belt. Through the open cockpit door he watched Reg and his co-pilot check the instruments. Two pilots – typical of American-built aircraft. What bloody luxury, he thought.

The RAF was miserly with its crewing of heavy bombers. By day the American B17s, with their multiple 50-calibre defensive armament and two pilots on board, pounded the Germans, but by night it was the RAF Lancs and Halifaxes, with their bigger bomb loads, smaller crews and solo pilots, doing the pounding. RAF flight engineers sat on fold-down seats next to the pilots to help with the throttles and instruments during the critical take-off phase, but after that the pilots were on their own.

The logic of the single-pilot policy was that every pilot trained meant one more aircraft over the target. A two-man cockpit crew was judged to be simply a waste of resources, since the night-fighter cannon shells or exploding flak that would kill or maim one pilot would almost certainly do the same to a man sitting a couple of feet to his right.

The Dakota's twin Pratt & Whitney rotary engines whined and spluttered, missing several times before coughing throatily into life and then settling into a solid, comforting rhythm. The sound was nothing like the chorus of the four V12 Merlins on Berlin's Lancaster, but his mouth was dry as it had been every time he'd waited for the ground crew to pull the chocks away from the tyres so he could begin the long taxi out to the runway.

Reg was as good a pilot as he claimed and their take-off was smooth and uneventful. Once the aircraft levelled off, the woman who had been sitting in the back brought Berlin coffee in an enamel mug. There was chicory in the coffee concentrate, and sweetened condensed milk helped cut the bitterness.

'I'm Valmae. I'm Reg's fiancée.' She was wearing one-piece mechanics coveralls dyed black. 'Sorry about the awful coffee, but it's all we can get.'

'I've had worse.'

Valmae handed him a grey woollen blanket. 'In case you get a bit chilly when we get up higher. It might be a bit itchy, I'm afraid – army surplus.' She smiled. 'I think you and I are the only things on board that aren't military surplus, Mr Berlin.'

'It's just you, Valmae.'

'Call me Val. I thought the police was a reserved occupation?'

'We were actively encouraged not to enlist but my brother was with the Eighth. He went missing after Singapore fell and I thought I ought to do something.'

'He come home?'

Berlin shook his head. 'Army still can't trace him. He was in a military hospital sick as a dog with malaria when the Japs took over and that's the last anyone heard of him.'

'That's tough, Mr Berlin, I'm sorry. But at least you're back and in one piece.'

'That's right, Val,' Berlin said, 'At least I'm back.'

'And you flying with us today means Reg & Val's Trans-Continental Airways lives to fly another day.'

'Business a bit slow?'

'You could say that. Reg loves flying. Before the war he was a sales clerk in Myer's shoe department, and he can't go back to that life. But there's a lot of cheap aeroplanes around, and even more pilots.'

'Ex-military types like Reg?'

'Yep. We have to fight for every passenger and parcel. Reg thinks maybe we should move to Broken Hill or the Alice. Or maybe Asia.'

16

'Sometime it's hard to find your place in the world again, Val.'

'Yes, that's what Reg says. You'll let me know if I can get you anything else, won't you.'

Berlin nodded and Val went back to organise coffee for the crew.

That was another problem with war, what came after. Some men came home with skills that could easily translate into civilian life, and others didn't. Some men wanted nothing more than to go back to the life they'd known before, and others were hooked on a thirst for adventure or the constant adrenalin rush of danger. These were men who had been trained to take and to hold, and to efficiently kill anyone who got in their way – skills essential to survival in Rommel's and Monty's North African desert or the rotting green hell of New Guinea, but ill-suited to a civvies' life with the war two years done.

Berlin glanced out the window at the wispy, low cloud and the patchwork of fields far below. Around five thousand feet, he estimated. He wondered if Reg would be following the railway line to Albury. Berlin had taken that trip once, by train from Melbourne to Sydney and then on to Brisbane to board a troopship. And he knew the stops to Wodonga by heart now from the recent spate of robberies along the northern line: Tallarook, Seymour, Euroa, Violet Town, Benalla, Wangaratta, Barnawartha.

He picked up the manila folder. The top sheet was a single-page typed report on the Wodonga loco sheds pay office robbery. Transcribed from a telephone call with the local police, there was enough detail to confirm it was the same gang responsible for the dozen or so other robberies briefly outlined in the file. Five masked men riding motorcycles and armed with submachine guns had carried out the raids, all targeting Victorian Railways office payrolls.

Coincidentally, many of the robberies had taken place in areas where the Kelly gang had run wild almost seventy years before.

This Kelly-country link and the way the gang ran rings around the police was starting to give them a larrikin appeal to a public starved of adventure since the end of the war. Their last raid had been at Glenrowan, over a month ago, and while the local cops may have taken Ned Kelly down at Glenrowan in 1880 they were having a lot less luck these days.

The gang was ruthlessly efficient, Berlin had to give them that. So far no one had been killed, and until this morning no one had been injured. The gang leader usually fired warning bursts of submachine-gun fire into the air to ensure compliance, but this time it looked like the paymaster had decided to be a hero and then it had been on for young and old.

A piece of flimsy, onion-skin foolscap paper was stuck to the back of the report. It was a memo from the deputy police commissioner to the state premier. The typed letters were in faded blue, indicating it was a third or fourth carbon copy. The head of the railways wanted the robberies resolved quickly and the deputy police commissioner was guaranteeing results. The name 'Hargraves' was handwritten at the top in the purple ink favoured by the deputy commissioner and the words 'heads will roll' were underlined.

Berlin recognised Hargraves' scrawl on the bottom of the page. It was a list of detectives and all the names had been crossed through except for Berlin's. Had it been left in the file by accident or had Hargarves included the underlined memo on purpose? Berlin wondered.

After a battlefield retreat early in World War I, French officers selected a half-dozen soldiers at random and had them shot by firing squad in front of their battalion. *Pour encourager les autres*, 'to encourage the others', was the rationale.

Either way it was obvious to Berlin that his head was on the chopping block and he didn't like his chances of solving the case in a hurry. He didn't know a single soul in Wodonga and detective work was all local, all about knowing who the bad boys were and having a stable of reliable fizzes – underworld informants who were always ready and willing to sell out a friend or accomplice for a fiver, or a chance to duck a court appearance or avoid a belting in the police cells.

They hit turbulence over Benalla. Through the open cockpit door he could see Reg with his hands on the joystick, fighting to keep the Dakota under control. The aircraft jerked and shuddered, buffeted by swirling winds and sudden downdrafts that smacked hard into the fuselage like a blow from a fist.

Berlin's fingers closed around the empty Benzedrine inhaler in his pocket. It was hard for him to imagine he had once sat in the front seat of an aircraft even bigger than this and held the controls, skilfully guiding his lethal cargo to its point of delivery. It was a different place and a different time. And I was a different man, he said to himself.

FIVE

The Royal Air Force had Charlie Berlin and twenty-eight thousand or so young volunteers like him on loan from the Australian government for the duration of the war. And Berlin, like the rest of them, had what he felt was a perfectly reasonable fear of dying.

While the RAF may have agreed that it was reasonable to be afraid of dying, to talk about it or do anything to avoid it was considered a sign of LMF, or Lack of Moral Fibre, and this wasn't tolerated. People who displayed LMF quickly disappeared and were only ever spoken of again in hushed whispers. LMF could manifest itself in suspicious physical injuries that took a pilot off flying duties, a flight engineer weeping in the Chaplin's office or an air gunner bailing out, unordered and unseen, over enemy territory, preferring to live out the war in a POW camp than be blown to pieces by the cannon shells of a German night fighter or burnt to death trapped inside a plexiglass turret.

The day-to-day routine in a Bomber Command squadron swung wildly between life and death. Between operations the men trained at their various specialities, attended briefings on how to survive ditchings in the freezing waters of the Channel and listened to airmen who had escaped German captivity. They heard the airmen describe what would happen should they have to bail out over enemy territory, and wind up in the dreaded aircrew interrogation rooms of Dulag Luft in Frankfurt.

For off-duty airmen there were movies, drinks in the mess or at the local pub, and sometimes leave passes to London. To expend their youthful energy, there was football or cricket, carnal wrestling with the station WAAFs or rolling in the hay with lusty Land Army girls, who were kept slim and fit by long days harvesting crops and tending sheep and cattle.

Then there would be a phone call from HQ, or a motorcycle despatch rider would race through the station gates, and an op would be called – and suddenly everyone understood that this might be their last day on earth. In a few hours' time they would be sitting high over Germany on top of ten thousand pounds of high explosives and a couple of thousand gallons of petrol with massed anti-aircraft guns and night fighters shooting at them.

After briefings and preparations sleep was impossible, so kitted out for twenty thousand feet, they laughed and joked in the crew-ready room and casually filled their thermoses with coffee while hiding their terror. Some prayed or wrote letters home, and all were keyed up and exhausted by the time the green GO signal was flashed from the control tower. Dozens of idling Merlin engines were throttled up and the bombers began rolling through the twilight, taxiing to the long, undulating concrete runway and what lay beyond.

So the aircrew put on brave faces, stuck out their chests, kept their chins up, maintained stiff upper lips and, in a state of outer physical rectitude and inner mental turmoil, soldiered on. Many coped by drinking too much, whoring, fighting, gambling and driving fast cars. Some coped by visiting the station medical officer for pharmaceutical solace. Air-force research had suggested the amphetamine Benzedrine provided the ideal mix of optimism and aggression for aircrew to achieve peak efficiency in prolonged periods of stress. Benzedrine pills were readily available from the station medical officers for those in need of a little more alertness, improved reaction times and increased stamina, and for those wanting to feel that perhaps death wasn't an inevitability. Some took these wakey-wakey pills occasionally, and others took all they could and then raided their escape kits for more when the MOs cut off their supply, worried by signs of excessive aggression or unrealistically high spirits and mania.

After the war Berlin, like all the others, swore blind he had taken no pills and had made it through the terror on steely resolve and strong moral fibre. But this wasn't strictly true, and after his fiancée dumped him he had gone back to the drug, using legal over-the-counter Benzedrine inhalers from the local chemist or pills freely available from his doctor. For those with the urge for something stronger, cocaine and morphine could be had at a price from St Kilda sly-grog merchants, although Berlin had resisted this temptation.

And Berlin was tempted on his first week back on the beat. A nine-year-old running late on her way to school was struck and killed by a tram and he had helped carry her shattered body off the roadway. He drank for three days straight, and when grog and the drug both failed to ease the pain he tried drowning himself in sex with a series of lonely war widows. Driven on by the manic hypersexuality the Benzedrine unleashed in him, he existed in a downward spiral of anonymous naked bodies, sweat and tears, until the awful night he recognised a face from his training days staring at him from a black-banded, framed photograph next to a woman's bed.

Around midnight a uniformed constable in Pascoe Vale found him vomiting into the gutter and he spent the night in their lock-up. In the morning they called Russell Street and then tore up the charge sheet, giving him back his personal belongings, including an empty inhaler. He kept it in his pocket as a reminder of a place he never wanted to go again.

SIX

The Dakota bounced three times on the Albury runway before settling. As the tail came down Reg yelled, 'Sorry 'bout that!' through the open cockpit door. They taxied quickly towards a run-down hangar, where Berlin could see a couple of vehicles waiting. When they finally came to a stop, Reg switched off the engines and walked out of the cockpit.

'Bit of a gusty crosswind there, Charlie. I've done better landings on strips chopped out of the jungle with Japs shooting at me.'

Berlin shook his hand. 'No worries, mate, at least now I can chalk up thirty safe landings.'

Outside the aircraft a quarter-ton Chevy truck was waiting to pick up the cargo. Just past the truck Berlin saw a tan four-door Dodge sedan with a uniformed constable standing next to it. He was wearing one of the old British-bobby-style Sudweeks police helmets. As Berlin walked across the tarmac the constable came to attention and saluted.

'Constable Roberts, DC Berlin. Welcome to Wodonga, sir – I mean Albury, we have to drive back over the river to Wodonga.'

Roberts looked about eighteen or nineteen, tall and solidly

built with pale skin, blue eyes and a smattering of pimples on his chin. Berlin noticed a small shaving nick on his jaw. The constable's neatly pressed blue tunic was done up to the neck, the buttons brightly polished. His black shoes had a parade-ground shine that almost matched the gloss of the Dodge. The two men shook hands.

'Pleased to meet you, Constable. You're not expecting Dugout Doug by any chance, are you?'

The constable looked flustered. 'I'm sorry, sir, I don't understand.'

'All the spit and polish. General MacArthur has returned from whence he came, son. I'm just a cop up from the big smoke.'

'My sergeant wanted to make sure we did things by the book. I'm to be your driver while you're in Wodonga, sir.'

'That's very nice but I'm not sure I'll be needing a driver.'

'I'm afraid Sergeant Corrigan insists, sir.' The constable appeared to be a little uncomfortable, avoiding Berlin's eyes.

'Fair enough, no skin off my nose.'

'Shall I take you to your hotel?'

'If we're going by the book I think I'd better have a look at the crime scene first.'

'Yes, sir.' Roberts snapped another salute.

'Let's drop the saluting. And what's with the hat?'

'We were issued with the new flat caps, sir, but not enough to go round.'

'I guess that means you're the most junior constable at the station.'

'There's just four of us, plus the sergeant. I've been here a year.'

'Always a bastard being the junior. I know what that's like. You get all the worst jobs around the joint, right?'

'That's the truth!'

'And picking me up is probably one of them.'

The constable smiled. 'I don't mind. Maybe, I hope – I mean, I might learn something.'

Berlin decided he liked the lad. 'Not planning on spending your whole career in uniform, then?'

'No, sir.'

'Fair enough. Lesson one is that the scene of the crime is usually where most of the answers are. I want to see what these bastards have been up to, so I suggest we get moving.'

'Shall I get your luggage first, sir?'

Berlin held up the folder. 'Travelling light today.' He took a cigarette from the packet of State Express 333s in his coat pocket. As he reached for the box of matches, Roberts pulled out a shiny metal Zippo lighter and flicked it open. He cupped his hand around it and Berlin caught the sweetish smell of lighter fluid on the breeze before the flint sparked and the wick caught. He leaned forward and lit his cigarette. 'Lesson two, Roberts. Don't try too hard. I'm just a bloody detective constable. Now let's get going, shall we?' Berlin winked at the constable.

Roberts opened the passenger door. The vehicle had leather upholstery and the interior was immaculately maintained. Berlin whistled. 'Very nice. A bloke could get used to this. Army surplus?'

'Yes, sir. Staff car. Used to belong to a colonel. A lot of the vehicles running locally are ex-military, too.'

'That so?'

'Oh, yeah. There's tons of military surplus around here, Mr Berlin, because of all the big army camps we had nearby. The local farmers can get surplus trucks and tractors or they can have a go at pulling a plough with a Bren gun carrier. They were going for fifty quid not long back.'

Bren gun carriers were small, open-topped, lightly armoured scouting and transport vehicles. Their twin caterpillar tracks were intended to take them over rough country, and with their V8 engines a farmer's flat wheat fields would be no challenge.

'They reckon some cove up by Yackandandah's using a General Grant tank with the turret knocked off. War ends one day and the next there's a million tons of stuff nobody wants. Stuff made for killing people and now that's over, thank God.'

'There's a lot of people out there trained for killing people, Roberts, and for a lot of them it's not over.'

Roberts' helmet was knocked off as he slid into the driver's seat, and he tossed it onto the rear seat before starting the engine. As the Dodge rounded the back of the hangar a startled Berlin exclaimed, 'Well, bugger me!'

A twin-tailed, four-engine aircraft was parked on the concrete apron. Suddenly Berlin's mouth was dry again, there was that familiar hollow feeling in his stomach and his hand found the inhaler in his pocket.

'That's what you flew, sir, right?'

'Very similar, Roberts,' he said, after a pause, 'but that's a Halifax, I was in Lancasters. The old Halibag was a good aircraft though. Rugged as hell. What's an RAF heavy bomber doing way out here?'

'After the war some demobbed RAAF boys in England got tired of waiting for a ship home so they bought it as military surplus and flew her back with paying passengers. It's mostly used for hauling cargo now.'

'Smart buggers.' And braver than me, Berlin thought. Twelve thousand miles – and most of it over water – wasn't something he'd have fancied.

They drove out of the airport gate and onto the gravel roadway.

'So how'd you know I was a pilot? Your sergeant been checking up on me?'

'He made a call when we heard you were headed up here.'

'And what did he find out?'

Roberts stared straight ahead at the road without speaking.

'It's okay, you can tell me, and it's just between us.'

Roberts glanced across and studied Berlin's face for a brief moment. Sizing me up before he answers, Berlin decided. Fair enough too, it was the smart thing to do and the kid looked smart. Just how smart, he would judge from the answer.

'They said you were a good copper but a loner and a bit bomb-happy, you know, screwy.'

Berlin took the cigarette from his mouth and flicked the butt out the window. 'Sounds about right.' Probably a bit of an understatement, truth be told. 'Anything else?'

'They said we were to report back to Melbourne right away if you went off the rails.'

Berlin smiled. 'I'll make sure you're the first to know.'

He glanced out the window back towards the airport disappearing in the dust behind them. The Halifax stood out clearly among the silver aircraft hangars and low scrub. At this distance it could have been a Lancaster, and it looked totally out of place. No more than me, Berlin decided.

SEVEN

Almost every evening of the war, hundreds of heavy bombers formed up at assembly points in the night sky over England, before heading towards the Channel and occupied Europe. After extinguishing their navigation lights over the coast, each aircraft was on its own, travelling at a specified height and speed until it arrived over the target. Once there, German parachute flares, searchlights and the glow of the flames twenty thousand feet below allowed the pilots a glimpse of their companions in the bomber stream for the first time in hours.

After its first mission, the airfield mechanics christened Berlin's Lancaster bomber, *T for Tango*, 'The Berlin Express'. The station control-tower log showed the aircraft as last away on a run to Stuttgart and first back on the airfield circuit seven hours later. Some suspected Berlin of squibbing the mission – dumping his bomb load over the Channel and stooging aimlessly about for several hours – but target photographs from the bomber's camera soon put that to rest. *T for Tango* had dropped its load of high explosives and incendiaries right on top of the pathfinder markers, and no one could argue with that.

Jock, the mid-upper gunner, described Berlin's style as 'the three Gs': 'Get there, get it done and get the fuck out'. It was also how Gary, the shy young Canadian navigator, described it to Gwen, the pretty blonde WAAF who drove the big Dodge crew bus from the ready room out through the deepening twilight to the waiting bombers. But he left out the expletive because Gwen was a nice girl.

Each morning, Gwen and the other WAAF drivers collected the surviving aircrew and ferried them to debriefings with the station's intelligence officer. They served hot coffee to the men waiting to be interviewed and tried not to look too deeply into the red-rimmed and still-terrified eyes of those who clutched their enamel mugs tightly in both hands to stop the shaking. Gary was happy when Gwen was the one who served him coffee, and she always smiled and sometimes gently patted his hand. He was secretly in love, and desperately hoping to have sex with her before he was killed.

The airmen all knew they were going to be killed because that was the way it was. Aircrew attrition, which was how the RAF described the ending of young men's lives before they'd even got themselves a driver's licence, was currently running at 15 per cent. The airmen called it the chop rate, and as a completed tour was thirty missions, even the most mathematically impaired could work out the odds.

Night after night the radar-controlled night fighters, searchlights and massed anti-aircraft guns of the Kammhuber defensive line, which stretched across Europe, waited hungrily for the bombers. And every morning more FTRs were chalked up next to the aircraft listed on the big board in the ops room. 'Failed to return' was air-force speak for the annihilation of a twenty-ton Lancaster bomber and its seven-man crew.

But over the next few weeks observers of the board began to notice the steady and regular early return of *T for Tango*. They quizzed the mechanics about any modifications Berlin might have had made to the four massive Merlin engines, but the mechanics shook their heads. Berlin's crew just shrugged and said it was the three Gs – just get there, get it done and get the fuck out.

And as the early returns mounted on the board, *T for Tango*'s crew began to wonder if they were actually going to make it – going to do their thirty, be rated TOUR EXPIRED, given leave and then posted to a cushy training squadron, and maybe even get to blow out the candles on their twenty-first birthday cakes.

A newly qualified wireless operator, who cheerily jumped aboard *T for Tango* to do his familiarisation on a Bremerhaven run, was wide-eyed, white and shaking when they got back. After he'd finished vomiting up what looked like everything he'd eaten in the last week, a couple of mechanics took him behind a fuel bowser, gingerly stripped off his flight suit and uniform and used a fire hose to wash the stinking mess off him. His flight suit and trousers and even his newly issued sheepskin-lined flying boots all had to be burnt.

They gave the man several triple whiskies in the sergeants' mess. In borrowed overalls and with a trembling voice, he described a mad dash to the head of the bomber stream and then on to the target through probing searchlights, massed anti-aircraft fire and night fighters, dodging between falling bombs and crippled aircraft spiralling downwards in flames.

'He's bloody mad. The man should be put away. They're all mad, every one of them. If they weren't praying out loud they were cursing to high heaven and when we got to the target all I could hear in the headphones was that bastard in the cockpit chanting, "Do it! Do it! Do it!" And then when we heard, "Bombs gone" from the nose I thought the fucking wings were going to come off, he turned her so hard.'

They didn't notice Berlin walk into the mess in his blue RAAF uniform, darker than their RAF uniforms, with the 'Australia' flash on the shoulder. He ordered a whisky at the bar and turned to watch the group gathered around the shaken wireless operator.

'Then we go back, right through the bomber stream,' the man continued, 'through all these falling five-hundred pounders and bits of blown-up burning Lancs, and the tail gunner picks up a night fighter over Holland and screams for him to corkscrew port, and I swear, ten seconds later we're upside down and the kite is creaking and banging and kit goes flying all over the place and he has all the damn throttles full to the gate. How those bloody engines didn't tear themselves right out of the mountings I'll never, ever know. Mad. Totally fucking mad.'

At the bar Berlin took a bottle from the steward. He walked across to the group and topped up the wireless operator's whisky. The rim of the glass, shaking in the man's hand, rattled against the neck of the bottle. Berlin steadied the glass and looked down into the man's pale face and terrified eyes.

'You're still alive, aren't you, mate? Go and have a look at that list of FTRs on the board – those poor buggers aren't.'

The brass knew about Berlin's tactic of racing to the assembly point and working his way to the head of the bomber stream, and he was repeatedly threatened with court martial for breaking formation but he knew it wasn't going to happen because it would take him off flying duties. With Bomber Command's continuing heavy losses every pilot was needed, especially one who made his target every time.

Berlin ignored mechanical problems that gave other pilots an excuse to turn back. He was intent on ticking off the ops in his logbook and getting his crew to the end of their tour. He received no promotions or medals even though he had earned them, but that didn't bother him. He figured it was better to be a live sergeant pilot with a 'satisfactory' rating than a dead flight lieutenant or wing commander with a posthumous Distinguished Flying Cross.

Berlin and his crew stayed alive and they did their twenty-nine ops. On number thirty, over the docks at Kiel on a beautiful moonlit night, Berlin lined up on the target indicators and said to himself, 'Looks like we're going to make it,' and that was the last thing he remembered. He learned after the war that other aircraft in the bomber stream had reported seeing his Lancaster exploding in mid-air. *T for Tango* was listed as lost, with no survivors.

Berlin came to in a pine forest, swinging in his parachute harness, hooked high up in the branches of a massive tree. If the angry farmers on the ground had been armed with guns instead of pitchforks and shovels, they would have killed him on the spot. The Volkssturm home-guard soldiers who eventually cut him down were all old enough to be his grandfather but they still beat him to a bloody pulp before dragging him through the streets of the burning target city. They turned him over to the Luftwaffe, starting him on his journey towards that freezing, sleeting morning on a muddy Polish roadway.

EIGHT

'You got a first name, Constable?'

Roberts was a careful driver and he concentrated on negotiating a sharp bend before answering.

'You can call me Bob.'

'That make you Robert Roberts, Bob?'

'I was registered Robert Rob Roberts, after Robert Burns and Rob Roy. My old man had a skinful at the time.'

'People do silly things when they're pissed.'

'Yeah, but my old man had a skinful most of the time and he was a nasty bastard when he was drunk. My mum was surprised he passed the army physical, but she was glad to have him out of the house.'

'Where is he now?'

'Somewhere in the Middle East. He was an AA gunner and a Jerry Stuka dropped a bomb right into his gun pit. Everyone else got clear but they reckon there wasn't even enough left of him to put in a sugar bag. They just filled in the hole and stuck a cross on top. We got the telegram on my thirteenth birthday while I was blowing out the candles. Best present I ever got.'

'Fair enough. How come there's no local detective here?' Berlin asked, changing the subject.

'Went mad and we shot him.' The constable smiled at his joke, then caught himself and glanced across at Berlin. 'Sorry, Mr Berlin, I didn't mean . . . I mean he's been off on medical leave for months, bad liver.'

'Bit of a drinker?'

Roberts shrugged. 'I wouldn't know.'

That was good, Berlin thought. The boy was discreet.

A few minutes later they were approaching the Albury city centre.

'That's the railway station coming up. Nicer than Wodonga's, that's for sure.'

Ahead on his left Berlin could see a sandstone and red-brick clock tower topped by a steeple, rising over a long, low single-storey building. Wrought-iron lacework held up a tin-roofed verandah that ran the length of the station. It was an impressive building. Berlin hadn't seen the outside before but he knew what the inside looked like.

When the railways first came to Australia in the 1870s, New South Wales decided on the standard rail gauge of four feet eight and a half inches while Victoria chose the broader Irish gauge of five feet three inches. This became a problem when the lines reached Albury and Wodonga, and the incompatible gauges meant that passengers travelling between Melbourne and Sydney were forced into a mad scramble to change trains.

Berlin remembered his midnight arrival at Albury station on his way to war. He remembered the soot and the steam and the confusion, the shrill note of the stationmaster's whistle, and the squeal and clang of metal on metal as the railway carriages were shunted into position. Bleary-eyed soldiers, sailors and airmen hauling cumbersome canvas kitbags made their way across the windswept platform, stumbling and grumbling and cursing. Harried ladies behind the counter in the noisy refreshments room thrust cups of hot tea and soggy white-bread sandwiches and the infamous railway pies out into a sea of grasping hands.

Just before the station the constable made a smooth right turn into a wide street bordered by low-rise stone buildings.

'This is Dean Street, Mr Berlin, Albury's main street.'

Trucks, farm utes and the odd pre-war sedan were parked on both sides of the road and there were a few pedestrians, mostly women in floral dresses and a couple of men wearing suits and broad-brimmed hats.

Roberts pointed over to the right. 'That's the best picture theatre, the Regent. There's also a rollerskating rink and a couple of good dances on a Saturday night. There's a lot of pretty girls in Albury.'

'I'll take your word for it.'

Dean Street was as wide as Russell Street in Melbourne, but a lot quieter. It was midmorning so most of the men were at work, leaving the women to do the shopping. They passed some fine-looking pubs and a number of commercial buildings – substantial two- and three-storey brick constructions with wide awnings shading the footpaths. Several of the buildings boasted masonry towers, attesting to the financial success of insurance and pastoral companies and indicating that Albury was a town built on a solid economic base. The tower above the post office had a clock to mark the time, though no one on Dean Street seemed in much of a hurry to be anywhere.

There was a slender white obelisk sitting high on a hill at the far end of the street. 'What's that thing?'

'That's the war memorial on top of Monument Hill. Built back in the twenties. It's lit up at night and you can see it from most places in town.'

Berlin stayed silent. He hated war memorials. He didn't need to be reminded of the mates he'd lost.

The road veered left, skirting a river. Berlin studied it: surprisingly wide, bordered by tall gum trees and willows with their drooping, leaf-laden branches skimming the grey-green surface of the swiftly moving water.

'The mighty Murray.'

Berlin was amused by the tone of pride in the constable's voice.

'You should go fishing if you get a chance, Mr Berlin. The river's full of redfin and huge Murray cod and big freshwater crays you can pull out by the bucketful.'

'Not much of a fisherman, I'm afraid.'

The Dodge followed the curve of the road as it ran down towards the Murray and then they were on the bridge that crossed the river border between New South Wales and Victoria. The car rumbled across the thick wooden planks of the bridge, rattling the heavy metal bolts and startling a flock of waterbirds that took to the sky at the noise. They crossed over a second rattling bridge and then the town appeared.

'Welcome to beautiful Wodonga, Mr Berlin. This is High Street. The police station is straight up ahead.' Roberts shook his head. 'Dean Street it isn't.'

Berlin had to agree. Wodonga had even more of a country town feel than its neighbour. Many of the shops lining the main street were of wooden construction and most were single storey, though with the same wide corrugated-iron awnings for shade. They passed the usual mix of haberdasheries, hardware stores, grocers and greengrocers, butchers with sawdust-covered floors and cafés with painted signs advertising mixed grills, light refreshments, Peters Ice Cream, Jusfrute cordials and soft drinks on ice.

Berlin pointed to a tall concrete tower ahead in the distance. 'Another war memorial?'

'Water tower. Tallest thing in town, about a hundred feet high. Holds seventy-five thousand gallons. We've got that, a stock saleyard, a train station, one lousy picture theatre and not much else. Thank God Albury is just across the river.'

'You've got yourselves an armed robbery.'

Roberts smiled. 'That's right, I suppose things are looking up.'

NINE

Roberts made a right turn off High Street onto South Street, passing a small post office with a row of red telephone boxes out the front. He drove a short distance before parking the Dodge outside the fence bordering the loco sheds, in front of a mangled wire gate with a sign that read VICTORIAN RAILWAYS – NO ENTRY.

A neat little two-door pre-war Austin 8 Tourer with a canvas soft-top was parked across the road. Berlin had seen a lot of vehicles like it in England, as well as the four-door hard-top model. The RAF used them as staff cars, painted matt grey-green with air-force roundels on the front mudguards. This Austin was in perfect condition, with sparkling chrome bumpers, a brand-new canopy and a shiny light grey paint job.

Roberts led Berlin between large goods carriages, over a maze of crisscrossing steel railway lines. At the sound of a loud whistle the constable put out his hand and stopped Berlin. A locomotive hauling empty goods wagons lumbered past them in a cloud of steam and smoke. Berlin watched the thick wooden sleepers that supported the steel rails flex in their bed of stone ballast as the massive engine passed over them. From the cab of the locomotive a grim-faced man wearing denim overalls and a soft cap stared down at them, ignoring a friendly wave from Roberts.

'Miserable-looking bastard,' Berlin said after the last wagon had rattled past.

'That's Cec Champion. He's got a right to be miserable, Mr Berlin. His oldest son was a commando – got captured in the islands and the Japs cut his head off with a sword. Someone took a photo and it turned up in the wallet of a dead Nip. It was in the papers a while back. Cec is a fireman – he shovels coal all day and drinks all night, poor bugger.'

Berlin remembered seeing the photo in *The Argus* – a bunch of grinning Japanese soldiers holding rifles taller than themselves gathered around a kneeling blindfolded young lad. A soldier stood behind him, stripped to the waist and holding a long, curved sword in a two-handed grip. It was an image guaranteed to stop a father smiling forever.

When the tracks were clear Roberts led the way across to the main section of the yards. The locomotives, the buildings and even the railway workers, with their oilcans and giant spanners, were the same shade of drab grey. Black ash and cinders crunched under Berlin's feet as they passed stationary engines that sighed and groaned like great beasts and emitted irregular, sudden bursts of steam that swirled around the massive steel driving wheels.

A tall, corrugated-iron building that reminded Berlin of an aircraft hangar housed a soot-blackened locomotive and tender and several other engines parked over deep pits. Further along the tracks another locomotive was being swung around on a giant turntable for the trip back to Melbourne. Behind the maintenance area was a long row of low buildings that housed administration offices and storerooms for freight. Roberts led Berlin towards a doorway surrounded by several uniformed police officers.

A battered flyscreen door marked PAY OFFICE lay in the dirt, torn off its hinges. The policemen looked on while another man crouched down, examining the ground. The man was rangy and lean, his skin a shade of deep blue-black Berlin had never seen before. He was wearing a faded flannel shirt, old overalls and battered army boots. The sleeves had been ripped off the shirt and his arms were all muscle and sinew. Berlin watched as he carefully flicked ash and dirt aside with his index finger and tilted his head to one side to study the ground. Berlin and Roberts joined the group just as the man stood up and shook his head.

'No good, Boss. Tracks all mixed up long time. Too many policemans walk all round, bugger 'im up.'

'Call yourself a fucking blacktracker, Jacky, you useless Abo bastard.' The speaker wore a police uniform with sergeant's stripes.

Berlin saw a hard glint in the dark-skinned man's eyes just before he smiled. The man's teeth were startlingly white against his black face.

'Jacky him no fucking blacktracker, Boss. I tell you, Jacky woodcutter. Dis blackfella him tree feller.'

Berlin laughed at the joke and the group turned towards him. No one else seemed to get it.

The black man's eyes locked on Berlin's for a brief moment. Then he broke his gaze, squatted back down and examined the ground some more.

'Berlin, get your arse over here.'

Berlin walked across to the sergeant, who slowly looked him up and down. Probably pushing forty, Berlin guessed, and pushing it hard. The red, perspiring face and protruding belly said the sergeant liked a good feed and the drink that went with it.

'So you're the DC sent up from town to show us how to do it? I'm Corrigan, and I'm in charge here.' He pointed at the stripes on his sleeve to make his message clear. 'And just so we understand each other, Berlin, you're here under sufferance to investigate this robbery so I don't want you giving me any trouble. Do your job as quick as you can, keep your trap shut and your nose out of things that don't concern you and then bugger off back to the city.' Corrigan pulled a wrinkled handkerchief from his pocket and mopped his face. Then he lifted his cap and ran the sweaty cloth over his bald head.

'You're the boss.'

'You got that right, Berlin.'

'And I'll be more than happy to get out of your hair as soon as I possibly can.'

Corrigan's eyes narrowed slightly as he tried to work out from the tone of Berlin's voice whether he was having a go at him.

'Young Roberts you've met, and don't you go teaching the boy any bad habits. Over yonder are constables Hooper and Eddy.'

The two policemen nodded towards Berlin and then went back to watching the blacktracker. They both looked bored.

'First Constable Hogan is minding the desk back at the police station. You'll meet him later.'

'I can't wait.'

Corrigan stared hard at the detective constable, trying to work out if he was taking the piss again but he couldn't read his expression.

'Any chance you can fill me in on what happened here, Sarge? And then I'd like to take a look at the damage, get an idea of the lay of the land.'

The sergeant led him into the pay office, walking right over the broken screen door. Berlin took one last look around outside. Constables Hooper and Eddy were now leaning on a wall out of the sun, smoking and chatting, and Berlin saw the squatting blacktracker scoop something shiny from the dirt and casually pocket it. He glanced up and saw Berlin watching him.

'Two bob, Boss. My lucky day, eh? Baccy money, okay?'

Berlin shrugged. With several thousand pounds missing, who cared if some bloke scooped up a two-shilling coin from the dust.

Inside the dingy, low-roofed office a couple of flyspecked bulbs in the ceiling illuminated three wooden desks and several cane-bottomed wooden swivel chairs. A grimy electric jug sat on a bench in one corner, near enamel mugs and a bag of sugar with a teaspoon in it. Flies buzzed noisily round the lip of a tin billycan half-full of milk. A massive Remington typewriter and an adding machine lay on the floor, amid a scattering of foolscap pages, buff pay envelopes, overturned inkwells and some shiny brass shell casings. Berlin's nose wrinkled at the familiar smell of burnt gunpowder.

'Made a right brothel of the place, didn't they?' the sergeant said. 'Fancy a brew, Berlin? Roberts, get the water on, boy.'

The young constable took the jug outside to look for a tap while Berlin studied the office.

'Can you tell me what happened, Sarge?'

'Not a lot to tell, really. Since the robberies, the paymaster's been varying his routine from payday to payday – this time he wanted the payroll brought in a day early. So we got the cash out around five this morning, before the bank officially opened for business.'

'Who's we?'

'Paymaster and his offsider, me and two constables.'

'Armed?'

'On payroll escort I always issue revolvers. And the paymaster had a little automatic, not that it did him any good. Anyway, we get here around quarter past five, drag the cash inside and then me and my boys head off home for breakfast. Right in the middle of my porridge there's a phone call and by the time we get back here it's all over.'

'Nice timing.'

'You can say that again. Five blokes on motorcycles, according to the paymaster's offsider, army-style mechanic's coveralls and Tommy guns. One of them fired a burst into the ceiling to get everyone's attention.'

'It would definitely do that.'

'That's the clerk's version anyway, what he told Constable Hooper. The paymaster, name of Owen McGill, might say something different but he's unconscious over at Albury Base Hospital.'

'He get shot?'

The sergeant shook his head. 'No, but he made the mistake of going for his gun and then trying to tackle one of them. Knocked the bloody screen door off its hinges and they were rolling around outside in the gravel until one of the other bastards biffed McGill in the face with a gun butt.'

'That must have hurt.'

'Too damn right. If you stand on anything crunchy round here it might be one of his teeth. Silly bugger'll be drinking Bonox for breakfast, lunch and tea for the next few months, they reckon.'

'Where's this paymaster's assistant? I need to have a chat with him.'

'Gone home, probably needed to change his trousers. His name's Janeway. Roberts can organise for him to come in to the station for an interview.' The sergeant smiled. 'You'll probably enjoy that. Now if you'll excuse me I need to go and shake hands with the wife's best friend.'

There was a bulge in the back pocket of the sergeant's trousers that even his jacket couldn't hide. Probably more in need of a quick belt from that hip flask than a piss, Berlin guessed. Roberts came back with the jug and plugged it in.

'Moody bastard, your sergeant.'

'He'll be better after . . .'

'After he takes a leak?'

Berlin had worked with a lot of coppers who were moody and irritable all morning until a quick visit to the dunny or a trip outside to 'pick something up' restored their equilibrium.

Roberts put the billycan up to his nose, sniffed and grimaced. 'Want me to pop over to the station tearooms and see if I can get us some fresh milk?'

'That'd be good.'

Alone in the office, Berlin scanned the room carefully. Something crunched under the piles of paper on the floor as he moved around. Teeth? he wondered. But when he bent down and lifted the papers he saw that he'd stepped on a pair of wire-rimmed glasses. Great, he thought, a bespectacled paymaster with a little automatic taking on bandits waving Tommy guns. That was never going to end well for the paymaster.

The centre of the Masonite ceiling was blackened and pitted, probably from the burst of Tommy gun fire. Berlin studied it for a minute or two before turning his attention back to the floor.

There was a lump under a scattered pile of pay envelopes near one of the desks. He moved the envelopes aside with the toe of his shoe, revealing the paymaster's little automatic pistol. The gun was a .32-calibre Browning, compact but at close range quite deadly. As he bent over to pick it up, he heard footsteps outside the office. He straightened up and was slipping the automatic into his pocket when someone called from the doorway, 'Hold it right there, copper.'

Berlin turned towards the voice and was blinded by a brilliant white flash.

TEN

Berlin's hand tightened around the butt of the gun. His pupils had contracted at the brightness, and the figure in the doorway was only a silhouette at first. Slowly the details began to emerge. It was a woman and she was holding a camera with a round silver flash reflector mounted on one side.

'Sorry, DC Berlin, too good a shot to miss.'

The woman pressed a button on the back of the reflector and the used flashbulb fell to the floor. She was wearing high-waisted, loose-fitting trousers with a matching jacket, and a figure-hugging argyle jumper underneath. Berlin had never liked trousers on a woman. It might have been okay during the war, when women had to do men's work, but all that business was over now.

'And who the hell might you be?'

There was a canvas satchel slung over the woman's shoulder. She rummaged inside for something and Berlin used the time to study her face. She was slightly tanned, with shoulder-length auburn hair, full lips and prominent cheekbones. Probably in her mid-twenties, Berlin decided, and quite beautiful. His eyes dropped to her chest and when they came up again she was staring straight at him.

'You just window-shopping or planning on making me an offer?'

Berlin was taken off guard by her comment but recovered quickly. 'I'm not in the market at the moment.'

'If you say so, Charlie.' She handed him a business card. 'Or do you prefer Charles? Charles is a bit formal though, don't you think?'

'I prefer DC Berlin.' He glanced at the card. 'I didn't know *The Argus* had women crime reporters, Miss . . . Green. Oh, I see – social diarist.'

'You can call me Rebecca. And why can't a woman cover crime?'

'Sometimes things can get a bit ugly, Miss Green.'

'I could tell you tales from the Melbourne social scene that would leave you white and shaking, DC Berlin. And I was up in Darwin when the Japs attacked the last time. I know what a person looks like when a bomb's gone off on top of them.'

'What the hell were you doing in Darwin?'

'Developing and printing reconnaissance photographs for the RAAF. Leading Aircraftwoman Green, Women's Auxiliary Air-Force Photographic Section.' She saluted Berlin casually. 'Retired.'

'That's a pretty ropey salute.'

'Probably why I stayed an LAC. Attitude problems, they said. I just thought I had a low tolerance for dills.'

Berlin smiled. 'And you're covering this story for *The Argus*, Miss Green?'

'Somewhat of a grey area there actually, DC Berlin. You ever heard of Russell Drysdale?'

Berlin shook his head.

'He's a painter. Used to live around here and came back during the war. Did some wonderfully evocative paintings of servicemen in the area, very distinctive style. Good landscapes too – won the Wynne this year.'

'Won the Wynne, eh? Good for him.'

'Anyway, I want to do something a bit more serious than debutante balls and weddings so I talked my editor into letting me do an arts piece on Drysdale and here I am, the only city reporter on the spot to cover a major payroll robbery.'

'So you're not officially covering the story for *The Argus*?'

'Well, let's just say I'm here officially for *The Argus* and right now I'm covering the story.'

'Alright, let's just say that.'

'Good. And it's a great story – this motorcycle gang racing around the highways and byways at will, staging hold-ups like a modern-day Kelly gang, and the police falling over their feet trying to stop them. It's got page one written all over it.'

'You're an ambitious young lady, Miss Green.'

'Nothing wrong with wanting a by-line on the news pages, DC Berlin, instead of way down the back with the society snaps of shower teas and engagement parties.'

'Won't you be taking a job away from a man who needs it – someone with a family to support?'

'And who's going to support me, DC Berlin? As soon as the war was over we were all suddenly supposed to go back to knitting, and cleaning and cooking dinner for hubby and making babies, and being grateful for it. That's not going to be enough for a lot of women, and not for me, that's for sure.'

'How's your editor going to take all this, when he finds out what you're really up to?'

'If I bring back a good enough story on this motorcycle gang then he'll just have to grin and bear it. So have you managed to solve the crime in the five minutes you've been here?'

This woman was really starting to annoy him, he decided. 'Why would I tell you if I had, Miss Green?'

'Well, for starters, because there are two ways to write the caption for the photograph I just took. "DC Hot on the Trail of the Kelly Country Crime Kings – Arrests Expected Soon", or "Incompetent Copper Stumbles Through Crime Scene – No Leads Yet". Which would you prefer?'

'Kelly Country Crime Kings?'

'I'm looking for a hook, DC Berlin, an angle for the story. I need a nickname for the gang – what do you think?'

'I think you'll be back on the debutante circuit in no time with that one, Miss Green. But I'm only really interested in whether you're going to keep out of my way, or whether I have to phone your editor and let him know what you're up to.'

'Let's not go getting our knickers in a twist, DC Berlin. I think we might be able to help each other out here. And please call me Rebecca.'

'I really don't see how you can help me, Miss Green . . . Rebecca.'

'Well, in return for being kept informed about the progress of your investigations I might have something you'd find very interesting.'

'And what might you have that I'd be interested in?'

'Aside from the obvious, would a photograph of our gang of robbers in action this morning fit the bill?'

ELEVEN

The Wodonga police station was housed in an old single-storey, tin-roofed brick bungalow on High Street. It was a rabbit warren of cramped offices piled high with paperwork, and Roberts led Berlin through to a small room at the back.

'This is where you'll be working, Mr Berlin. I tidied it up as much as I could.'

An empty desk, a chair, an ice chest, a sink and an electric jug took up most of the space in the room. With the two men inside there was barely room to move.

'Maybe I should set up shop in one of the cells, Roberts.'

'It is a bit cramped, Mr Berlin, I'm sorry about that. It's sort of actually the tearoom, but it's the best we could do given the short notice. Sergeant Corrigan moved into the detective's office a while back.'

Berlin dropped his folder on the desk. 'It's fine.' He thought about the tiny space given to the navigators on the Lancs – and they'd had to read maps and find their way to a target halfway across Europe and back again, at night. All he had to do was solve some robberies.

He opened his wallet and took out a ten-shilling note. That only left him with three pounds so he'd need to get to the bank at some stage. 'Any chance you might be able to dig me up a sandwich, Constable Roberts? Ham, cheese and tomato.'

'No worries, Mr Berlin, there's a café just up the street.'

Ten minutes later Roberts was back with two brown paper bags. One held a ham, cheese and tomato sandwich and the second a vanilla slice. The lad *was* smart.

Berlin ate lunch at his desk, reading witness statements and pinpointing the location of the gang's robberies with brass drawing pins on a wall map, looking for a pattern or a common thread. But the only thing that the sites had in common was that they were all connected to the railways and they were all on the northern line, which he already knew from the file.

He was grateful for the interruption when Constable Hooper put his head round the office door. 'The paymaster's offsider is here, DC Berlin. I'll send him straight in, shall I?'

Vivian Janeway was around twenty-five, very thin and awkward, with pale skin, a prematurely receding hairline and a nervous tic under his left eye. The slow and deliberate way the man moved his angular body reminded Berlin of a praying mantis. Janeway was neatly dressed in a three-piece suit with a Windsor knot in the pale blue tie that matched his pocket handkerchief. When he sat down opposite Berlin he nervously folded his hands on the desk. His nails were manicured, Berlin noted.

'No need to be nervous, Mr Janeway, we just need you to answer a few questions. My name's Berlin, Charlie Berlin.'

Janeway nodded his head rapidly.

'Ever been in a police station before, Mr Janeway?'

'No, never, why do ask – what's that got to do with the robbery?' The answer was blurted out in one long, continuous breath.

'No reason. I was just making conversation.'

Berlin had picked Janeway as a queer the moment he walked in the door. He was almost certainly lying about never having been in a police station before but Berlin couldn't blame him. What was it about the gentleness of some queers that drove his fellow policemen into such fits of rage? Berlin knew Janeway would have been beaten bloody in the cells on more than one occasion, just for sport on a quiet Saturday night.

'Just tell me what happened, Mr Janeway, and take your time. Can I get you a cup of tea?'

Janeway shook his head. 'No, thank you, I'm fine. I've already told the local police what happened, Mr Berlin, when they spoke to me earlier, just after the event. I'm sure you could look at their notes. Mr Hooper, the gentleman who interviewed me, was very precise in his questioning. He seems to be very good at his job.'

Berlin opened his notebook. 'Sometimes we forget things, Mr Janeway – witnesses, I mean. What you went through must have been quite nerve-racking. I've read the notes but sometimes things come back to us later so I find it helps to go over it again.'

'Very well, Mr Berlin.'

'For instance, Mr Janeway, I've been wondering why you didn't hear the motorcycles coming and just lock the money in the safe.'

'That's easy. As I told Mr Hooper, the first sign we had of the robbers was when one of them burst in the door of the pay office and told us to put our hands up. It was after that we heard the bikes smashing through the gate into the yard.'

That fitted the pattern, the leader going in first on foot, ahead of the motorcycles.

'Your assailant, you described him to Constab . . . Mr Hooper as six feet, medium build, wearing black-dyed coveralls, army boots, brown leather gauntlets and a balaclava, that right?'

'Yes, exactly.'

'And he had a very big gun.'

'Yes indeed, a Thompson submachine gun, the M1928 model .45 ACP calibre, with the 100-round drum magazine.'

'That's a remarkably precise description, Mr Janeway.'

'The M1928 is easy to pick because of the front handgrip, Mr Berlin. They took it off the later M1928A1 models to simplify manufacture and reduce costs. We used the earlier model quite extensively until the Owen Machine Carbine became readily available.'

'We?'

'I was in the army, Mr Berlin.'

Berlin looked up from his notebook. 'Yes, of course. And the robber fired his M1928 into the ceiling, is that correct?'

'That's right. Owen – Mr McGill, the paymaster – was somewhat tardy in complying with his instructions.'

'I'm guessing firing that Thompson had the desired effect.'

'The noise was dreadful, deafening. I fell to the ground and covered my ears.'

'You hadn't heard gunfire before? In the army?'

Janeway searched the tone of the question for any hints of sarcasm or irony or disbelief but found none. Policemen were usually easy for Janeway to read but this Berlin fellow was different. He wasn't looking at him with disgust and he was treating him with respect. Janeway relaxed a little and decided he wasn't going to get a beating today.

'I heard gunfire in training, of course, Mr Berlin, and in New Guinea. But that was outside, and in the jungle. It's very much louder in an enclosed space, surprisingly so.'

'You were in New Guinea?'

'Yes, Mr Berlin. Over there it was mostly just the odd sniper shooting at us from a distance, though sometimes we were mortared, or bombed from the air. I was in the Quartermaster Corp so we were usually many miles from the real hand-to-hand fighting, you understand.'

'Of course.' Berlin made a note on the pad on his desk. 'Can you tell me what led to McGill winding up in hospital?'

Janeway briefly pursed his lips before he spoke. 'Stupidity is what it was, plain and simple. After they took out the last of the money we were alone with the leader of the gang for a brief moment. Mr McGill took out his pistol but the man saw him and knocked it out of his hand. I thought Mr McGill's action rather ill-considered under the circumstances. Then he tackled the robber and they fell out the door. They finished up wrestling in the dirt in front of the rest of the gang.'

'You didn't think to pick up the pistol, Mr Janeway?'

'It was five against two, Mr Berlin, and besides, I'm a pacifist.'

'War can do that to a man.'

Janeway again searched the comment for sarcastic or derisory undertones but it sounded like this Berlin fellow had made it simply as a statement of fact.

'One of the other robbers then struck Mr McGill with the butt of his weapon. The leader seemed quite upset by this.'

'Upset?'

'Perturbed that Mr McGill might be seriously injured, I suppose is a better description. He yelled at his mate that he shouldn't have done that – that no one was supposed to get hurt. He told me to call an ambulance immediately, which I did, of course. Then they took off.'

'Do you think you could possibly identify this man, perhaps by his voice?'

Janeway had carefully noted the colour of the robber's eyes and the shape of his lips through the openings in the balaclava, and the pitch and cadence of his speech. He knew he would have absolutely no trouble in identifying him but this Berlin character, nice as he seemed, was still a police officer. He shook his head. 'I'm sorry, Mr Berlin, but I very much doubt it.'

Berlin stood up and shook Janeway's hand. 'Thank you very much for coming in, Mr Janeway. I appreciate your assistance.'

'Thank you, DC Berlin. I'm happy to help in any way I can.'

Hooper stuck his head in the doorway a few minutes later. 'Creeping Jesus has left, I see.'

'Who?'

'Janeway. We call him Creeping Jesus round town. Shirt-lifter you reckon, DC Berlin?'

'I wouldn't know.'

'Bastard gives me the willies.'

'That's funny, Hooper,' Berlin said, 'he speaks quite highly of you. Can you get me Albury Base Hospital on the phone, please?'

TWELVE

The charge nurse at the hospital told Berlin that McGill was still unconscious, and almost certainly had concussion. She volunteered the opinion that even when he regained consciousness he probably wouldn't know if he was Arthur or Martha for a few days.

Berlin spent the rest of that afternoon on the phone, talking to the detectives at Wangaratta about the robberies. The details were the same in every location: five men in balaclavas, motorcycles, Tommy guns, shocked witnesses. These guys certainly had their routine down pat. They got in, got the money and got out, and until this morning no one had been hurt.

At around half-past five Berlin realised the other coppers had gone for the day and went looking for Constable Roberts. The boy had the Dodge parked out front and as he climbed into the passenger seat, Berlin saw a couple of brown paper parcels in the back, tied with string.

'I picked you up some shaving gear and soap from the chemist. Plus underpants, singlets and a towel from the haberdashery. They'll send the accounts to the police station.'

'That's going above and beyond, Roberts. Keep it up and you'll be police commissioner before you turn forty.'

Roberts grinned. 'Jeez, Mr Berlin, I wasn't planning on waiting that long. Want me to run you out to your hotel now?'

'That sounds good. I've got a meeting later. You know a pub called the Diggers Rest Hotel?'

Roberts started the engine. 'As a matter of fact that's where we're headed, Mr Berlin. The sergeant organised you a room there and the publican's wife is a pretty good cook. Plus they're very flexible when it comes to the licensing laws.'

'Even for coppers?'

Roberts turned the car across the street. 'Especially for coppers.'

Berlin offered the constable a cigarette but the boy shook his head.

'What do we know about Rebecca Green, Roberts?'

'The lady with the camera?'

'That's the one. I'm supposed to meet her to look at a photograph later.'

'Blew into town a few days back. Says she works for *The Argus* down in Melbourne. She's been driving all over the countryside in her Austin, asking a lot of questions.'

'About the robberies?'

Roberts nodded. 'And some painter. She's a bit of a looker.'

'If you say so.'

'A few of the blokes round here have tried putting the acid on her, but she's knocked them all back. Sergeant Corrigan reckons —' Roberts stopped himself.

'Sergeant Corrigan reckons what?'

Roberts shifted uncomfortably behind the steering wheel.

'The sergeant reckons she might be one of those . . . you know, since she wears trousers most of the time and won't have a bar of any of the blokes.'

'A lesbian?'

'I suppose so.'

Roberts was blushing. 'C'mon, Constable, you'll need to toughen up if you ever intend to work in the big smoke.'

'Oh, cripes,' Roberts said. 'This is all I bloody need.'

Berlin glanced over at the constable, who was staring straight ahead, shaking his head slowly from side to side. A horse-drawn, two-wheeled cart was moving rapidly towards them on the opposite side of the road. As it drew nearer Berlin leaned forward and squinted. 'What the hell is that?'

The driver was standing upright in the cart, holding the reins with his right hand and swaying from side to side with the motion of the vehicle. He was dressed in flowing white fabric that wrapped around his body, had a shiny metal helmet on his head and was enthusiastically waving his galloping horse on with a sword that looked like it was made from half a broomstick.

The cart went speeding past them and Berlin could see two silver milk churns in the back.

'That's Trev Casterton, our local milkman. He gets a bit pissed and every so often decides to practise for the milkos' Roman chariot race at the Albury Show. Nicks a bed sheet off someone's clothesline and whacks on a brass helmet he pinched from the fire station.'

'He looks like he's more than a bit pissed,' Berlin said.

'Generally gets on the turps as soon as he finishes his milk deliveries, gives it a real hammering some days. Someone usually phones the station when he finally passes out and I have to go and collect him and drive the cart back to the dairy.'

'You want to go get him now?'

'If you don't mind. He looks like he's about ready to keel over.'

They caught up with the charioteer a mile down the road. The horse was calmly grazing on the grassy verge and Trevor Casterton was curled up on the floor of the cart, snoring contentedly, his arm wrapped round an empty milk churn. The two men got out of the Dodge.

'Can you handle a horse, Mr Berlin?'

'Are you pulling my leg, Roberts?'

'You should have a go.'

'I'm a city copper, and apart from duty at Flemington Racecourse on Melbourne Cup Day, I've never been near a horse in my life.'

'It's easy, you'll see. The dairy's straight ahead out on the Tallangatta road and Jesse knows the way, and she'll actually be looking forward to getting home.'

'Who the hell is Jesse?'

'That's Trev's horse, she's a darling. You just have to hold the reins and give her a "gee-up" and a "whoa" and she'll do the rest – trust me.'

'I do trust you, Roberts, but I'm not here to upset the smooth running of Sergeant Corrigan's station, so if it's your job to take Jesse home you should hop to it.'

Roberts was right about the horse wanting to get home, and with the Dodge following behind they got to the dairy without incident. The milko was singing happily to himself as Roberts helped him onto a battered couch on the dairy's porch to sleep it off. Berlin slid over to the passenger side as Roberts walked back to the car.

'One more chorus of "Old MacDonald Had A Farm" and I was about ready to throttle the bugger.' He put the car into gear and backed the Dodge carefully out onto the roadway. 'She handles well, eh? You can take her any time you want, you know.'

Berlin wasn't likely to take Roberts up on the offer. He didn't own a car and he hardly ever drove these days. And he never, ever drove with passengers. Berlin had sworn he wouldn't take responsibility for another person's life again for as long as he lived.

THIRTEEN

The two-storey Diggers Rest Hotel was out on the causeway connecting Albury and Wodonga. Built in the 1860s and set well back from the roadway, it was a solid-looking stone structure, flanked by stands of eucalypts and fronted by a gravel car park. Since it was past six, the front door of the hotel was shut and the windows of the public bar were dark, but for a closed hotel the car park was remarkably busy. Half a dozen utes and farm trucks were lined up, nose in to the hotel's verandah. Two stock horses, still saddled, were tied up to a verandah post and a couple of wiry red cattle dogs snoozed under a wooden seat.

Roberts drove the Dodge cautiously across the gravel and turned right at the end of the row of parked cars. He stopped next to a white open-topped jeep with MILITARY POLICE painted under the windshield. A couple of khaki slouch hats lay on the front seats.

'Trouble inside, you reckon?'

Roberts shook his head. 'Sergeant Whitmore and one of his offsiders from out at the Bandiana Army Camp. He cruises through town around closing most nights to keep an eye on things and then hangs out here for a bit. It's one of his regular watering holes. Let's get inside, you must be hungry. After we get you sorted I'm off home for tea.'

'Let me shout you a beer first.'

Roberts shook his head. 'No thanks, I'm teetotal. I took the pledge when I turned eighteen. My mum wanted me to, and with the old man, you know . . .'

'Fair enough. How about a lemon squash then?'

Roberts opened the driver's side door. 'Sorry, but my landlady doesn't make allowances for latecomers. If I'm not there right on time then the dog gets my dinner.'

A single bulb lit up a sign above the side door, HOTEL GUESTS ONLY. Roberts knocked and for a minute Berlin thought Sergeant Corrigan had opened the door.

'Berlin, right? You met my brother, Barry, this morning I think. The local sergeant. We're twins. I'm Vern, Vernon Corrigan.'

Berlin put out his hand then realised that Vernon Corrigan's right arm stopped at the elbow.

'Hand grenade. Happened back in militia training. Held onto the bastard of a thing a wee bit too long.' He winked and smiled. 'Used to be a bit of a larrikin in my youth, DC Berlin, but now, as Barry likes to say, I'm "armless".'

Berlin could smell whisky on Corrigan's breath and the smile on his face didn't match the look in his eyes, which was hard, calculating and bitter.

'Come on along down to the dining room and we'll fix you up with a drink and some tucker. She's steak tonight, and boiled spuds and caulie with white sauce . . . Lil!' he yelled at the top of his voice. 'One more for tea. It's the Melbourne copper.'

'That mean I get the good beef?'

'It's all good here, sport. The wife's a cracker cook and your tea's the arse end of a steer that was grazing down by the Murray not too long back. Can't get fresher than that. Good beef's my speciality and I get it at the right price.'

Berlin hung his coat and hat on a hook in the hallway, alongside some jackets, caps and scarves. He wondered about leaving the little automatic in his overcoat pocket, but decided in a country town it would be safe.

Corrigan led him down the corridor and into a parlour. The room contained a couple of sagging sofas, a radiogram, an upright piano and a coffee table strewn with copies of *Picture Post* magazine and tattered *Beano* and *Magnet* comics. Linen-covered copies of *Khaki and Green*, *H.M.A.S.*, *These Eagles* and other army, navy and air-force wartime annuals lined a bookshelf. The books, published by the Australian War Memorial, were full of paintings, sketches and photographs of servicemen and women on active duty, accompanied by stories, poems and uplifting essays. They were meant to reassure the anxious families left behind that beauty and creativity flourished amongst the slaughter.

Two small boys, aged around five and six, were sitting on the floor in front of the radiogram, listening intently to a radio serial. They were wearing pyjamas, dressing gowns and slippers, and their wet, neatly combed hair and shining faces, along with the smell of Sunlight soap, suggested they were fresh out of the bath.

'Them's me lads,' Corrigan said, 'plus we've got a new bub – a wee girl. Now you little buggers, soon as Biggles is over get off to bed. And make sure your mum gives you your Hypol first.'

The boys groaned and inwardly Berlin groaned with them. He remembered the disgusting ritual of the tablespoon of greasy, grey cod-liver oil his grandmother had forced on him and his brother every evening in autumn and winter.

Through a set of glass doors there was a private dining room with a fireplace, a dozen or so tables and a bar along one wall. Men drinking alone occupied half the tables, while a couple of blokes in faded plaid shirts, dusty moleskin trousers and worn-down, elastic-sided riding boots were sitting together eating dinner. Drovers just back from delivering a mob of cattle to the saleyards, Berlin guessed – the owners of the horses and dogs outside, and possibly the source of the hotel's freshly slaughtered steer at a good price.

Two men in army uniforms were leaning on the bar. The older of the pair stood well over six feet and was wearing standard-issue khaki trousers and a military tunic with sergeant's chevrons on the sleeves. His belt, webbing and pistol holster were white, indicating he was with the Provost Corps – the military police. The younger man next to him, a private, was wearing the standard-issue khaki belt.

'Get you a drink there, DC Berlin?' Corrigan shouted as he slid behind a buxom barmaid with platinum blonde hair, who giggled and loudly whispered, 'Behave yourself!' when he patted her rear.

The sergeant turned and looked in Berlin's direction when the landlord called out his name. Berlin noted the triple row of ribbons over the left chest pocket of the sergeant's tunic. He felt he was being sized up as competition by a man who thought he owned the bar. It was a look he'd seen before in pubs and more often than not it finished in a fight. The sergeant had the casual grace of a man relaxed and comfortable in his own skin. His face had the appearance of having run into a fist or two in the past and Berlin was surprised when it was split by a friendly but slightly cocky grin and a wink, before he turned back to his drink.

'Maisie here pulls a good beer if you fancy one,' Corrigan continued, 'and there's whisky and some bourbon I got in for visiting Yank officers back in the good old days.'

'A whisky'll be fine,' Berlin said.

Corrigan glanced under the bar. 'We've got gin too, I think, if bloody Sergeant Whitmore there hasn't drunk it all, and there's sherry for the ladies and poofters, not that we get many of those.'

'Probably more than you imagine, Vern.' As the sergeant spoke he turned and smiled at the stockmen, raised his glass in a toast and then emptied it. He turned back to the bar and held up the empty glass. 'Can you gimme another, Maisie? There's a good girl.'

'You bloody calling us poofters, mate?' One of the stockmen pushed his chair back and was getting to his feet.

Whitmore turned to face him and shrugged. 'Long, lonely nights on the track with just a mob of cattle, your faithful dogs and only each other for company. Flickering firelight, star-filled skies. Young love is bound to blossom.'

The second drover was on his feet now. 'Fuck you, arsehole.'

Whitmore smiled. 'I think you've made my case. But I fancy someone a wee bit younger, and a tad better looking.'

The younger drover was sizing up the sergeant. 'You're pretty tough with that gun on your hip.'

As Whitmore began undoing his webbing belt, Corrigan placed a short iron bar on the counter top.

'Take it outside, gentlemen. I don't need any trouble in here.'

'Look after this lot for five minutes, will ya Private Champion?'

Whitmore handed his pistol holster and webbing to the second soldier, unbuttoned his tunic, neatly folded it and laid it across the back of one of the chairs. Berlin was expecting a more muscular torso and was surprised at how slim and pale the sergeant's body was under his singlet.

The two stockmen were halfway to the door leading out to the parlour when Whitmore called after them.

'Boys, I fear I may have done you both a disservice by calling you poofters and I apologise.'

Both stockmen turned, the older of the two slowly shaking his head. 'That'd be right you gutless prick, trying to weasel your way out of a blue.'

'I can clearly see now that you boys aren't poofters at all,'

Whitmore continued. 'You two would have to be the biggest pair of cow fuckers I've ever seen.'

The older drover lunged towards the soldier, pushing a table sideways. Beer splashed from a glass, there were angry murmurs and a distressed, 'Fair go, cobber,' from the man who had lost his drink. A couple of the drinkers leapt up and fronted the drover, holding him back.

Corrigan smacked the iron bar down hard on the counter. 'Take it outside boys, *now*!'

Whitmore smiled at the woman behind the bar. 'Maisie, darling, give Terry there another beer on me, will ya. And don't forget my gin and tonic, there's a good girl.' He glanced across at Berlin, his eyes full of mischief, before following the two stockmen out the door.

Behind the bar Corrigan held up a bottle of Johnnie Walker and Berlin nodded.

FOURTEEN

'I'm Lily, Vern's wife. Here's your tea, Mr Berlin.'

Lily was a slight, almost bird-like creature, with thin, wispy red hair plastered to her head by the heat of the kitchen. Berlin thought that she was either forty or had lived a very hard thirty. He decided it was the latter. There was a tired, resigned look in her eyes and fading evidence of a bruise on her right cheek. She put two plates on the table in front of him.

'Thanks, Lily. Looks good.'

The smaller plate held two slabs of white bread heavily smeared with butter. On the dinner plate was an inch-thick piece of steak with blackened edges, half a dozen boiled potatoes and a soggy mass of cauliflower drowning in white sauce.

'There's salt and mustard over on the sideboard. Pudding's puftaloons with golden syrup. I'll bring it along in a minute. You having a drink?'

'Vern's organising me a whisky, thanks.'

Lily glanced at the bar where Corrigan was whispering something in the ear of the barmaid, who was laughing. Berlin saw Lily's eyes tighten at the corners.

'Enjoy your tea, Mr Berlin.'

Berlin walked over to the sideboard for a pot of hot English mustard and the saltshaker. Back at his table he smeared a yellow dollop of mustard over his steak and sprinkled the potatoes liberally with salt.

Berlin made a habit of eating everything on his plate. He'd known starvation once and had sworn he would never be hungry again. He was freshly back from the war when a young waitress had tried to clear away a plate that still held a crust of bread and Berlin had barely stopped himself from plunging his fork into her hand.

The dinner plate was wiped clean and a second whisky half gone when Rebecca Green came through the glass doors. Every eye in the place followed her as she crossed the room to Berlin's table. He studied her as she walked, estimating her height to be around five feet eight, give or take an inch or two. She had an easy, languid, almost insolent gait.

A couple of the drinkers nudged each other and whispered. Someone laughed.

'In their dreams and my nightmares. Mind if I join you?' She pulled out a chair and sat down before he could answer. Lily appeared beside her a moment later.

'Will you be having something to eat, Miss Green?'

'Not tonight thank you, Lily, but I wouldn't mind a cup of tea. How about you, Berlin?'

He drank the last of his whisky and smiled. 'Sure, why not.'

Lily seemed pleased. 'That's settled then, two teas it is. And your pudding's on its way, Mr Berlin.' She gathered up his empty plates. 'I must say I like a man with a good appetite.'

'Me too.' Rebecca smiled at Berlin. There was a playful glint in her eyes, and her tone made Lily blush. Lily picked up Berlin's plate and hurried back towards the kitchen.

Berlin decided he'd ignore the comment.

Rebecca took off her jacket and slipped it over the back of her chair. 'Bit of a stoush going on in the car park when I pulled up.'

'Really?'

'Sergeant Whitmore from out at Bandiana going at it with a couple of blokes. There's a man who doesn't mind a fight.'

'Is he winning?'

'Didn't look like it to me. He was on his knees vomiting his guts out when I came inside, so probably not. Might need to call the cops.' She smiled at him across the table. She had that glint in her eye again. 'You don't happen to know where I can put my hands on a policeman at short notice, do you, DC Berlin?'

He stood up. 'I think I'd better take a quick look.'

Berlin really didn't know whether Sergeant Whitmore needed his help or not but he wanted to get away from Rebecca Green for a moment. He wasn't used to having to match wits with a woman and he found her banter strangely unsettling.

FIFTEEN

'Lost something?'

Whitmore was on his knees, running his fingers through the gravel. He glanced up.

'Mostly my dinner. But I dropped something in the excitement. Nothing to worry about, just a bit of a lucky charm.' He got slowly to his feet, pausing halfway to brush gravel dust from the knees of his trousers.

'Fag?'

Whitmore looked at Berlin, spat, nodded and took the offered cigarette. Berlin lit the cigarette and his own with the same match. Whitmore took a deep drag and then coughed and spat again. The two men leaned back against the jeep and smoked in silence. Berlin could hear the murmur of the river and the croaking of frogs somewhere in the distance. Whitmore raised one shoulder, twisted his body and grunted.

In the darkness Berlin could just make out the damage to Whitmore's face – a split lip, a quickly blackening eye and gravel rash on one cheek.

'You right? Looks like those blokes gave you curry.'

'Nah, I reckon it was a draw. That young 'un had a good right on him though.'

'You often go looking for trouble like that?'

Whitmore grinned and then grimaced and touched his split lip. 'There's nothing like a bit of a blue to round out the evening.'

'If you say so.'

'You're the copper who flew up from town, right?' The soldier put out his hand. 'I'm Sergeant Whitmore, Pete.'

'DC Berlin, Charlie.'

The two men shook hands. Whitmore's grip was firm but Berlin found his hand surprisingly cold. 'I noticed you had a hell of a lot of ribbons on your tunic, Pete.'

'Yeah, my aunty Gwen runs a haberdashery, I get 'em wholesale. Scuttlebutt round town says you had a war too, Charlie – over in Europe. You get any medals?'

'Just the ones we all got for showing up.'

'A pilot and a POW to boot, I hear. It all sounds very glamorous.'

'Not a lot of glamour from where I was sitting.'

'So, tell me about it. What rank did you reach?'

'I was just a sergeant. Promotion to warrant officer and beyond always seemed to escape me.'

'Good job, too. Pissy rank, WO. Like they say – not really an officer and not quite a gentleman.'

'Where'd you serve, Pete?'

'Up in the Guinea, and the Solomons for a bit. Independent company, then commandos.'

'What does an independent company do?'

'Travels light, lives off the land, hits the enemy where they least expect it.'

'Tough going?'

'Bit of a bugger. A bloke had to fight the jungle as well as the Japanese. Bugs and germs and worms and strange wogs and shitty food and wet rot and tinea and weird fungal infections that made a man look like a mangy dog and smell worse.'

'You in any of the big battles?'

Whitmore shook his head. 'Like I said, hit and run was more our style. Half a dozen blokes staking out a possie on some shitty bush supply track and blasting whoever stumbled past. Empty a mag or two from the Owens, chuck a couple of hand bombs and then piss off quick before the Sons of Heaven could work out who or what'd hit 'em. "Shoot and shoot through" was our motto.'

'Get there, get it done and get the fuck out.' Berlin didn't realise he'd said the words out loud.

'That's the story, Charlie.'

'You coming back inside for a drink, Pete?'

'Nah, probably give it a miss. I know my limit.'

'Yeah, me too.'

'Doesn't stop a bugger going past it, of course, but what's a man gunna do. Reckon you can send Kenny, the young bloke, out? Might have to let him do the driving tonight.'

'Sounds like a good idea. I'll see you later then.'

Whitmore studied Berlin's face for a moment before he smiled. 'Wodonga's a small town so I don't doubt it, Charlie, old son.'

SIXTEEN

Berlin couldn't see the young soldier anywhere in the dining room. He stopped Lily, who was passing by balancing several plates of food.

'The young bloke who was at the bar, the soldier, Kenny, know where he went?'

'He took some empty plates out to the kitchen for me. He's a good lad. Let me fetch him for you.'

'I'll do it, you've got your hands full. Kitchen's through here, right?'

Berlin turned and walked through a narrow passageway. The hotel's kitchen was a large room with a long wooden table in the middle. A huge, black slow-combustion wood stove was set into one wall and there were two large refrigerators and several benches stacked with dishes and cooking utensils.

He almost ran headlong into the young soldier. The boy's face was flushed and he looked upset. Behind him Berlin caught a glimpse of blue fabric and black hair as someone disappeared through a screen door at the rear of the kitchen, slamming it behind them.

'Your sergeant's out in the car park. He's ready to leave.'

The boy pushed past him without speaking.

Rude little bugger, Berlin said to himself.

Back at the table, Rebecca smiled when Berlin sat down. 'Want to go halves on your dessert?'

Berlin looked at the plate of fried scones swimming in golden syrup and shook his head. 'Order your own. I don't like sharing food.'

'Not a good start for someone hoping to see a photograph of the robbers in action. Or wanting to get into my pants, for that matter.'

The comment caught Berlin off guard again. He knew how to handle tarts, but this woman wasn't a tart, even though she talked like one. 'What makes you think I want to get into your pants?'

'Give me your hand.'

Berlin stared at her warily.

'C'mon. I won't bite.'

Berlin slowly extended his left arm across the table. She took his hand, turned it over and placed her fingertips on his wrist for a moment.

'Well, that confirms it. You're a bloke and you definitely have a pulse – that seems to be the criteria for lustful desire in every man I've ever met.'

Berlin moved his arm away, disturbed to find he had enjoyed the touch of her fingertips. 'I'm still not sharing.'

'Suit yourself. But I'm a woman of my word so here's the photograph.'

She lifted her satchel onto her lap and undid the snaps. Under the flap were slots for pens and a place for an ID card.

'Is that a motorcycle dispatch rider's satchel?'

'Yep. Got it in an army disposal store for five bob.'

'Don't you have a real handbag? A purse?'

'It holds everything I need, it was cheap and I think it looks good. Is there a problem?' She fished in her bag and pulled out an envelope.

'No.' He'd never met anyone quite like her before – blunt and plain-spoken like a man but everything else about her was all female, except for the damn trousers and that satchel.

He carefully studied the blurry black-and-white, eight-by-ten inch photograph she handed him. It showed three motorcycles with sidecars turning left just as they raced out of the loco-shed gateway. Two of the motorcycles had a passenger in the sidecar but the third only had a rider, obviously the one holding the loot. The five bandits were wearing dark coveralls, leather gauntlets, black balaclavas and motorcycle goggles. The driver of the lead motorcycle had his head turned towards the camera.

'Where exactly did you take this?'

'Right outside the gates of the loco sheds, just after they grabbed the payroll.'

'And you just happened to be waiting, all on your Pat Malone, at the scene of the crime at exactly the right moment?'

She smiled. 'Old press photographer's motto for a perfect picture – just set your lens to *f11* and be in the right place at the right time.'

'I don't know what *f11* means, Miss Green, but I need to know if your being there was just dumb luck or something else.'

'You think I'm an accomplice to these wicked deeds, DC Berlin? I'm flattered.'

'I don't know much about you, Miss Green.'

'I'm over the age of consent if that's what you're getting at. And it's Rebecca, remember.'

'You talk about sex a lot, Miss Green.'

'I'm not all talk, DC Berlin.'

'If I give you some of my pudding can we change the subject?'

Rebecca started to laugh, and then she looked into his eyes and saw a hint of the pain that lived there and stopped.

'I only want a taste. Puftaloons with golden syrup aren't really my favourite.' She picked up a spoon. 'That Lily is one hell of a good cook.' She dipped her spoon into the dessert bowl. 'And as to me being outside the gate of the loco sheds this morning, I guess it was just good timing.'

Berlin figured she wasn't being straight with him about being at the right place at the right time and, as it turned out, she also liked puftaloons a lot more than she'd let on.

SEVENTEEN

After she'd helped him polish off the puftaloons, Rebecca had excused herself to listen to the ABC news on the radio. Berlin was usually perfectly happy with his own company so he was surprised to find himself wishing she'd stayed a little longer.

He ordered another whisky after she left, and then another after that. Berlin's rule was nothing before two in the afternoon and nothing after midnight. He only drank whisky, preferably Scotch, but he was willing to be flexible. He only drank in pubs and when the pubs were shut, in sly grog joints – if he could find one that wasn't full of drunken coppers. Chater had once asked him why he didn't just buy a bottle to keep at home and Berlin said he'd tried it and discovered that once you opened the bottle, whisky didn't keep.

Around half-past nine he asked Corrigan for his room key and followed the landlord out through the parlour. The hallway floor and stairway banisters both showed signs that they had been painted at some stage in the distant past, but there was little evidence remaining. Upstairs, numbered bedrooms lined both sides of a narrow corridor and on a doorway at the far end the word

BATHROOM was painted in flaking gold letters on frosted glass.

'Dunny's down there to the left of the bathroom. The stove in the kitchen heats the water for up here so it's hottish in the bathroom from around six in the morning and there's a sink with cold water in your room. You need to supply your own soap and towels but if you're short I can lend you some.'

'Thanks,' Berlin said. 'Constable Roberts organised that for me.'

Corrigan opened a door marked 4. 'It's not the bloody Hotel Windsor, but it's clean.'

The room was about twelve feet by eight feet, the floor covered with chipped and flaking green linoleum. There was a fireplace, a double bed with a couple of grey army blankets and a single pillow, a wooden chair and a battered bedside table with a reading light. A shabby wardrobe, which might have been the twin of the one in his room back in Melbourne, leaned against one wall. In the corner, near a window covered by a flyspecked brown roller blind, was a white enamel washbasin with a single tap. Above it was a small shelf holding two water glasses, and above that a mirror.

'No animals allowed, Mr Berlin,' Corrigan said, 'but even if you did have a cat there ain't really room enough to swing it anyway.'

The parcels that had been on the back seat of the Dodge were on the end of the bed.

'The wife must have brought those up. Anything else you need?'

'Can I borrow some Nugget and a shoe brush?'

'Don't bother about that. Just leave your shoes outside the door.'

Berlin didn't trust anyone else to polish his shoes. He glanced at Corrigan's empty sleeve. 'I don't want to put you to any trouble.'

'No trouble for me, mate, the wife'll do 'em. She's already got the kids' school shoes to do anyway plus my boots, so one more pair don't make no never mind.'

'Okay.' It was late and probably not worth arguing over, Berlin decided.

'Breakfast's downstairs at seven sharp: porridge, bacon and eggs, steak and eggs or chops and eggs. But you can have a full mixed grill if you want something substantial.'

'It's sounding more and more like the Windsor every minute, Vern.'

When Corrigan had gone, Berlin raised the roller blind and looked out. His window had a view over the hotel's parking area, out across the roadway and down towards the tree-lined riverbank. Rebecca Green's little Austin was the only vehicle left in the car park.

He walked back to the bed and opened his parcels. One held a shaving brush, soap, a safety razor and Gillette Blue blades, a toothbrush and a tin of toothpowder, a comb and a jar of Brylcreem. The other package contained socks, singlets, underpants and a towel that was carefully cradling a familiar-shaped bottle.

Berlin broke the metal seal, worked the cork free, poured himself a large glass and took a drink. For a teetotaller Constable Roberts had made a good choice – Haig & Haig's Dimple whisky was Berlin's favoured drop. It seemed the boy was well on track for rising through the ranks of the Victoria Police, since the first thing a bloke needed to do was suss out his superior officer's weaknesses. Of course, if Roberts had been a little more astute there might have been a Benzedrine inhaler nestled among the Chesty Bond singlets and underpants.

Berlin wandered down the corridor to the lavatory. It had the familiar carbolic smell of Phenyle disinfectant and in the bathroom next door he could hear water running in the bath and the sound of a woman singing softly. He walked back to the bedroom and reluctantly left his shoes outside the door.

In the room he took off his suit and hung it neatly in the wardrobe, draped his shirt over the back of the chair and pulled off his singlet, socks and underpants. He opened the window, pulled the shade down and got into bed. He lay there wondering if it was Rebecca he had heard singing in the bath. His watch told him it was just over an hour to midnight, and he reached for the glass and the bottle of whisky and drank himself to sleep.

At least he thought he was asleep. Sometimes he wasn't sure but Jock's voice was strong and clear and definite. Wilf, the flight engineer, was leaning on the mantelpiece smoking that pipe he thought made him look older. Across the room Lou, the rear gunner, stood at the window, carefully scanning the star-filled sky and wondering aloud why Orion was upside down. The men were wearing their flying suits and sheepskin-lined boots and Berlin was embarrassed by his nakedness. Mick, the knockabout radio operator, and Harry, the cockney bomb-aimer, were listening as Jock, the mid-upper gunner, cracked jokes in his Glasgow accent and told his stories of growing up in the Gorbals, fights with razor gangs and beatings from seven-foot coppers from the highlands with fists like hams. Young Gary, the Canadian navigator, was morose as usual, still pining for Gwen. He kept complaining about being dead and Berlin tried to explain to him that being alive was no picnic either.

Then the rooster in Lily's chook pen crowed, and through the open window shade the brightening sky told Berlin dawn was close.

EIGHTEEN

Berlin felt like death. His head was throbbing, his mouth dry. A hair of the dog would fix that but it was the weariness in his soul he didn't know how to fix.

He washed and dressed then tiptoed down the creaking stairs in his socks, searching out the kitchen and his shoes. The kitchen was warm from the slow-combustion stove that had burned all night. A large black kettle bubbled on its top and there was a teapot ready on the table. Berlin found his shoes in a neat row of work boots and tiny school shoes. They were beautifully polished and there were no signs of any residual Nugget in the stitching or on the eyelets. He slipped them on and as he tied the laces he thought he could hear a woman sobbing.

Berlin took his hat and overcoat from the rack in the hallway and let himself out of the hotel's unlocked side door. There was no sign of frost, but his breath condensed in the chill air. Reaching into his overcoat pocket for his gloves, his hands touched the cold metal of the small automatic.

Walking briskly, it took him twenty minutes to reach the entrance to the loco yards on South Street. The sky was brighter now and he could hear the raucous early-morning warbling of magpies and currawongs. In the loco sheds, massive steam locomotives snorted and wheezed and there was the clanging sound of a metal shovel in a coalbunker, followed by loud cursing in a Glaswegian accent. Jock?

Standing across the road from the entrance, he tried to judge where Rebecca Green had been when she took the photograph. Then, turning right, he followed the road in the direction the gang had taken after the robbery. The train tracks were on his left now and on the right, on a slight rise, he passed a fuel depot with huge cylindrical petrol-storage tanks.

The road ended at a small creek, where the train tracks crossed the trickle of water on a wooden piling bridge – a motorcycle and sidecar would have no trouble passing under it, he judged. There were no tyre tracks, as cattle on their way to the saleyards had recently churned the earth and sand. Berlin made a concentrated effort not to tread on any of the fresh cowpats. The trail was cold here and he looked up to the early-morning sky and saw the last faint outline of fading stars. No wonder Lou was confused by the stars – they looked so different from those in the Northern Hemisphere. On impulse he turned right, stepping over a trampled, rusting barbed-wire fence, and walked slowly out across the flat countryside, startling the occasional sleepy rabbit foraging among the thistles.

Berlin stopped when he could no longer see any sign of habitation. There was just a thin stream of smoke coming from the direction of the creek, perhaps a stockman's camp. For a moment he thought he could smell Wilf's pipe. A rabbit popped its head out of a burrow some twenty feet away and stared at him, blinking. He took the pistol from his pocket and checked the magazine – it was full. He cocked the weapon and slowly raised his arm to take aim. The rabbit stared at him, its nose twitching. One gentle squeeze of the trigger was all it would take and Mr Rabbit would be maggot food.

Berlin hated the thought of maggots. If there was one saving grace in that march through the snow and ice of the worst European winter in a hundred years, it was the snow and ice. The bodies of people and animals that littered the roadways and fields were frozen solid, sleeping in their white cocoons, and they would stay that way, free from any signs of decay, till spring. Even the young Wermacht soldiers summarily hung from lampposts as deserters by roving bands of German military police had a sad, unconscionable beauty when a light snowfall dusted their uniforms.

Berlin struggled to get the images out of his head. He felt the muzzle cold against his right temple. One gentle squeeze of the trigger was all it would take. How long would it be before they found him? Would a drover's dog sleeping by the creek jump up at the sound of the shot and come to investigate? Or would the crows pick out his eyes before they found him here, sprawled among tussocks of weedy grass and thistles and cow shit?

Berlin saw the white cap of the mushroom from the corner of his eye. It was smallish but there was a bigger one just beyond, and a bigger one beyond that. He took the pistol away from his head. There were dozens of mushrooms. He de-cocked the pistol and slipped it back in his pocket. Bending down, he pulled one of the larger mushrooms from the ground, shaking the stem free of soil. He turned it over and examined the dark brown ribbed gills underneath. He rubbed the cap gently with his thumb and checked it for any sign of yellowing, but found none. Yellow was a sign that the mushroom wasn't safe to eat – his grandfather had taught him that.

Berlin lined his upturned hat carefully with his handkerchief and harvested the best looking of the fungi until his hat was overflowing. When he had as many as he could manage he realised he had lost his way, but the loud whistle of a steam locomotive gave him a direction to head towards. After another few minutes, the glint of the morning sun on a steel petrol-storage tank confirmed it.

As he walked, Berlin imagined his breakfast. He would chop the mushrooms and fry them gently in butter, or even better, bacon dripping if there was any, just like his grandfather had done for him. Some salt and pepper and maybe a dash of Worcestershire sauce and more butter at the end and freshly chopped parsley from the hotel's garden and under it all thick-cut fresh white bread toasted golden brown. He smiled at the thought that a hat full of field mushrooms had brought him back from a very dark place.

In the hotel kitchen Lily insisted on preparing the mushrooms for him. Berlin sipped hot, milky tea at the large table and watched as she cooked his breakfast just as he wanted, but with chopped bacon and even more butter. He insisted she share them and she fetched a second plate and more cutlery.

'Are you sure they're not poisonous?' she asked as she buttered the toast.

'I'm pretty sure, Lil, but what does it matter? They look so good it's worth the risk, don't you think?'

'I'm game if you are, Mr Berlin.'

But he noticed she gave him a couple of minutes' head start, watching him closely before beginning to eat.

NINETEEN

Constable Roberts was waiting in the car park just before nine. The Dodge had been washed and polished and the tyres blacked. Roberts opened the passenger door and saluted.

'You're not just aiming for deputy commissioner, are you, Roberts? You're planning on going all the way. But we can drop the chauffeur business for now, I can open my own doors. Hop in.'

As the constable walked round to the driver's door, Berlin slid into the passenger seat and reached for his cigarettes. He offered Roberts one and lit them both.

'Oh, and thanks for rounding up the shaving kit and the other stuff for me. The whisky, too.'

Roberts started the engine. 'No worries, Mr Berlin. Do you want to go to the police station first off?'

Berlin shook his head. 'Let's just stooge around for a bit, I need to get my bearings.'

There was a small dip where the hotel's car park met the road, and Roberts stopped the car there while several cattle trucks rattled past on their way to the saleyards.

'I know you're going to have your hands full driving me about and reporting back to Sergeant Corrigan . . .'

The constable stared straight ahead, waiting. Berlin was glad that the boy hadn't tried to deny it.

'But I'm going to need your help. A copper's only as good as his local knowledge, the word on the street, the stuff he gets from his informants – but I don't have that knowledge here. I get the feeling that you're someone who knows how to keep his eyes and ears open. I'd like to know what you think.'

'Well, Sergeant Corrigan thinks . . .'

Berlin shook his head. 'I'm not interested in what the sergeant thinks, Roberts.'

The constable looked at Berlin for a few moments before speaking. The man who'd stepped off the aeroplane in Albury wasn't quite what Roberts had been expecting. He'd figured a big-city detective and a bomber pilot would be a brash know-all but this Berlin character was nothing like that. He was hard to read and he played his cards close to his chest, that was for sure. There was violence in him too, even though he seemed easygoing, and he certainly looked like he could handle himself in a stoush. Roberts was chuffed that Berlin was asking for his help. No one else at the police station was interested in his ideas or opinions.

'Wodonga's a small town, Mr Berlin, and pretty much everyone knows everyone else and all their business. We get a lot of stockmen through because of the saleyards, but mostly they're only trouble after they get paid. On the whole the soldiers out at the army camps are pretty well behaved, well, in public anyway. Sergeant Whitmore and his MPs keep them in line.'

'So you think this gang's not local?'

Roberts shook his head. 'There's a bunch of builders out at Bonegilla who've been getting into a bit of trouble lately. They might be worth looking into.'

'Bonegilla?'

'Bonegilla and Bandiana were the biggest of the army camps round here during the war. Bandiana is pretty much the only one still fully operational, though. They've got huge repair and storage depots for vehicles and weapons – trucks and tanks and artillery and stuff. And besides all the mechanics they've also got engineering and ordnance people based there.'

'What was the attraction of Wodonga?'

'It was far enough from the coast to be safe from Japanese planes taking off from aircraft carriers, and with the change of railway gauges at Albury it meant you could ship stuff north or south pretty quickly in an emergency. They had lines running out to the camp in both gauges.'

'And Bonegilla?'

'That's out past Bandiana, near the Hume Weir. It was this massive training establishment with barracks and mess halls and a hospital. The two camps had ten thousand people based there between them but now Bonegilla's been scaled right back and a lot of its facilities are being turned into a reception place for all those displaced persons and migrants who'll be coming out from Europe soon. I reckon this town will be a bit of a shock for them.'

'Trust me, Roberts, some of the places these DPs will be coming from would be an even bigger shock to you. What's the gen on these builders?'

'Lot of work for tradesmen out there, getting the camp up to scratch, and this mob turned up a couple of months back. Half a dozen of them, and real hard bastards. Probably ex-military, but that's nothing new. They drink too much, cause a lot of trouble. And some of the local girls have had problems with them.'

'Anything else?'

'Some of them ride around on motorcycles.'

'That sounds like a pretty good reason to make Bonegilla the first stop of the day.'

Five minutes after they left the outskirts of Wodonga the flat countryside gave way to bare, gently undulating hills with outcrops of lichen-covered rock. They passed a pub on the right side of the road and then, behind sagging barbed-wire fencing, rows and rows of neatly parked military vehicles appeared – there looked to be thousands of them.

Roberts slowed the Dodge down. 'That's Bandiana.'

On both sides of the roadway Berlin could see canvas-topped khaki and jungle-green four- and six-wheeled military trucks, jeeps, small-tracked Bren gun carriers and large tanks. There were also rows of canvas-wrapped objects in the distance that he reckoned were probably field guns. He twisted in his seat for a better view as they drove past a long double row of brand-new, six-wheeler Studebaker trucks.

Berlin whistled. 'That's amazing.'

'Oh, that's nothing. Stacks of equipment has already been sold off and they've still got warehouses further back crammed full of stuff. They say at the peak of the war there were maybe fifteen, twenty thousand tanks and trucks and jeeps and bits and pieces parked around the joint.'

The ranks of vehicles seemed to go on for miles and then finally the fences ended and Bandiana was behind them, and they were back in open country. Somewhere far ahead Berlin saw the glint of sun on water, but before they reached the weir they arrived at Bonegilla.

Roberts turned the car off the main road and into the driveway of the army camp. They stopped at a small guard post where a soldier in a slouch hat and khaki battle dress was sitting outside in the shade, reading a copy of the *Australasian Post*. As Berlin wound down his window the soldier glanced over the top of the buxom swimsuit girl on the magazine cover and asked, 'You right?'

'You've got a bunch of carpenters here, I'm told.'

'We got carpenters, plumbers, tilers. Take your pick.'

'Riding motorcycles.'

'Oh, those bastards.' The sentry folded his magazine and stood up. 'Down that way about half a mile and then hang a left at the dunny block and keep going till you run into a bloody great pile of dead marines, you can't miss 'em. And watch yourself with those blokes, if there's trouble you're on your own.'

TWENTY

Roberts drove slowly, following the guard's directions. The camp was sprawling, with sealed roads and street names, but had a desolate, forlorn feeling. There were people around, soldiers and civilians, but not enough to make the place look or feel lived in.

As they drove down the rows of wood and corrugated-iron sheds and barracks, the lethargy of the camp sentry became a common theme. Soldiers and officers ambled across parade grounds or in and out of the buildings, and any saluting Berlin saw seemed casual, or even downright resentful.

'This must be a bastard of a place in summer.'

'That's the truth, Mr Berlin. You get those hot, dry days when it's a hundred and twenty in the shade and there's willy-willys whirling down the main street and you can feel all the water being sucked right out of you. And then in winter you freeze your nuts off and the wind blows right through a bloke, no matter how much stuff you're wearing under your coat.'

They turned left and drove another couple of hundred yards before Roberts slowed the car. 'I guess this has to be the place.'

Dead marines were empty brown beer bottles, and the height

of the pile indicated Berlin would be dealing with men who liked a drink or seven. Roberts pulled the Dodge up next to a half-finished corrugated-iron building. As he climbed out of the car, Berlin could hear the buzzing of blowflies and caught the stink of urine and worse coming from the bushes near a battered ex-military truck.

The sound of hammering stopped and a tall, red-haired man wearing a khaki work shirt, shorts and battered boots stepped into the doorway. He was in his late twenties, with an acne-scarred, weather-beaten face, and he was holding a hammer loosely by his side.

'Morning. Nice day for it.'

The man studied Berlin's face before speaking. 'What the fuck do you want?'

'I'm not looking for any trouble, sport, so let's keep it polite.'

Roberts glanced across at Berlin. His voice was even but there was an icy tone that indicated while he might not be looking for trouble, he'd be up for it if it came along.

'My name's Berlin. I'm a police officer and I want to talk to you.'

'I figured you weren't one of the foremen 'cos those bastards know better than to come bothering us.'

'I've got a few questions. Won't take long.'

'You bloody got that right, copper, 'cos I don't know nuthin', haven't seen nuthin' and I'm not sayin' nuthin'.'

'You got a name?'

'What's it to ya?'

There was a long silence and then another figure appeared in the doorway.

'Problem, Blue?'

The red-haired man shook his head. 'Nothin' I can't handle, Stumpy. Just some Johns nosing about.'

The second man was dressed in a plaid shirt, shorts and boots, with a battered slouch hat on his head. He had long, greasy hair, a beard and eyes that twitched constantly, even though he was in the shade of the shed.

Stumpy whistled and three more men appeared from somewhere behind the hut. Two carried hammers and the third was holding a piece of steel pipe. Berlin could smell beer and tobacco and a distinct lack of care about personal hygiene.

Roberts moved around the car to stand beside Berlin.

'Bringing up reinforcements, copper? I think you and the boys brigade yonder are a little outnumbered.'

Stumpy pulled a half-smoked roll-your-own from the mess of lank hair over his right ear and took a box of wax-tipped, green tropical matches from his shirt pocket. A match flared, lighting up the shadow under his hat brim, and Berlin saw the patch of smooth white flesh on his temple. Stumpy noticed Berlin staring and rubbed the patch of skin with a dirty finger.

'Woodpecker. Bastard almost took my head off.'

'Woodpecker's a Jap light machine gun, Mr Berlin,' Roberts said.

Stumpy snorted. 'Very good, give the lad a teddy bear, every child player wins a prize.'

The one named Blue grinned. 'Your mum get you *The Boys' Bumper Book of Machine Guns* for your birthday?'

Berlin sensed Roberts starting to move towards the two men and put out his hand.

'Let it go, Roberts,' he said quietly. Then, 'His old man got knocked by the Afrika Korps, so why don't you give it a rest.'

'That so?' Blue said. 'In that case, I apologise, Constable. If we hadn't drunk it all for breakfast I'd offer you a beer.'

'He could pour it on his Weet-Bix,' the man with the steel pipe said and the others laughed.

'Leave it.' The tone in Blue's voice killed the laughter.

'There've been some robberies around the area.'

'It's a hard, hard world but like I said, seen nothin', heard nothin', saying nothin'. Same thing goes for my boys.'

'I hear you blokes ride motorcycles.'

'And?'

'They parked around here someplace?'

Blue shook his head. 'Too many dubious characters about the place, foremen and officers and the like. We leave the bikes somewhere safe during the day.'

'Any chance we can get a look at them?'

Blue spat on the ground. 'Buckley's. But if you come back with all your mates and all their mates and maybe those nancy-boy MPs from Bandiana, we can discuss it again. For right now I reckon you should just fuck off, we need to get back to work. These palaces for the reffos aren't going to build themselves.'

Berlin studied the hut for a moment. 'My brother was a carpenter. My guess is he'd say those walls aren't all that square.'

Blue shrugged. 'As if I give a rat's arse. I never said we was real carpenters. They needed blokes to nail 'em together and me and the boys were looking for a job in the open air where no bugger gives you grief.'

'Looks like you found that, then.'

'Yeah, well I had a good long look in the positions vacant pages when I got demobbed and there weren't a whole lot of jobs advertised for a bloke who was good with a bayonet.'

'Maybe you could have got a job in a slaughterhouse,' Roberts said.

Blue spat on the step. 'No thanks, sunshine, I already had one of those.'

TWENTY-ONE

'Where do I find Sergeant Whitmore?'

'He expecting you?' The sentry at the entrance to the Bandiana camp was reading a copy of the *Australasian Post*, too.

Berlin held his police ID out the window.

'Righto, down to the end there and then follow the signs to the Provost Office, you can't miss it.' The soldier turned his attention back to the magazine.

Berlin wanted more background on Blue and his boys. Since they were ex-army, he figured Whitmore might be just the man to help.

Roberts stopped the car outside a low wooden building with a verandah. The soldier leaning on the verandah had an MP armband around his right arm, just above the elbow and below his corporal's chevrons. He was rolling a cigarette.

'Sergeant Whitmore about?' Berlin asked.

The corporal indicated the office with a tilt of his head.

'Why don't you wait with the car, Roberts,' Berlin said as he headed up the wooden steps. He knocked on the door and went in.

Whitmore was sitting with his feet up on a wooden desk, reading a copy of *The Border Morning Mail*. The office had three desks, half a dozen filing cabinets, a notice board with some flyers pinned to it and an old ice chest in one corner. Behind Whitmore's head, a large Japanese battle flag with a red rising sun on a white background was pinned to the wall. There was a samurai sword in a black lacquered scabbard mounted beneath it.

Whitmore looked over the top of the paper at Berlin. 'Morning, Charlie. Seems like the government is dead keen on bringing in this forty-hour week, and according to the dairy farmers it will be the end of civilisation as we know it.'

'I'd be happy if I could get mine down to sixty.'

'Pull up a pew, mate. You're just in time for tea. The lad's got a brew on.' He walked over to a side door and yelled, 'Private Champion! I hope that bloody tea is strong this time, none of that witch's piss you've been making lately. We need two clean cups and see if you can find some of that fruitcake your auntie sent. We've got visitors.'

'Champion? Is that Cec Champion's boy?'

'Yep. Young Kenny. He's a good lad.'

Whitmore was limping slightly as he walked back to his desk, and the soldier winced as he sat in his chair.

'Last night catching up with you?'

'Must be getting old, Charlie. Time was I could eat blokes like that for breakfast and still take down a copper for morning tea.'

'Then I guess I'm glad you're past it.'

Private Champion came into the room with a tray. There were two enamel mugs, a teapot and a plate with several thick slices of fruitcake. He put the tray on the sergeant's desk and turned to Berlin. 'You want milk or sugar?'

'Milk and two, thanks. It's Kenny, right? We bumped into each other in the pub last night, remember?'

The private nodded, but seemed preoccupied. 'Sorry about that, I was in a hurry.'

'I heard about your brother. I'm sorry. I lost my brother up north, too.'

'Yeah, thanks. I'll take a cup out to Bob, shall I?'

'That'd be nice.'

'That's us now, Charlie,' Whitmore said, 'the nice army. No more celestial Sons of Heaven to slaughter and from next year we become a real standing army for the first time. Don't know why since we won two world wars with just the blokes who showed up when the shooting started. Now there'll be new uniforms and a new command structure and even more buggers to salute. All they'll probably keep is the flag and the hat.'

'You staying in?'

'I'll be army to the bitter end, old son, and you can quote me on that.' He raised his mug in a toast. 'To absent friends, Charlie, and brothers.'

Berlin lifted his. He sipped his tea then reached for a slice of the fruitcake. 'You from around here, Pete?'

Whitmore shook his head. 'Country New South Wales, Bathurst. Like Mo McCackie, I'm just a boy from the bush.'

Berlin smiled. He'd seen the comedian Roy Rene do his act on stage at the Tivoli theatre more than once. Rene would walk on stage as Mo McCackie, dressed to the nines like every wannabe local gangster and street corner spiv, and deliver the 'just a boy from the bush' line to uproarious laughter from crowds who had heard it dozens of times already.

'Family still there?'

'No family to speak of. Never knew my mum, she ran off when I was just a bub. Pegged out not long after – Spanish flu.'

That would make Whitmore a bit under thirty, Berlin calculated, but he looked a lot older.

'The old man raised me on his own. Had a hardware store and I had a bit of a knockabout time growing up. It was grouse, riding horses and building forts in the bush and shooting rabbits with my pea-rifle. The Depression knocked the hardware store and the rest of Bathurst on the head and the old man and me hit the road. I guess I was twelve or thirteen.'

'Must have been tough.'

'Nah, not really. I was still a kid so it was all a bit of an adventure. Missed a meal occasionally but we got by okay and I got to meet a lot of interesting people. I missed out on school, too, which I figured was no loss. If the old bloke scored a job for a couple of days in some country town he had me down at the library or the Mechanics Institute catching up on my reading. And when we camped by a railway line the passengers would sometimes chuck out their newspapers and magazines for us. Kept us up on the day to day.'

'Where's your old man now?'

'Dead. Died a long time back. We were jumping the rattler in north Queensland, trying to get onto a goods wagon. They slow down on the curves and I'd just got on board and turned round to give the old man a hand and an express train going the other way came out of nowhere and cleaned him up.'

'Jesus.'

'Yeah, one moment we're laughing and yelling and I'm calling him a slow old bastard and our fingertips are just touching and the next minute I'm a bloody orphan.'

Berlin didn't say anything.

'I was on my Pat Malone until the stoush with the Jerries started and I joined up. Then when the Japanese jumped in I wound up with one of the independent companies, like I said, since I was a bit too independent for the regular mob. Me and the jungle got along okay so I managed to make it through to VJ Day pretty much in one piece.'

Berlin noted that Whitmore always used the word 'Japanese'

rather than the almost universal 'Jap'.

'When it was over they asked for volunteers to go to Japan as part of the occupation force, so I put my hand up. Not a lot to come back to in Aussie and anyway, I was a bit scrambled in the head after some of the things I'd seen and stuff we had to do.'

'How was that? Japan, I mean?'

'Amazing. And awful. The Yanks gave the Commonwealth Occupation forces the shitty end of the stick, but what else is new? Our mob got Hiroshima Prefecture – you know, where they dropped the first atom bomb. It was a lousy job, bad quarters, supplies were crook and the locals were all shell-shocked. The Japanese have immense respect for authority and the higher-ups had been giving 'em all this bullshit about how well the war was going right up to the moment their hometown was vaporised, along with most of their friends and families.'

On the forced march back into Germany from his POW camp in Poland, Berlin had passed through towns and cities pulverised by Allied air attacks. As bad as the destruction was, nothing he'd seen had come even close to the newsreel footage of the devastation of Hiroshima and Nagasaki after the A-Bombs.

'Tell you one thing, Charlie, I was glad I did what I did up north because when you see what an occupying force can get up to in a defeated country you'd never want to have enemy soldiers strutting around Melbourne or Sydney or Brissy. You give one man total power over another and it gets ugly real quick.'

Berlin's mind flashed to a slush-covered Polish roadway but he quickly forced the thought out of his head.

'Pick any bloke in any pub,' Whitmore continued, 'pick the one who's all smiles and jokes and bloody hail fellow, well met. Tell him he can do what he likes to anyone in the room and no one would lift a finger to stop him or ever breathe a word about it and he'd have the barmaid naked and bent over a table in about ten seconds flat or he'd get a knife from the kitchen and cut off some bastard's cock or gut him or chop off his head. Trust me on that.'

'Stuff like that happen in Japan?'

'Human nature is human nature, Charlie. To make us kill the Japanese they had to make us hate the Japanese, which wasn't too hard since your average Aussie already had a head start disliking all Asians. So they filled the fellers up with a lot of horror stories and some were true and some were bullshit. A lot of blokes in the Commonwealth Occupation Forces hadn't seen action – joined up or finished training too late – but they knew blokes who got knocked: family friends, relatives and such. Plus all that stuff about what happened to the POWs under the Japanese had come out.'

'The Japs started it, didn't they?'

'That they did and the Imperial Nipponese army did some bloody horrendous stuff and they deserved all they got and then some. I never once regretted pulling the trigger up north but every second bastard on both sides has a wallet with a photo of Mum and Dad or the wife and kids and pretty much everyone's homesick and frightened.'

Berlin wondered if his brother had been homesick and frightened. His brother had been a soldier, a man like Whitmore, someone who did his killing up close, seeing the results of his actions. Berlin's killing happened after, after 'Bombs Gone' crackled in his headphones and he wrenched the aircraft around with its engines screaming. That was all the screaming he'd had to listen to.

'Look, Charlie, I'm not saying some of our blokes treated the civilians in Japan anywhere near how they would have treated us if they'd had the chance but, you know, I saw a few pretty nasty things over there and the funny thing is I always thought we were supposed to be the civilised ones.'

TWENTY-TWO

While Berlin sipped his tea he could hear shouting and the familiar sound of boots on a parade ground. Whitmore finally put his mug on the tray, leaned back in his chair and folded his hands behind his head. 'We've had the tea and the cake and you know more about me than I do about you so we should probably get down to tin tacks, what d'ya reckon?'

'Truth is, Pete, I wanted to pick your brains.'

'Might be slim pickings, digger, but fire away.'

Berlin opened his folder and handed over the photograph.

Whitmore studied the picture for a minute and then shook his head. 'Can't really help you, mate. Picture's a bit blurry. You get it off your Miss Green?'

'Yes, but she's not my Miss Green.'

'You two had your heads pretty close together at the pub last night. Put in a decent bit of spadework, Charlie – take her to the pictures, buy her a nice bunch of flowers and a box of Winning Post chocolates, and you never know your luck. I've seen blokes worse looking than you score big with the sheilas.'

'Winning Post, you reckon?'

Whitmore grinned. 'Yep, works every time.' He studied the photograph carefully. 'Harley-Davidsons, looks like, army issue. Nice bikes.'

'So if they're military bikes and the blokes riding them are waving Tommy guns about, logic says there might be a military connection.'

Whitmore handed the photograph back. 'If you're talking about the army, Charlie, logic has very little to do with anything. And there are a hell of a lot of demobbed ex-soldiers out in civvy street who know how to handle a Tommy gun. Probably one or two Tommy guns floating about, too, given how soldiers feel about snaffling the odd souvenir.'

'That's what I wanted to talk to you about. What do you know about some carpenters with motorcycles out at Bonegilla?'

'Me and my boys have had the odd set-to with those bastards, but now they know the limits. Just another bunch of demobbed diggers having trouble getting themselves sorted.'

'Since they're ex-military, any chance you can dig up some background on them for me?'

'Happy to try, old son. I can get their real names easy enough, but having someone hunt through army records down at Vic Barracks for more info could take a while.'

'Whatever it takes. I can't go home till I've got this sorted.'

'Lucky you, stuck in Wodonga, the Paris of the north. Of course, that's assuming Paris has an arse end.'

Whitmore stood up and reached for his slouch hat from on top of the filing cabinet.

'Fancy a bit of a tour of the camp? Since you're looking for military-type motorcycles I want to show you something.'

He smiled when Berlin picked up his folder.

'No need for that, she'll be safe in here while we're gone.'

Berlin smiled back. 'She'll be safe in your jeep too, right?'

'Charlie, old son, nothing and no one is safe in my jeep, as you are about to find out.'

Outside, Berlin walked round to the left side of the parked vehicle and was stopped by a whistle from Whitmore.

'Other seat, mate, it's a Yank vehicle, remember. Bastards put the steering wheel on the wrong side.'

They left Roberts sitting in the Dodge with a couple of copies of *Man* magazine. Whitmore pointed out the massive repair workshops and giant storage sheds full of all kinds of transport and attack vehicles, then he took the jeep off road, speeding up and bouncing through rutted and churned countryside and in and out of the neat rows of trucks and jeeps. Berlin grabbed on to the windscreen as the jeep bucked and tossed, nearly throwing him out of his seat.

'Warned ya, Charlie!' Whitmore yelled. 'Run a tank or two across the old vegetable garden and you bloody know about it.' Berlin could see from the grin on his face that Whitmore was having a good time.

They skirted a parade ground where a corporal was berating a small squad of marching soldiers, screaming comments about their mothers, grandmothers and the legitimacy of their births, before driving into one of the large warehouses.

'You're looking for military Harleys, so here you go, take your pick.'

Under the corrugated-iron roof of the warehouse, Berlin was staring at row after row of neatly parked olive drab motorcycles, all looking brand-new.

'Three hundred and ninety-seven bikes,' Whitmore said, 'and you're welcome to count 'em if you want. And these are just what we have on hand after flogging a heap off.'

'Who to?'

'Local and interstate army-surplus dealers and a couple of police departments. Pretty much anyone with enough cash. Might be a list somewhere but I don't have it.'

'So this gang's bikes could have come from anywhere?'

'Sorry, but that's the drum. Wangaratta police came up and checked the inventory when this whole business started. My blokes have no missing motorcycles or weapons, nothing unaccounted for. Same goes for the Bonegilla camp but that's pretty empty anyway, what with them getting it ready for the reffos.'

'What's the local feeling on the DPs being billeted here? You think there might be trouble?'

'These people are gunna be Balts and Dutchies and Poles and Hungarians. Probably even some krauts. And most of them won't speak any English. Strangers make some of the locals nervous, Charlie,' Whitmore said, 'even just people from the big smoke, regular Aussies, such as yourself.' He smiled. 'No offence intended.'

TWENTY-THREE

Whitmore slid the jeep to a sudden, jarring stop outside the Provost's Office. A couple more MP jeeps were parked in front of the building and three corporals were waiting on the verandah, smoking.

'Detective-Constable Berlin, meet the boys: Cliffy, Boof and Spud. Corporals Mackris, Bailey and Murphy to their mums.'

The three soldiers nodded to Berlin. Berlin recognised Corporal Mackris. He was the one who had been abusing the soldiers out on the parade ground.

'Charlie here's up from town looking for those blokes tearing around the countryside on motorcycles, giving Railways a headache and scaring the shit out of the populace.'

The men all looked fit, and Berlin noted their relaxed stance and casual arrogance. He also noted that, like Whitmore, they were all wearing multiple rows of ribbons.

'Lot of fruit salad up on that porch.'

'You got that right, we oughta get the mess to whip up a pavlova.'

'You blokes all serve together?'

'Just me and Boof. But we all saw the same kind of action.'

'Life must be a bit dull now compared to what you were doing up north?'

'That's the army for you, Charlie. It's all battle or boredom – just filling in time till the next stoush.'

'You reckon another one's on the cards?'

'Go and have a chat to Captain Bellamy sometime.'

'Who's Captain Bellamy?'

'Boss cocky out at Bundaroo Downs. Big sheep and cattle property. Been in his family since this town was a pup. He's a local councillor and just lately he's been putting together a sort of homemade private-army-cum-militia – the Bushman's Battalion. If you're interested in a band of roving nutcases you should probably check them out.'

'And they're armed?'

Whitmore nodded. 'Farm guns mostly, shotguns and hunting rifles. Plus some ex-military .303s. They drill on Bellamy's land. There's around thirty of them in the group, give or take, depending on the weather and what's on at the pictures. Anything with Humphrey Bogart or that Veronica Lake sheila showing at the Melba usually puts a real crimp in the rollcall.'

'Motorcycles?'

'Bound to be a few. Like I said, anyone could buy 'em.'

'Why a militia?'

'He reckons he's getting them ready to protect property, the local populace and womenfolk against commies, trade unionists, immigrants and the yellow peril sweeping down from Asia.'

'Is he serious?'

'Dead serious. Real captain in the first war, lost a leg at Pozières. Went over to Germany in '37 or '38 for a stickybeak and came back saying Hitler had the right idea about how to run a country. Obviously he's had his head pulled in for the last ten years but just lately the Prime Minister has been getting on his wick. Got a bee in his bonnet with all the industrial trouble we've been having recently, and now with the PM wanting to nationalise the banks.'

Berlin had been reading a lot of fiery newspaper editorials on those subjects lately. 'You have any feelings on that one way or the other?'

'Not me, Charlie, I'm just a soldier. I try to stay out of politics – it's a mug's game. Anyway, our Captain Bellamy did okay during the war selling livestock to the government to feed the troops but things got a bit tough after the war ended.'

'All good things must come to an end.'

Whitmore grinned. 'For some people. From the sound of it, Bellamy must be getting back on his feet though. I've heard he's been splashing the cash about recently.'

Berlin mentally added Bellamy to his list of suspects.

'One last thing, Pete, the local cops are a little outgunned, so if I run into some real trouble down the track any chance I can count on you and your men for a bit of support?'

Whitmore shook his head. 'Nothing I'd like better than to sign my boys up for a bit of adventure, Charlie, but unfortunately this is a civilian matter. So I'm afraid you're out there all on your lonesome.'

'Just thought I'd ask.'

The two men climbed out of the jeep.

'Thanks for the tour and the tea, Pete.' They shook hands.

'Anytime, Charlie. Us NCOs got to look out for each other cos no other bugger will.'

Roberts backed the Dodge out and as they headed down towards the sentry post he glanced over at Berlin. 'Where to now?'

'Back to town, I need to make a phone call to Melbourne.' He pulled a cigarette from the pack in his pocket and lit a match. 'What do you know about this Captain Bellamy and his militia?'

Roberts laughed. 'The Bushman's Battalion? They're a real bunch of drongos, those blokes.'

'But they're drongos with access to vehicles and weapons, and a need for cash to build up their army, Roberts. At this stage we can't rule anybody out.'

'Right you are, Mr Berlin.'

Berlin took a deep drag on his cigarette. 'You get any of that fruitcake with your cup of tea?' he asked.

Roberts smiled. 'A couple of pieces. Kenny and me both play on the local footy team, in the reserves.'

'What's your position?'

'Ruck-rover.'

'I'd have pegged you as too big for a rover and too short for a ruckman.'

'We don't win a lot of matches, if that's what you mean. Kenny's our full-forward. Got a handy boot on him. Kenny's a good bloke, bit quiet, but, you know . . . his brother and everything. You play?'

'I used to.'

'We've got an away match on Saturday, if you're interested.' He glanced over at Berlin. 'And if you're still here, of course.'

'Thanks for the vote of confidence, but I don't think there's much chance I'll be getting this mess all squared away in a couple of days.'

Back at the police station Berlin picked up the telephone on the front desk and had the Wodonga operator connect him to Melbourne. No one answered the phone in the detective squad office and he remembered that it was lunchtime on a payday, which meant everyone would have already left for the pub.

Berlin went out for a sandwich and when he got back he found a pile of folders on his desk. The Wangaratta police had sent up every single piece of paper they had on the robberies. They were obviously happy to wash their hands of the whole investigation.

He sat down at his desk and began to read, scanning every page carefully, but there was nothing new in the files – just confirmation of what he had been told on the phone.

He left the office at half-past five, passing the noise and frantic activity of several pubs where patrons fought to get served in the half-hour that remained till closing. Berlin considered joining them but changed his mind. On the walk to the Diggers Rest he found himself wondering if Rebecca would be in for dinner. But there was no sign of her when he got there, so he ate alone.

TWENTY-FOUR

The gravel driveway from the front gate to the old Bundaroo Downs homestead was lined with a neat row of tall English oaks, which cast long shadows in the mid-morning sun. A single-storey brick structure surrounded by a wide, flywire-screened verandah, the house had a dam behind it, several steel water tanks and a windmill. Set further back were workshops and sheds, an assortment of trucks and farm machinery, and a kennel with a mob of kelpies on chain runs. The dogs began yelping and jumping at the approach of the car.

As they drove up to the front of the house, Roberts let out a soft whistle. 'Now, *she* is nice.'

'She' was a sleek, pale blue two-door automobile parked in the driveway. The car had white sidewall tyres, covered rear-wheel wells, a matching blue visor over the windscreen and hooded headlights. And anything that wasn't shiny blue duco was sparkling chrome.

Roberts slowly pulled the Dodge up alongside. Berlin had very little interest in cars, but this one did have beautiful lines.

'Imagine getting to drive her, Mr Berlin. Chevy Fleetmaster, the latest model and brand-new. Can't be too many in the country and she wouldn't come cheap.'

'Whitmore said that things were looking up for Bellamy recently.'

Roberts glanced over at Berlin but quickly looked away. 'I guess they must be.'

They climbed out of the car and the screen door on the verandah swung open. A tall man in jodhpurs, riding boots and a fitted tweed jacket stood in the doorway, leaning on a walking stick. He was smoking a pipe.

'Morning, Roberts.'

The constable took off his helmet. 'Good morning, Captain. This is DC Berlin, up from Melbourne about those railway robberies.'

'Welcome to Bundaroo Downs, DC Berlin. I'm Frederic Bellamy.'

Bellamy was around fifty, with a wiry build, thinning hair and a weathered, tanned face. The tweed jacket was neat and clean but the lapels were fraying slightly. With rationing still in force, a lot of people's clothing was in a similar state.

'Nice to meet you, Captain. Any chance I can have a quick word?'

Bellamy tapped his pipe against the doorpost. 'Sergeant Corrigan said we could expect you. Cook put the kettle on when she saw your car coming through the gate.'

Berlin hadn't mentioned visiting Bellamy to the sergeant. Over breakfast at the pub he had asked Lily Corrigan how long she thought it would take to drive out to the captain's property. Roberts was certainly right about this being a small town.

'Young Roberts here was just admiring your new car.'

Bellamy took the pipe from his mouth. 'I'm partial to the Studebaker when it comes to trucks but for my money on long drives Chevrolet is always the way to go.' He called down to the constable, 'You can have a look inside if you want, Roberts.'

The boy was beaming. 'Thanks very much, Captain.'

'Best you keep away from the sheds there, laddie. Those damned dogs bite.'

Berlin glanced at Roberts, who nodded to acknowledge that he had heard.

Bellamy turned and walked in through the screen door, without offering to shake hands. Berlin followed, noticing that the older man's limp was quite pronounced and that his left leg thumped loudly as it hit the floorboards. Bellamy led him down the verandah to a square, wicker table with matching cane chairs. He swivelled around and lowered himself into one of the chairs, sitting with his leg outstretched.

He indicated the outstretched leg. 'Boche machine gun at Pozières took it off in 1916. Did you serve, DC Berlin?'

'Air Force, Europe.'

'Quite,' Bellamy said. 'On operations?'

'Bomber Command. And I was a POW.'

'Really? How interesting.'

'You seem surprised, Captain. I thought it was all over town.'

'I'm not one for local gossip, DC Berlin. Ah, here's the tea.'

A stout, older woman with a white apron and maid's cap placed a tray onto the wicker table. The teapot, milk jug, sugar bowl and teacups were delicate bone china, white with a blue floral pattern. There were scones on a matching plate.

'Nice china.' Berlin carefully picked up one of the cups. It reminded him of his grandmother's wedding china. She had kept it locked away in the crystal cabinet for 'best' but Berlin had never ever seen a 'best' occasion arise.

'It's Meissen, bought it in Dresden, on my trip.'

'I'd heard you toured Germany before the war, Captain. I don't think you'd recognise Dresden now. Flatter than a pancake when we got done with it.'

'Germany will rebuild, DC Berlin. But it must do so quickly or the world will fall to a red tide of Bolshevism.'

'As I recall, it was Russian tanks that flattened the wire round my POW camp and liberated me.'

'Chamberlain and Churchill both made a mistake in not allying with Hitler against Stalin after France fell. Stalin was always the real enemy. Mark my words, we'll all pay for that before too long.'

There was a brief flurry of barking from the direction of the sheds. Bellamy glanced out through the balcony louvres but the racket stopped as quickly as it had started.

'Help yourself to a scone.'

Berlin put a couple on his plate. 'Good-looking property you've got here.'

'I'm the third generation on this land. My grandfather started the property, my father built this house with his own hands – even made the mud bricks – and now we run over two thousand sheep and cattle and horses.'

'I guess that was a big help in the war effort.'

'My leg kept me out of active service this time, but we did our bit against the Japs, providing wool for yarn and fleeces to line your flying jackets and boots, and mutton and beef to line the belly. Bloody Yank soldiers complained constantly about the mutton, of course. All they wanted was beef and pig meat. But Bundaroo Downs did well by the Empire.'

'Looks like you did okay, too.'

'If you mean the new car outside, I've earned that. A man is what he makes of himself by his own efforts and I have nothing of which I need be ashamed.'

TWENTY-FIVE

Bellamy put his cup and saucer back on the table. 'And now we have the pleasantries out of the way, DC Berlin, what do you want?'

'I'm investigating this motorcycle gang and the robberies round here.'

'And not getting anywhere, I hear.'

'Early days yet.'

'So what help do you think I can offer?'

'I've heard you've got yourself a group of armed men and you're giving them military training. I was wondering if you thought any of your men might be getting together after meetings to try out their new skills and do a little fundraising.'

'What I'm doing is in no way illegal and I can assure you my recruits are of the highest moral character. Men who love their country and respect the law. And men who are willing to uphold the rule of law when others fail.'

'So you think running a private army in peacetime is a good idea?'

'At the moment this is a free country, thanks to men like me.'

He paused briefly. 'And you, of course, but it is always wise to be prepared. There are already ominous signs.'

'Such as?'

'Our current prime minister is a damned socialist who wants to nationalise the banks and refuses to outlaw the Communist Party. We have unionists constantly striking and holding our ports and railways to ransom and disrupting the manufacturing industry, and lawless thugs are roaming our highways with impunity.'

'The lawless thugs are my area. And as you say, this is a free country so people have the right to form unions and strike.'

'Rubbish. Chifley should put the army in the factories and on the docks with orders to shoot to kill any man who strikes or disobeys a lawful order to go back to work.'

'You don't think that sounds a little . . . I don't know, fascist?'

'The Germany I saw in '38 was a clean, well-run, ordered, safe, happy and efficient society. Our attorney general at the time, Mr Menzies, was quite taken, as was I, with the almost spiritual quality in the young Germans' willingness to devote themselves to their nation. Very impressive.'

'Made a big impression on me too, and a lot of blokes I used to know. Having seen that devotion in action I reckon it's something we could well do without in this country.'

'The British Government was as much to blame for the war as Hitler. Perhaps there were some . . . extravagant actions on Hitler's part, but the war was forced on him and the German people.'

Berlin put a half-eaten scone back on his plate. It took a lot for him to lose his appetite but Captain Bellamy had achieved it. 'I witnessed some of Hitler's *extravagances* firsthand, Mr Bellamy, and I don't want to see anything like that again as long as I live.'

Bellamy's neck turned red around his collar. 'That is your view, DC Berlin, but if the government can't or won't protect what is mine then I will do it myself, side by side with others who share my views.' He stood up, using the cane to keep his balance. 'And now if there is nothing else you wish to discuss . . .'

Roberts was still sitting in the Chevrolet when the two men came out through the screen door. He climbed out and closed the door carefully. 'She's a real beauty, Captain.'

'How are we fixed for Saturday, boy?'

Roberts gave two thumbs up. 'We'll eat 'em alive, just you wait. Did he tell you he used to captain the local team, Mr Berlin?'

Berlin shook his head. 'That so?'

'A long time back. I was Best and Fairest in 1913. Haven't played since, of course.'

Bellamy leaned on his walking stick and the two men studied the vista.

'Quite impressive, Mr Bellamy.'

'What you see out there is the result of one hundred years of grit and hard work, DC Berlin. There was nothing here when my grandfather arrived, and his nearest neighbour was thirty miles away.'

'Seems like you'll be getting new neighbours soon,' Berlin said. 'Out at Bonegilla, those displaced persons.'

'The dregs of Europe, in all likelihood. It's good British stock we should be encouraging to emigrate here, but the socialists think we should settle for foreigners and their spawn. And Jews. They come empty-handed, with nothing to offer us. Still, a source of cheap labour may make some of our local layabouts wake up to themselves.'

Berlin found himself wishing that German machinegunner had lifted his aim a foot or two. 'Start the car, Roberts, we need to be going.'

Bellamy put out his hand. 'I'm sorry I couldn't have been of more assistance, DC Berlin.'

For a moment Berlin considered ignoring the outstretched

hand but finally he shook it. 'Every little bit helps, Mr Bellamy. Thanks for your time.'

In the car, Berlin lit a cigarette to kill the taste of the Captain and his scones. Roberts stopped the Dodge at the point where the road from Bundaroo Downs met the main highway.

'Okay, Constable Roberts, what did you find out?'

Roberts carefully checked for traffic in both directions and then drove out onto the highway. He was pleased as punch that Berlin had expected him to do some sniffing around while he'd been talking to Bellamy. He felt that they were working as a team.

'I took a bit of a quick squiz at those sheds of his.'

'He said to watch out for the dogs.'

'Him using the dogs to warn us off was what got my attention.'

'That's a nice bit of detective work, Roberts. Always stick your nose in where people don't want you to. You didn't get bitten? We heard a bit of a barney.'

'I grew up with dogs back home in Benalla, we get along fine. Just give them a bit of a pat and share your devon and tomato-sauce sandwiches around and everything's jake.'

'Find anything interesting?'

'You mean like half a dozen army-surplus Harley-Davidsons with sidecars loaded up with Tommy guns and cash?'

'That would be nice.' Berlin quite liked the idea of putting Captain Bellamy into handcuffs.

'No such luck, I'm afraid. Most of the farm machinery is pretty run-down and all the sheds were padlocked. One had an open window so I climbed in.'

'And?'

'Lot of tools and iron plating and welding gear lying about and something big hidden under a tarp, so I took a peek. Captain Bellamy and his amateur militia have got themselves a Bren gun carrier tucked away in there.'

'Might be using it to pull a plough.'

Roberts shook his head. 'I don't think so. They're welding steel plates on to enclose it completely and there are gun ports on all sides. Turning it into a baby tank, I reckon.'

Berlin smoked and watched the passing countryside. Was Corrigan going to phone ahead to everyone he planned on interviewing? And was he warning his mates so they could lock up sheds or maybe move incriminating items out of sight before Berlin got to them? And what was Bellamy up to that he needed his own tank?

'When we get back to town, Roberts, I'm going to buy you another sandwich, and then I'm going to kick your arse.'

'What have I done wrong?'

'When you picked me up from the airport yesterday you said Wodonga had a water tower, a stock saleyard, a train station and bugger-all else. Turns out there's a damn sight more going on around here than you let on.'

Roberts smiled. A ute loaded with hay bales passed them going the other way, leaving a fine mist of dust in its wake. The Dodge crested a rise and just ahead in the haze, a crow picking at the carcass of a dead fox took off suddenly, swooping down low across the bonnet of the car. Berlin jerked backwards into his seat with a swift intake of breath and Roberts thought he felt him shudder.

'Just a crow, Mr Berlin.'

'I hate those bastards.'

Roberts wanted to ask why, but from the look on Berlin's face he thought better of it. Berlin didn't speak again on the rest of the ride into town.

TWENTY-SIX

Sergeant Corrigan and his brother Vernon had their heads together at a back table when Berlin walked into the Diggers Rest dining room just after seven. He got himself a whisky from Maisie at the bar, and when he glanced over in the direction of the Corrigan brothers the sergeant was watching him. Berlin wasn't sure if he should take this as an invitation to join them for a chat, but he walked across the room to the table anyway. The sergeant was finishing off a beer and he belched and licked his lips. 'Bloody marvellous. First for the day.'

'If you say so, Sarge.' Berlin took a sip of his whisky.

The sergeant ignored the comment but there was a hard look in his eye. The table was set for three. Both the Corrigan brothers were drinking beer and there was a half-empty glass of what looked like sherry on the table.

'You have a productive afternoon, Berlin?'

If Roberts was reporting his movements back to the sergeant he already knew that most of it had been spent at his desk.

'You could say that. I've been through all the files on all the robberies and now I know exactly how much I don't know.'

117

'Shall I tell Melbourne that if they ask?'

'Maybe you should. They might replace me with someone more experienced and then I'd be out of your hair.'

Berlin caught a quick worried look exchanged between Vern Corrigan and his brother.

'You've met Captain Bellamy, I believe,' said the sergeant.

Bellamy was standing behind Berlin, leaning on his cane. 'Indeed. DC Berlin and I had words earlier in the day.'

Berlin stepped aside and Bellamy settled into the empty chair.

'Dear me, dear me, not ruffling the feathers of the local populace, are we, Berlin?'

'I can't do my job without ruffling a few feathers, Sarge.'

'Get us another beer will ya, Vern, and a sherry for the captain. You want another, Berlin?'

The question was asked grudgingly, but in a country pub an offer to shout a drink was expected. Berlin had spotted Rebecca Green at a table on the other side of the room and her nod and smile was a definite invitation. He took this as a welcome opportunity to escape. 'I've got one going already, thanks, and I'm supposed to be meeting someone. I'll leave you gentlemen to your dinner. Have a pleasant evening.'

Berlin crossed the room, and put his hand on the back of a chair at Rebecca's table. 'Mind if I join you, Miss Green?'

'Desperate times call for desperate measures, DC Berlin. And of course if anyone more interesting shows up I can always ask you to move on.'

Berlin was about to push the chair back in when she smiled. 'For goodness' sake, I'm pulling your leg. And will you call me Rebecca so I don't feel like a middle-aged spinster? Now sit down and get yourself some of this roast chicken, it's delicious. I don't understand why you people in the city think chicken is only for Christmas.'

She was wearing trousers again, but this time with a soft-pink silk blouse. There was a string of pearls around her neck. Berlin liked the way the blouse clung to her figure.

Lily walked past, balancing three plates heaped with chicken and vegetables. Rebecca caught her eye. 'I've just been telling DC Berlin here how good your chicken is.'

Lily put a plate down in front of him. 'This was for Vern, but he can wait.'

'Hope for your sake it's not the one with the ground glass in it,' Rebecca said quietly after Lily moved away. 'I'm pulling your leg again, in case you were wondering.'

'I worked that one out all by myself. You a country girl then, Rebecca?'

'Ballarat country enough for you? My dad was a photographer, we had a camera shop and studio there. Weddings, portraits, pictures for the local paper, you know the kind of thing. Plus developing and printing everyone's holiday snaps.'

'And that's how you learned to take photographs?'

'I helped Dad out in the darkroom and at weddings. It was a good little business till the war. Then my dad had to go away for a while so we closed up shop and Mum opened a café and milk bar.'

'Bit of a change from photography.'

'Actually it was a lot of fun. Mum turned it into a malt shop when the Americans built their big bases outside town. She did okay selling hamburgers and hot dogs and milkshakes. I used to help out whenever I came home on leave. I discovered that if I kept the right number of buttons undone on my blouse and bent over the fridge to dip the milk in just the right way, I was able to pretty near double our takings.'

'I can see how that would happen.'

Rebecca grinned. 'Don't tell me you're shocked, DC Berlin? Even in country towns, it was all sex during the war. At one stage we had US marines based there to recuperate after Guadalcanal. Those boys were out to live life to the full, and who could blame them?'

'And I'm sure plenty of the local girls were happy to accommodate them.'

Berlin smiled when he said it but his tone was flat and Rebecca caught an edge of hardness to his voice. She let the comment pass.

'The Yank army engineers lent the town council these big water tankers to wash out the doorways and gutters before sunrise every day. Used frenchies would clog up the street drains on a Sunday morning and the ponds in the parks were full of them. The soldiers from New York called them Coney Island whitefish. It wasn't all that uncommon to find one hanging off the café's front doorknob when I came to open up.'

'We called 'em Yarra trout,' Berlin said, 'down in Melbourne when we saw them floating in the river. So did you have a boyfriend back then?'

'One or two. Nothing serious, though. A war's not a time for getting serious. What about you?'

'No boyfriends.'

Rebecca smiled. It was the first time her mysterious DC had cracked a joke.

'But I did have a fiancée, for a bit.'

'She didn't Dear John you?'

'First letter I opened when I got back to Australia. I was expecting to see her on the dock but she'd just left a letter for me with her mother.'

'That's cold.'

'I thought so. She'd up and married some Yank army sergeant and was long gone. Bloke was a mapmaker by day and played saxophone by night at the Chevron Club on St Kilda Road. She's living in a place called Palo Alto, outside of San Francisco, apparently.'

'Sorry to hear that. War is a bastard on everybody.'

'That's the truth. A real bastard.' Berlin sipped his whisky. Over the top of his glass he saw Rebecca was watching him.

'Better eat your chicken before it gets cold, Charlie.'

Berlin was surprised when he looked down at his untouched dinner plate. How long had it been since food hadn't been his number one preoccupation? And why was he looking at Rebecca's silky blouse and wondering exactly how many of those buttons she would have to undo to get his mind off his dessert?

Rebecca watched him as he tucked into the chicken. The man opposite her was in real pain, and it was from more than just a broken relationship. He was damaged and he was trouble and nothing would ever be easy with a man like that.

After she'd made the print of the motorcycle gang in the Albury newspaper's darkroom, she'd also made a print of the shot she'd taken of him in the railway yards pay office. As the image of his face appeared under the red light, in the swirling developer solution, she told herself she should run a mile the next time she saw him, but for better or worse she knew she wouldn't.

TWENTY-SEVEN

Dessert was a steamed pudding with strawberry jam, and Berlin had just finished his when Sergeant Whitmore and Private Champion came in for their nightly visit.

Cec Champion was slumped in a chair at the side of the dining room with an empty beer glass in his left hand. He studied Whitmore for a long time and his jaw worked rhythmically, as if he was giving something a good chewing over.

Rebecca was watching him.

'You might want to check your watch, DC Berlin,' she said.

'What?'

She indicated Champion with a nod of her head. 'It must be a quarter to eight on the knocker because Cec Champion over there is about to blow his stack. Apparently it's a regular occurrence when he's had too much to drink.'

Berlin turned around at the sound of a chair being pushed back. Champion was on his feet, swaying slightly. The beer glass was at his side, with the dregs running out onto the leg of his grimy, coal-dusted overalls. He was breathing heavily, still making the chewing motion with his mouth, and his eyes were fixed on the two soldiers at the bar.

'Whitmore, you cunt, you are a fucking dirty low fucking Jap-lover and you should be bloody ashamed of yourself.'

The words were slurred and Cec drew himself up to a semi-erect position, bracing himself on the table with his right hand. Whitmore, leaning on the bar, kept his back to the room. Kenny Champion turned around to face his father. 'C'mon, Dad. Give it a rest, will ya.'

Cec Champion kept his eyes fixed on the back of Whitmore's head. 'You shut your hole, boy. The Japs cut your brother's head off and you stand there drinking with a bloody Jap-lover. You should be ashamed of yourself, Kenny, you useless little shit.'

Whitmore turned and put a restraining hand on Kenny's shoulder as he started towards his father. The boy looked back at him and Whitmore shook his head.

'Let him get it out, son.'

'Bastard goes off to Japan after the war to give those murdering yellow slanty-eyed devils what for and then he turns all lovey-dovey and gets himself a slant-eyed girlfriend. My boy is dead in a hole in the stinking jungle and Sergeant fucking Whitmore is eating rice and shacking up with his killers.'

Berlin got up from his chair, but before he could reach Champion, the man had thrown his empty beer glass towards the soldier. It was a drunk's ineffectual throw, left-handed, and Whitmore leaned casually out of the path of the missile, which shattered on the front of the bar. Champion was off-balance from the throw, and Berlin caught him as he started to fall.

'You might want to think about calling it a night, mate,' he said quietly, still holding the other man up.

Champion stared at Berlin in confusion. 'Who the fuck are you?'

'I'm just a bloke saying you should go home and sleep it off.'

Champion shook himself free of Berlin's grasp and straightened up.

'I'll go when I'm bloody good and ready.'

'I think you're ready now, mate.'

Champion fixed his gaze on Berlin, weighing up his options. After a moment he turned, set his sights on the doorway and slowly moved towards it, weaving unsteadily but determinedly through the silent patrons, bumping tables and chairs as he passed. Several of the drinkers lifted their beer glasses safely out of the way as they let him through.

As Berlin walked back to his table he glanced towards the bar. Whitmore gave him a brief nod. He sat back down opposite Rebecca. 'Jesus wept, I think I've had enough excitement for one night.'

'I'm sorry to hear that.'

Berlin looked at her and decided to ignore the comment. 'And he's like that regularly?'

She nodded. 'Gets a skinful and mouths off. Can't say I blame him, it's not like it's something you'd get over.'

'He's not the only person in the world to lose someone they loved in the war.'

'You must have known some people who got killed – are you over them?'

Berlin looked at her until she looked away.

'Sorry,' she said quietly.

There was a pot of tea on the table and Berlin poured two cups. 'That Cec Champion's usual performance? Going off at Whitmore, I mean.'

'Mostly, but he also thinks the army is now full of poofters, and the railways are run by idiots and the local cops are a bunch of clowns.' She paused and looked at him. 'He was mouthing off earlier in the week about what fools Corrigan and the railway paymaster were, planning to sneak the payroll in a day early.'

Berlin stopped stirring sugar into his tea. He could see from the way Rebecca was looking at him she was waiting for a reaction.

'That's interesting.'

'He probably overheard them planning it. Corrigan seems to conduct a lot of police business in the pub. And being the local drunk tends to make you a bit invisible to people.'

Berlin sipped his tea.

'He was telling anyone who'd listen that it put everyone working in the loco yard at risk, even the train crews. All that cash sitting there for a whole extra day with no one looking after it would be a real temptation.'

'Turns out he was right, eh? Funny that. Who was in the bar at the time, do you remember?'

Rebecca glanced around. 'Pretty much the usual crowd. Maybe a couple more. I wasn't paying that much attention.'

'You were paying enough attention to be parked outside the loco yard's gate Wednesday morning with a camera ready.'

'Let's just say I'm not as green as I'm cabbage'y-looking.'

Berlin studied the faces around the dining room. Young Kenny Champion had followed his father out of the room and there were about a dozen drinkers left. When he looked back at Rebecca she was lighting a cigarette. She took a deep drag, blew smoke into the air and stood up.

'I don't know about you, but I think I'll call it a night.'

'Alright, sleep tight.'

She looked at him. 'You know, Charlie, the smart move for you a minute ago might have been to tell me I'm not at all cabbage'y-looking. You sleep tight, too.'

TWENTY-EIGHT

Berlin leaned on the bar next to Whitmore.

'Buy you a drink, Pete?'

Whitmore shook his head. 'No thanks, Charlie. I'm off the hard stuff tonight. This is just lemonade. I'm a bit crook in the guts.'

'Still hurting from your run-in with the stockmen?'

'Something like that. Anyway, thanks for sorting out the old bloke.'

Berlin shrugged. 'I didn't do much. Must be a bit hard on Kenny.'

'Kenny's a good kid, it's just he's stuck in the middle. He idolised his big brother.'

'That stuff true, about you having a Japanese girlfriend?'

Whitmore reached into the right pocket of his battledress jacket and pulled out a wallet. He opened it and carefully took out a small, sepia-toned photograph, handing it to Berlin. 'Her name was Hiroko.'

Whitmore, who looked a lot younger in the photo, towered over a beautiful and delicate dark-haired Japanese girl wearing a kimono with flowing sleeves and a sash round the waist. Whitmore was smiling for the camera as the girl stood demurely in front of him.

'She had a three-year-old daughter,' Whitmore said, 'and a husband who was in the Nipponese navy, in submarines. When she hadn't heard from him in two years she knew she wasn't going to. They didn't take many prisoners out of submarines, especially not the Japanese ones.'

'She's very beautiful,' Berlin said and handed the picture back. 'Wasn't fraternising with the . . . the locals frowned on?'

Whitmore smiled. Berlin had pulled himself up just before saying 'Japs'. Whitmore really didn't care if people called them Nips or Japs or slanteyes, he just chose not too, and Berlin had been sharp enough to notice. The bloke might have a bit of a slightly battered mug and a funny look about the eyes every now and again but he obviously had a brain ticking away under the old cranium. Not something you found all that often, in Whitmore's experience.

'We might have been part of what was called the British Commonwealth Occupation Force, Charlie, but it was still the bloody army so anything entertaining, educational or just plain fun was frowned upon. Hiroko was a schoolteacher with a kid to feed, living in what was left of her house after the A-bomb went off. It started off as lessons in Japanese for me and developed into . . . you know.'

'What happened to her?'

'She was killed about six months after I met her. Drunken Pommy officer in a jeep with no lights skittled her and the kid one night.'

'Jesus! Did they get the bloke who did it?'

'They didn't bother looking. It was just two more dead Orientals to the powers that be, and Hiroshima was already the biggest fucking cemetery you've ever seen. What a bloody horror show that place was, I tell you. What sort of bastard sits twenty thousand feet up in the air and drops bombs on people he can't even see – women and kids?'

'A bastard like me, I suppose.'

Whitmore glanced at Berlin. 'Sorry, Charlie, it must be the lemonade talking. I think I might hit the road, I'm feeling a bit ordinary.'

'Think you got crook from something you ate?'

'Who knows? Could be a bug from the jungle. Maybe amoebic dysentery, that one's a real bugger to shake. Gives you the Gillette trots – a bloke feels like he's shitting razorblades.'

'Can I ask you a question before you go?'

'In your capacity as a copper?'

Berlin nodded.

'Fire away, then.'

'Ever use a Tommy gun?'

'A time or two. Bloody good gun for the jungle, but heavy as buggery. Bastard to lug about but when you needed to chop up a bunch of crazy Nipponese rushing your position, screaming Banzai, it did the business.'

'Weren't our Owen guns better, because they never jammed?'

'Don't kid yourself, Charlie, all machine guns jam at some stage. The Owen did it less than most, but even so they still only fired 9-millimetre ammo. They'd do some damage, but those .45-calibre slugs whizzing out of a Tommy could cut a bloke in half.'

Berlin looked upwards. 'Suppose I was to fire a Tommy gun up at that ceiling. What do you reckon would happen?'

Whitmore studied the ceiling for a moment and then looked back at Berlin. 'We speaking theoretically?'

'Yep.'

'Full magazine? Hundred-round drum?'

Berlin nodded.

'On repetition?'

'What?'

'Fully automatic. Weapon keeps firing as long as the trigger is down.'

'On repetition, then.'

'Okay, we've got lath and plaster up there, then the floor beams and the upstairs floorboards. No carpet, just lino, since Vern is a cheap bastard. And then, unless we have a very unlucky guest in the way, we have more lath and plaster on the upstairs ceiling, rafters and after that, a slate roof. Is it raining outside, theoretically?'

'Let's say it is.'

'Then in that case, Charlie, once the dust clears and your ears stop ringing you should probably move your drink a bit to the left.'

'Because?'

'Because there'll be rainwater landing in it, along with some very big chunks of plaster.'

'A pretty big hole then?'

'At least big enough to get your head through. That answer your question?'

Berlin nodded.

Whitmore picked his slouch hat up off the bar. 'Great. Now with my civic duty done I'm hitting the frog and toad.'

An hour later Berlin lay in his bed staring up at the roof, thinking. The ceiling of the Wodonga loco sheds pay office was half the height of the bar downstairs and, according to what Whitmore had said, should have been ripped apart by the bullets from the robbers' Tommy-gun bursts. But it had just been buckled and scorched. This had to mean they were using blanks – but why? And right now blank ammunition was probably harder to put your hands on than the real stuff.

TWENTY-NINE

The sudden shriek of the train whistle jerked Berlin back to consciousness, and he tried to work out where he was. The shriek was followed by the clang of timber and iron railway-crossing gates slamming shut in front of him. There was a clock up in the two-storey signal box, on the wall behind the big iron wheel that operated the gates. Berlin squinted in the bright sunlight – half-past ten. He had no recollection of exercising, washing and dressing but he must have done all those things then walked from the Diggers Rest to the railway crossing in High Street. He wondered if he'd had any breakfast.

The blackouts were happening less frequently these days. The doctors had been right about that. Now it was mainly the nightmares and flashbacks he had to contend with. Berlin heard a train whistle again. The locomotive was heading back from across the river, thick black smoke pouring from its funnel.

He turned his back on the crossing gates and walked towards the water tower. The streets were lined with cars and trucks and busy with Saturday-morning shoppers. Long lines formed in the butchers' shops, customers shuffling in and out on the sawdust-covered floors. Sweating, jolly men in blood-smeared, striped aprons swung cleavers down on carcasses spread on massive chopping blocks, or weighed out sausages and mince and fatty chump chops on their scales.

He passed a grocery store with brightly painted tin signs for Kinkara Tea, Lifebuoy and Sunlight soaps, Bovril and Keen's Mustard nailed neatly to the outside. Hardware stores had brooms and shovels and sacks of feed stacked out on the pavement, and the cake-shop windows displayed iced finger buns, lamingtons and neenish tarts.

People moved quickly, purposefully. At noon the shop doors would be shut tight and by ten past twelve Berlin knew he could fire a shotgun down the street and not hit a soul.

He ordered tea and raisin toast in a café. There was a greengrocer across the street, where men in leather aprons spruiked the quality of their tomatoes and carrots and beans. Berlin watched from his seat in the window and sipped his tea. When he'd finished a second pot of tea he ordered a sandwich to take with him, still not sure if he'd had breakfast.

On the walk to the police station he passed the Melba Theatre and a mob of boisterous children queuing up for the Saturday matinee. He smiled at the thought of the raucous cheering for the hero, the catcalls and foot stamping that would accompany any love scenes, and the laughter that came with the sound of Jaffas rolling down the wooden aisles. Harried usherettes with torches would battle to keep order, and at interval lines would form to buy Dixie Cups of vanilla ice-cream or sherbet bombs or chocolate frogs from the trays of the teenaged lolly girls standing in front of the screen in their short skirts and white jackets and caps.

He was tempted to join the line, figuring a newsreel, some cartoons and a cowboy serial or two might be the perfect way to spend the afternoon – but that wouldn't get this case solved and the brass off his back. Roberts had left the Dodge parked outside the police station and inside Constable Hooper had his head down close to a radio, trying to follow a Melbourne football match through a howling gale of static.

Berlin remembered the first football match he had attended. He was about five and still confused as to where his parents had gone and why he and his older brother were now living in Flemington with their grandparents. His grandmother kept the blinds drawn winter and summer and the house had a stale smell that had crept up his nose on the day they arrived and never left.

His gran spent a lot of time crying in her room and Charlie wondered if this was because of something he had done. One Saturday morning in June she had asked him if he would like to go to the football with his granddad and brother and Berlin said yes. He actually had little interest in football, but he was trying to say yes to everything his gran asked in the hope this might somehow stop her crying.

She dressed him in his best shirt and short pants, long socks held up with elastic sewn into garters, and his best boots. His little belted overcoat came down just to his knees and Berlin's spindly legs were blue with cold within minutes of leaving the house for the long walk to Windy Hill. As they lived in Flemington and his grandfather was a Scot, it was a moral that they would follow Essendon.

There was a reason the Essendon football ground was called Windy Hill, and Berlin's legs were soon shaking uncontrollably on the asphalt terrace where he and his grandfather and brother stood. At least it didn't rain, and Berlin took some comfort from the buttered milk arrowroot biscuits his gran had wrapped in greaseproof paper and popped in his coat pocket as they left the house.

There were no seats and little Charlie Berlin was a tiny figure lost amongst the surging, screaming, cursing crowd of men until his grandfather lifted him up on to his shoulders. Hidden among the crowd he had been sheltered from the worst of the wind, but now held up high in the icy breeze he could feel the chilblains already forming on his ears and fingers.

But the view was spectacular, even if he couldn't understand the on-field strategies and tactics. He understood, though, from the noise around him when a surging mass of towering giants in red and black forced the ball down the field and through the inner set of goalposts, that the Bombers were scoring. He soon learned he was for the Bombers and against the Hawks and the Demons and especially against Carlton – the Blues – and the old archenemy Collingwood, the baddest of the bad boys in the Victorian Football League.

And Berlin understood something else from that first afternoon of football, and that was that his grandfather was a special person. The crowd knew he was a policeman and a sergeant and they gave him room and respect, and kept their swearing to a minimum if they thought his grandsons were in earshot. They joked with his grandfather and winked at the boys but even the hardest of them, and there were plenty of hard men at Windy Hill, knew their place.

Berlin ate his biscuits at quarter-time and at half-time his grandfather let him and his brother share a hot meat pie doused in tomato sauce. He burnt his tongue on the steaming, salty gravy inside the crusty-brown pastry shell but said nothing, still marvelling at how the crowd of stamping, growling, hungry men in heavy coats and cloth caps, surrounding the pie stall, had parted for his grandfather.

After the final siren, when the crowds surged out on to Raleigh Street to pack the trams and trains and pubs, Berlin had already made up his mind that he would follow the Bombers and perhaps one day play for them, but he also knew with certainty that one day he would be a policeman.

THIRTY

'Message from Albury Hospital, DC Berlin.' Berlin looked up from his notes. Constable Hooper was standing in the doorway. 'McGill, the paymaster bloke, is conscious. I thought you'd want to know right away.'

'Thanks, Hooper. You have the keys to the Dodge?'

'Bob probably left them in it. You reckon the paymaster will be much help?'

'I'm hoping he can add a bit of detail to the picture. Maybe he's picked up some clue that no one else has. He's been a lot closer to these bastards than anyone else.'

On the approach to the bridge, a flat-bed truck and several farm utes were pulled over to one side, parked next to Bellamy's shiny blue Chevy. The driver's door was open and Captain Bellamy was behind the wheel, watching a dozen or so men lined up in two ragged rows. They were dressed mainly in work clothes and overalls but a couple were in suits. If he had to guess an average age, Berlin decided it might be closer to fifty than thirty. One was wearing an army-issue tin hat and they were all armed. Berlin counted seven Lee Enfield .303 service rifles in varying condition, four shotguns and a hunting rifle with a telescopic sight.

One of the men, wearing a slouch hat and a tattered battledress jacket with corporal's chevrons, seemed to know what he was doing but his exasperation was obvious as he tried to push the men into some sort of a military formation.

Rebecca's Austin was parked a little further down the road. The boot was open and she was bending down, rummaging for something. Berlin parked the Dodge in behind her. She smiled when she saw him and walked over to the driver's window.

'Hello, Charlie. Lovely day for a drive.'

'Or a little armed insurrection.'

'I don't think I'd give them that much credit. I reckon the nuns at my old school could give them a run for their money, guns or not. Just going to take one truck backfiring as it goes past and those blokes will drop their rifles and run for the hills.'

'You know what it's about?'

'Last Saturday of the month manoeuvres, they tell me. They're about to practise blockading the bridge. Just in case we ever go to war with New South Wales, I suppose. So where are you off to, or is that a state secret?'

'Paymaster has woken up so I'm going to see if he remembers anything.'

'Perhaps I'll see you at dinner. You can fill me in then.'

Behind them Bellamy's corporal began screaming at one of his troops. 'Right turn means you turn to your right, you idiot! That's the side your right hand is on. That's the hand you wank with. How hard is that to remember?'

'You manage to get that quote printed in *The Argus* and I'll buy you dinner *and* take you dancing.'

Berlin's arm was resting on top of the open window frame and Rebecca briefly touched his hand. 'Don't tempt me, Charlie, I'm a girl who likes a challenge.'

As he approached the Albury Base Hospital, Berlin felt his shoulders tighten, and after he parked it took all of his strength to get out of the car and walk up the steps to the main entrance. Hospitals held too many bad memories for him and he even tried to avoid driving past them if he could.

A male orderly was sitting on the steps smoking and Berlin asked for directions to reception. Inside the hospital the long corridors had that familiar sickly smell of disinfectant and ether and floor wax, making him swallow hard.

The matron on duty was wearing white stockings, white shoes and a white uniform starched so stiff Berlin figured if you hit it with a hammer the hammer would break. Her hair was pulled back in a severe bun under her veil and the hairstyle matched her mood. Berlin followed the matron into a four-bed ward. There was a steel cupboard beside McGill's bed with a bunch of limp yellow jonquils in a jam jar and a half-eaten bunch of grapes spilling out of a torn brown paper bag. Berlin pulled a grape from the bunch and ate it, earning him a disapproving stare from the matron.

The paymaster's head was swathed in white crepe bandages. His right eye was blackened and the cheek swollen.

'He's conscious and aware, Mr Berlin, but he has a fractured jaw and there also seems to be some hearing loss, hopefully only temporary. So unless you both know some kind of sign language, I can't see that you can get any information out of him.'

'You wouldn't have a pen and some paper, by any chance?'

'Nurse! Pen and paper.' The matron snapped the order without even looking round to see if there was a nurse nearby.

A wooden clipboard with several sheets of white quarto paper was thrust into Berlin's hand, along with a fountain pen. The nurse who gave it to him, a young, round-faced girl, moved to stand behind the matron, eyes down and hands folded in front of her. The matron didn't acknowledge the girl's presence.

Berlin unscrewed the cap of the pen and wrote DID YOU RECOGNISE ANYONE? on the paper. He handed the clipboard and pen to the paymaster, who stared at the writing. The paymaster squinted then looked up at the matron.

'Do – you – wear – glasses – for – reading, Mr McGill?' the matron asked, enunciating the question slowly and clearly as if speaking to a foreigner or someone who was a few sandwiches short of a picnic.

The man in the bed nodded.

Berlin remembered the glasses he had crushed underfoot in the pay office. This really was the icing on the cake. 'Fuck it!'

The junior nurse glanced at him wide-eyed, her cheeks flaring red, and the matron sucked in her breath.

'Young man, policeman or not we do not allow that kind of filthy language in my hospital.'

Berlin was debating whether to apologise or punch the matron in the throat when he heard the sounds of shouting and car engines, and moments later, someone running down the corridor. The orderly he'd passed at the main entrance slid in through the open doorway holding a thick, brown envelope.

'Bloke wearing a balaclava and riding a motorcycle just chucked this to me and told me to deliver it to this bloke quick smart. He took off and half a minute later a mob of blokes in utes, waving rifles, come driving in after him. I pointed them in the direction of the river and off they went. It was all a bit bloody exciting. What's in the envelope, you reckon?'

The envelope was hand addressed VICTORIAN RAILWAYS PAYMASTER, C/O ALBURY BASE HOSPITAL. Berlin tore it open. Inside was what he quickly estimated to be close to a thousand pounds in banknotes and a typed letter reading, SORRY ABOUT THE JAW. HOPE YOU GET WELL SOON. ALL OUR BEST. P.S. THE MONEY DIDN'T COME FROM YOUR PAYROLL SO YOU CAN KEEP IT. WHY DON'T YOU TAKE A

LONG HOLIDAY WHEN YOU'RE FEELING BETTER.

Berlin tossed the money onto the paymaster's bed and stuffed the envelope and note into his overcoat pocket.

'Excuse me, Matron, but I have to go after these bast—reprobates.'

Outside, a truck had parked the Dodge in. Berlin screamed at the driver to move, which only seemed to confuse him. By the time Berlin cleared the hospital car park and crossed the river there was no sign of the motorcycle or the militia.

He was trying to work out his next move when a figure on the roadway outside the police station flagged him down. Berlin slowed the car just enough for Roberts to jump on the running board and let himself into the passenger seat. The constable was still wearing his football jumper and black shorts under a khaki army greatcoat.

'Go straight on, Mr Berlin. They passed by me going like bats out of hell. Miss Green was bringing up the rear but she wouldn't stop. Can't have been more than five minutes ago.'

And five minutes was all it took. When Berlin caught up to Bellamy's men in the narrow cutting on the Tallangatta road, it was all over. Rebecca was laughing, but she was the only one.

THIRTY-ONE

Bellamy's men walked slowly towards them, surrounded by a mob of bleating sheep. The expressions on the men's faces ranged from anger to disbelief to embarrassment. The anger was probably because they were now unarmed and the disbelief and embarrassment almost certainly because apart from Rebecca and Captain Bellamy, none of the group was wearing trousers or boots.

Rebecca stopped beside the Dodge and turned around to take a photograph. Bellamy broke away from the line of men and limped slowly over to join them.

'Miss Green, I would really prefer if you didn't.' The Captain's jaw was set tight. He was obviously not a happy man.

She pressed the shutter button. 'It's a free country, Mr Bellamy. If you've got some pull with my editor or the Victorian premier you might be able to block publication but I can't see what grounds you'd have.'

Bellamy looked towards Berlin for help.

Berlin lit a cigarette. 'Public hygiene maybe, because people are going to piss themselves laughing if they ever get to see this.'

'Perhaps we should see what Sergeant Corrigan thinks,' Bellamy said and he moved back to join the line.

Rebecca knelt down to get a lower angle on the men, who were now moving away from them back in the direction of town. The militia were a sea of pasty white legs, saggy greyish-white underpants and drooping socks.

'Jesus wept, Rebecca. What the hell happened here?'

She got back to her feet, slowly winding the film on. 'A few minutes after you left for the hospital, a bloke wearing a balaclava zoomed past on a motorcycle in the same direction. He gave the troops the two-finger salute so they piled into a couple of utes and Bellamy's car and went after him. I followed them. Looks like the motorcycle looped through the hospital car park and went past us, heading back to the bridge.'

'He was dropping off a get well card for the paymaster.'

'How very thoughtful. Anyway, we turned round and went back over the bridge and through Wodonga and started to catch up to him a few miles out of town.'

Berlin knew those utes would only ever catch up to a bloke on a motorcycle if he wanted them to.

'My Austin was still at the back of the posse and when we came to the cutting the bike went up over the top on the gravel and we went through the middle, ploughing straight into this mob of sheep. Everyone gets out of the utes to clear a pathway and then we realise there's a bloke up on top of the cutting on each side of us and the main bloke on the roadway out in front of us, and they're all holding Tommy guns.'

'Sounds like a very well thought-out ambush,' Berlin said. 'You get any photos of them?'

Rebecca shook her head. 'Didn't seem smart to point a camera at someone who's pointing a gun at you. Makes no difference anyway. Same bikes as the loco sheds, same overalls and balaclavas. Next thing they order Bellamy's troops to drop their trousers and dump them into one of the utes, along with their boots and rifles. But they made an exception for the Captain and me. Then they told us all to start walking back to town.'

When the roadway was clear of sheep and half-naked militiamen, Roberts drove Berlin and Rebecca into the cutting. They found one ute, the Captain's blue Chevy and Rebecca's Austin. The ute and the Chevy had their bonnets up. The second ute, the one with the guns and clothing, was missing. Roberts got out and checked the vehicles.

'No keys in the ute or the Chevy and the distributor caps are off. Rotors are gone so they won't be moving any time soon. The Austin is okay though, they've left your keys and everything, Miss Green.'

'That was nice of them, eh Charlie?'

'Yeah, they're real gentlemen. Roberts, drive the Dodge back into town and pick up Bellamy on the way. Drop him out at his farm. I'll get a lift with Miss Green.'

'Righto, Mr Berlin.'

'And you were right about Bellamy's militia, Roberts, they're a right bunch of drongos.'

They found the missing ute a couple of miles further down the road. It had been backed through a wire fence into a farm dam with only the front end still clear of the water. Rebecca parked the Austin and they walked across to the edge of the dam.

A couple of pairs of trousers were floating on the surface. Rebecca took photographs of the scene while Berlin tossed clods of dirt into the dam and watched the ripples.

'You sure you didn't recognise any voices?'

Rebecca lowered the camera. 'Nope. Only one of them spoke anyway, one of the men up on top of the cutting. He did sound like he was dropping his voice, trying to disguise it. But he didn't have much to say really, just, "Drop your guns, boys, and your tweeds."'

'And no one gave him an argument?'

'Hell, no. Those Tommy guns are pretty persuasive. Everyone had their pants down in ten seconds flat.'

'Except you.'

'Takes more than a Tommy gun to get my pants down. At least a box of chocolates and maybe dinner and some dancing.'

'So are we talking Winning Post chocolates?'

Rebecca smiled, delighted that Berlin was going with the joke. 'You'll have to do better than that, Charlie boy. Cadbury's Milk Tray, if you don't mind.'

Berlin laughed and tossed another clod of earth into the dam. The ripples lapped up against the opposite bank, where the rotting carcass of a sheep lay half out of the water. A shiny black crow swooped down over Berlin's shoulder, startling him. The bird glided across the surface of the dam and landed on the remains, where it began to peck the matted wool and putrid flesh.

Berlin glanced up at the sky. It was starting to snow again so they were safe from the low-flying Russian ground-attack fighters for a while. The drifting snow reached his knees and Berlin had never known that a man could feel so cold. He pulled the dirty khaki greatcoat tight around his shoulders and turned back towards the Polish roadway and the girl, willing her, begging her, silently pleading with her to move before the SS officer pulled the trigger.

THIRTY-TWO

The Germans had built most of their POW camps as far east as possible, into Poland, Czechoslovakia and East Prussia, maximising the distances escapees would have to travel to safety. In early 1945 with the Red Army advancing, tens of thousands of Allied POWs were forced out of the camps, joining millions of refugees on the cluttered roadways, marching slowly westward back to Germany through the worst winter blizzards in a hundred years. Berlin's camp had been evacuated over two days, with the seven thousand prisoners split into more manageable groups of several hundred each.

On the seventh day of the march, the guards forced the column of shivering POWs out of the sleet and into the meagre shelter of a wooden barn left shattered by repeated Russian air strikes. It might have been around four or five in the afternoon but if the winter sun was still out there beyond the leaden clouds the POWs couldn't tell, and they cared even less. The horse-drawn army field kitchen was nowhere to be seen so the starving men knew it would be another night without food.

Berlin had found the potato a little over an hour after he and the other exhausted, freezing men had slumped gratefully down into the shelter of the barn. As he tried to sleep, something jammed into his back and he dug for it under the straw, expecting a stone, bewildered at finding a potato. It was hidden deep under the filthy straw and had somehow escaped detection by the hordes of refugees who must have used the barn every night.

His fist closed around the black lump and he slipped it into the pocket of his khaki army-issue greatcoat. Berlin was starving, like all the others, but he held onto the potato. Perhaps there would be worse to come, though he felt that if things became even just a little worse he would not survive.

The next morning the snorting of a horse woke them and there was a watery soup waiting in the big boiler of the field kitchen. Berlin joined the line of hungry men, his hand still closed around the potato in his pocket. Those with dysentery stayed a little longer in the barn, some sobbing in misery as they squatted and added another layer to the squalor that would greet whoever used the place for shelter that evening.

As the men waited, stamping their feet and swinging their arms to keep warm, Berlin checked the sky for any breaks that might give respite from the sleet and snow. Sunshine would be welcome to warm their freezing bodies but it would also make them easy targets for roaming Sturmoviks, the Russian aircraft responsible for their burnt-out lodgings and the rocketed trucks and tanks they passed along the road. The grey sky and snow-covered landscape merged seamlessly at the horizon, meaning they would at least be safe for the first part of the day.

Behind the barn a stand of fruit trees stood leafless and forlorn. Among the bare branches ravens were waking from rest. Berlin watched them, fat and sleek, eyes glinting, feathers shimmering through the winter mist. They would breakfast at their leisure while he starved, filling their bellies without the usual raucous squabbling over every morsel. It was a very good time for carrion eaters.

Around mid-morning Berlin heard gunfire from somewhere ahead of the line of POWs that was slowly shuffling westward. Single shots, spaced – pistol or rifle fire – not the steady, constant rumble of the Russian artillery far behind them. Sleet was falling again and the prisoners kept their heads down. Berlin squinted into the distance and could see the guards at the front of the column beginning to force the prisoners off the roadway and into the snowdrifts.

An order was coming down the line, passed from one guard to the next. Berlin could hear the word 'Juden' repeated. The guard for their section began pushing men off the road with his Mauser rifle, which he held horizontally at chest height. The POWs protested, groaned, resisted, preferring the ankle-deep slush of the roadway to the knee-deep snow of the drifts.

A thin, dark line appeared over the crest of the hill ahead, moving slowly towards them. As the figures drew closer they separated into two groups and Berlin heard an angry murmur from the POWs in front. On the right was a shuffling, stumbling line of people dressed in ragged striped tunics and pants, and in the middle of the road, out of the worst of the muck, was a smaller group dressed in black uniforms.

'Those bastards look like the fucking SS.' It was a shivering airman standing behind Berlin who spoke. He spat into the snow for emphasis. 'And them others, I think they're bloody four-be-twos.'

The German guards kept their backs to the column of Jews and SS men and Berlin wondered if they were more concerned with looking away from what was happening on the road than keeping an eye on their prisoners. Most of the SS men Berlin had seen since his capture had been neatly turned out in tailored black uniforms, but this group looked tired and angry, their clothes crushed and dirty. They carried rifles and holstered pistols or MP40 machine pistols, and several had whips or clubs.

Berlin was shocked at the condition of the shuffling, silent Jewish prisoners. Some wore battered shoes or wooden clogs but many were barefoot or simply had rags bound around their feet. Their clothing was threadbare – thin, tattered trousers and a shirt or tunic, some open to the wind and showing gaunt, skeletal torsos. Their hair was close-cropped or shaven, their vacant eyes sunk deep into sockets above protruding cheekbones. Berlin realised with a jolt that many of these walking scarecrows were women.

More shouting from near the front of the POW column and Berlin could make out a figure beside the road, someone who had fallen out of the line of Jewish prisoners. The man was on his knees, head bent forward. An SS soldier lifted his rifle and fired a single shot from about a foot away. The body jerked sideways and went limp, a red smear appearing on the snow near the head. The POWs were shouting now, screaming in anger at the SS while the camp guards nervously tried to calm them down.

A figure in the silently shuffling column opposite Berlin stopped and stared across at the POWs. It was a woman. She looked like she had just woken from a deep sleep and her eyes locked onto Berlin's. He found he couldn't look away. She must have been very beautiful once. She still was, despite the filthy striped tunic, cropped hair and drawn face, her lips blue from hunger and cold. How old was she? he wondered. A Jewess. The word 'Jewess' had intrigued him since he had first found it in Sir Walter Scott's *Ivanhoe* in the Essendon Public Library when he was ten. A real Jewess, his first, here among the filthy slush and detritus of war on a lonely Polish back road.

They continued to stare at each other, the Jewess standing quietly as the column moved slowly past her. A young SS officer, not more than twenty, was suddenly at her side, screaming. Berlin had enough Kriegie Deutsche from the camp to understand the words: 'Move your arse, you filthy Jew cunt.' The SS officer took his pistol from its holster, pulled the slide to cock the weapon and placed it against her temple.

'Please, oh please keep moving,' Berlin begged her silently. Behind her, in the distance he could see a raven circling. Closer, in painful detail, he could also see the silver death's-head insignia on the soldier's cap, the silver SS flashes on his jacket collar and a small scar on the corner of his angry mouth. The third finger on the soldier's right hand, the hand holding the pistol, was missing above the second knuckle.

'Please just keep moving, keep going.' Berlin was willing her to move with every ounce of strength he had. But the Jewess just smiled at him, a wondrous smile, deep and serene, as if to say, 'I chose my time. Remember me. You are my witness.'

Berlin saw the soldier's finger tighten on the trigger, the slide move back and the empty brass shell casing eject, tumbling end over end away from the gun. There was no sound, and then the girl was gone.

He continued to stare at the place where her face had been. The puff of smoke from the muzzle had been whisked away instantly by the chill wind. All around him the POWs were screaming at the SS officer, but to him their mouths worked silently. Berlin studied the steely grey sky and felt the wind and watched the raven circling, and he knew he would love the Jewess for all of his life.

'. . . Charlie?'

Rebecca was staring at him. 'Charlie, are you okay?'

Berlin looked around. The sky was clear but rain clouds were building on the western horizon and a chill wind was starting to blow. He pulled the overcoat tighter at the neck then thrust his hands deep into the pockets. 'It's getting late, we should be heading back to town.'

On their way they passed Bellamy's trouserless militia and Berlin's face was blank as he studied the line of shuffling, dispirited, miserable men. Rebecca glanced across at him and turned her eyes back to the road. The temperature always fell quickly around sunset on an autumn evening but right now there was a deep chill inside the Austin she couldn't quite put her finger on. But she knew as she looked at Berlin she'd never seen a more wounded man in her life.

THIRTY-THREE

Vern Corrigan knew his business. He looked into Berlin's face when he ordered the first whisky and then glanced under the bar to make sure there were a couple of full bottles standing by. He also checked that the iron bar was handy. Corrigan had seen that same look before, in Whitmore's eyes, and it always ended in trouble.

They shared a table, Rebecca nursing a gin and tonic and Berlin drinking whisky after whisky. He made polite conversation and drank. They ordered dinner and Berlin drank while they ate it, and then he drank some more and became silent. Behind the bar Maisie had started to keep a tally on a pad but Corrigan tore off the page, screwed it up and threw it away. Ten or twenty drinks, it made no difference. He would charge the local police double whatever was needed to pay for the booze and extra for the damage, and his brother would sign off without any questions.

Around nine a bloke who was old enough to know better decided Berlin ignoring the pretty girl at his table was a sign she might be available to someone who showed a little more interest. Rebecca shook her head as he approached the table, trying to warn him off, but he was either too drunk or too thick to recognise the signal.

The third time Rebecca said she wasn't interested, Berlin put his drink down, stood up and quietly asked the bloke if he was deaf or just plain stupid. The man was a head taller than Berlin and a few pounds heavier – and a very bad judge of character. Five seconds after the obscenity left his mouth his back was hard up against the wall on the other side of the dining room, feet desperately struggling to find the floor and Berlin's forearm jammed tight across his throat, cutting off his oxygen supply.

The whole room watched, and waited for Berlin's right fist, poised above his shoulder, to smash down hard into the terrified face. But he held the punch and kept his left arm in place until the choking man's hands came up slowly in surrender. Berlin released his hold, letting the man slide slowly down to the floor. He walked back to his table across a silent dining room.

After the incident Rebecca moved into the empty lounge with her cup of tea. She listened to the radio and flicked through magazines, feeling just as alone as she had been at the table with Berlin. He was gone, she knew, off someplace she couldn't follow or even understand. Rebecca was afraid, not for herself but for him. She had seen Berlin slip the pistol into his overcoat pocket at the robbery scene that first day, and she wondered if she should casually wander out to the hallway and check his coat.

She also wondered if she should go to his room and wait there. Wait in his bed to see if he wanted solace in her instead of the bottle. But something in Berlin's eyes said that all the sex in the world wouldn't ease his pain.

Berlin finally realised he was alone some time around midnight. The bar was empty, the barmaid gone, and the landlord was switching off lights. Corrigan walked across to the table with a half-full bottle of Haig in his left hand and a glass tucked under his right arm. He pulled the cork from the bottle with his teeth and put the bottle and glass on the table.

'One for the road,' he said. He splashed some whisky into his glass and filled Berlin's up to the top.

'You chucking me out?' Berlin said.

Corrigan shook his head. 'Wouldn't even think of it, mate, but I'm off to bed.' He tapped his glass against Berlin's and downed the whisky in one swallow. 'Turn out the lights if you can manage it, no problem if you can't. I'll leave you the bottle.' He walked across the room and tossed a log into the fireplace. 'It's gunna get bloody cold in here when this fire dies, just so you know.'

The fire and the bottle both died around the same time. Berlin's bed would be just as cold as the bar, but he remembered there was more whisky next to it. As he staggered to his feet he saw that Rebecca was asleep on the couch in the lounge. Someone had covered her with blankets and left a small radiator burning – probably Lily.

Why would she choose to sleep on the couch? he wondered. But she looked warm enough, and comfortable as he passed. He remembered where he was going and why and walked unsteadily towards the hallway. There was a lamp still burning on the reception desk and Berlin saw the outline of his overcoat on the wall rack. He stood at the foot of the stairs, one hand on the banister for support, thinking about the pistol in his coat pocket. Then he turned and took on the challenge of climbing the stairs.

The stair treads creaked and Rebecca stirred slightly. When her right hand confirmed that the eight cartridges from Berlin's pistol were still wrapped in the handkerchief tucked underneath her body, she went back to sleep.

THIRTY-FOUR

A gentle knocking woke Berlin at about three in the afternoon. By the time he had managed to wrap a blanket around himself and stagger from the bed to the door, the hallway was empty. There was a tray on the floor with tea, toast and scrambled eggs. There was also a packet of Bex aspirin powders.

He vomited up the first mouthful of egg, making it to the washbasin just in time. After rinsing his mouth out with tea he switched to dry toast, which seemed a better option. The Bex powders were touch and go for a minute but he kept them down. Then more toast and tea. He sat on the bed wrapped in the blanket, holding his cup in both hands to stop the shaking. Jesus Christ, why was Sunday always such an arsehole of a day?

He didn't trust himself to carry the tray down to the kitchen, so he left it outside the door. In the entrance hallway he slipped on his overcoat and felt the comforting presence of the automatic in the pocket. It had rained, but now the sky was clearing. Still enough cloud cover to cut out any glare, which was a good thing given how much his eyes were aching. He starting walking, feeling the damp gravel crunch under his feet. At the roadway he turned right.

Albury was as dead as a doornail, every shop on Dean Street locked or shuttered. Berlin walked up one side as far as the railway line and then back down the other. Crossing Olive Street, he looked up and saw the pale white finger of the war memorial on the hilltop ahead. He turned left to lose the sight.

St Patrick's Church had stood at the corner of Olive and Smollet streets since 1872, according to the sign outside. The doors were open and it was starting to drizzle so on impulse Berlin decided to go in. The sonorous chanting of Latin, the smell of incense and the ringing of small bells assaulted his senses, and he wondered what he was doing there. Hell, he wasn't even Catholic. He sat in the very back pew, pondering exactly how much dirt Saint Patrick must have had on the higher-ups in the Vatican to get every second Catholic church in the world named after him.

The place was empty apart from the first few rows and, given all the available space, he wondered why anyone would want to slide in next to him.

'Seeking solace, Charlie, or are you here for confession?'

Rebecca was wearing a long raincoat and she had a pale blue scarf tied over her head.

There was a noise off to one side and they both turned to look. A woman came out of a confessional booth.

'You can understand why so many Micks are attracted to the police force,' Rebecca whispered.

'I don't follow.' Berlin was feeling sick and his head was starting to ache again. Why hadn't he put some of the Bex powders in his pocket?

'The Catholic Church and the police have a lot in common. They're both about people sinning and then confessing their transgressions in a very small room.'

She had that right. Sticking a sinner in a small room with a couple of burly Irish cops was always the easiest way to get a confession.

'Back in Ballarat during the war our local Catholic church had so many confessions on Sunday mornings that the priests just sat on chairs a couple of feet apart with lines of Yank soldiers going out the doors. They even hauled an eighty-year-old priest out of retirement to help handle the overflow, and some of the boys used to tell me they'd make up the most outrageous stories just to see how he'd react.'

Berlin smiled. He was thinking of some of the things the boys got up to while training in Canada. He stopped smiling when he remembered how many of them were dead and gone.

'Of course, some of those young soldiers had a lot of confessing to do, Charlie. We had our fair share of shotgun weddings back then, and unmarried girls taking extended holidays to visit interstate relatives. And there were the girls who jumped in the local creek or wound up dead in an alley from a backyard abortion gone wrong. It wasn't all beer and skittles.'

Berlin was only half listening. He nodded his head from time to time to show interest but even that slight movement made him feel sick. After a while Rebecca stopped speaking and then some time later he heard the shuffling of feet. He looked up and people were making their way out of the church.

'The mass has ended, Charlie,' Rebecca said in a solemn voice. 'It's time for us to go forth and sin no more.'

When there was no one else left in the church they stood up and he followed her outside. The Austin was parked just across the street.

Rebecca pulled the scarf from her head and shook her hair to loosen it. 'Want a lift back to the hotel? It looks like it could rain again.'

Berlin glanced at the sky and shook his head. 'I'll be right, I need a walk.'

'You sure?'

'I'm sure. Besides,' he said, 'it's a very small car and I'm not sure I smell so good.'

Rebecca smiled. 'That's one of the things I like about you, Charlie – you are a master of understatement.'

It was dark and drizzling when Berlin crossed the river. His hands were in his pockets and his collar was up. He was starting to feel a little better at last and thinking perhaps Lily had something on the stove that he might be able to keep down. And he'd need to borrow her polish box to do some work on his shoes. Was Lily Catholic like Rebecca? he wondered.

And what was he? 'Presbyterian' was typed on his air-force papers and his fiancée had given him a small gold cross to wear with his identity tags – dead-meat tickets the boys had called them – but what was he now? Not Presbyterian, that was for sure. Berlin's God had died along with his crew in that fireball over the docks at Kiel. Berlin had tossed the cross, the identity tags and the engagement ring he'd saved so hard to buy into the Yarra on a drizzly Melbourne night just like this.

His head was starting to clear and he walked a little faster. Rebecca, church, sin and confessions were on his mind as the lights of the Diggers Rest came into view through the drizzle. But mostly confessions. Just before Rebecca had slipped into the seat next to him, Kenny Champion had left the confessional, and the young soldier looked like a very unhappy man.

THIRTY-FIVE

Berlin called Melbourne at half-past eight on Monday morning and got Hargraves on the phone.

'So nice of you to call, DC Berlin, you've been missed.'

Hargraves made the comment loudly, obviously for the benefit of the other men in the office. Berlin heard laughter and some derisive hooting.

'How was Chater's wedding?' Berlin wasn't actually all that interested but he really didn't want to talk about the motorcycle gang and his weekend.

'Pretty average, until the bride sprung him having a knee trembler with the bridesmaid in the dunnies at the reception. That's going to be one icy honeymoon. Last root Chater will be getting for a while.'

There was a pause. Berlin waited it out.

'And how was your weekend, DC Berlin?'

There it was. From Hargrave's tone Berlin knew he had all the details.

'We had a run-in with the gang on Saturday afternoon.'

'Oh, right, that would probably explain the picture on page six of *The Argus* this morning. And why I had my arse kicked round the top floor before my breakfast had a chance to settle.'

There was no noise in the background this time. Well, at least Rebecca was getting something out of all this.

'You know what, Berlin, you need to get your head out of the bottle, stop hanging around with the press – no matter how great the sheila's tits are – and get me a line on these arseholes.'

Twenty minutes later, Berlin found Roberts and the Dodge down the street at Toole's garage. A mechanic had just finished working under the hood. He lowered the engine cover, locked it, wiped the handle clean with a rag and winked at the constable.

'There you go, Bob, good as new.'

Berlin nodded to Roberts and the mechanic.

'Morning, Mr Berlin. Got us a new fanbelt. I thought I could hear the old one slipping.'

'Let's take her for a run then, shall we? I want to visit the crime scenes – all of them.'

The two men climbed into the car and the constable started the engine.

'Which one would you like to go to first, Mr Berlin?'

'Let's start with the furthest out and work our way back.'

Eight hours later, Berlin studied the countryside through the window as they headed back to town. They were running parallel to the main railway line and every so often they were passed by a goods train hauling wheat or freight, or a passenger service with its red dogbox carriages and buffet car strung behind the straining loco, briefly blanketing the roadway in rolling clouds of acrid, black smoke.

All the interviewing of witnesses, pacing out the robberies and reconstructing the events in his mind had produced very little of use. Careful inspection of the ceilings in places where shots had been fired confirmed his suspicion the gang was firing blanks.

These guys didn't leave any evidence behind and they were in and out so fast that their hapless targets didn't know what had hit them. Not one witness could give a decent description. Tall and solidly built were the common denominators, but the balaclavas meant no hair colour, and no one could report accurate eye colour or distinguishing marks – nothing new to go on.

The light was just beginning to fade and he glanced at his watch – four o'clock. It was getting cold. He turned up the collar on his overcoat and put his hands deep into the pockets. He was very tired – tired of waking up in the morning, tired of his days, tired of his nights, tired of drinking and tired of being sober.

'Wakey, wakey, Mr Berlin.'

They were parked outside the Wodonga Police Station. There were lights on inside.

'Sorry, Roberts, I must have drifted off.' It was just past six by his watch.

'Don't worry about it. It's boring country round here, and that's the truth. Looks like we've got a visitor.'

They were parked next to Captain Bellamy's blue Chevy.

'Bellamy and your sergeant seem to be —' The phrase 'thick as thieves' didn't seem appropriate. 'Good mates.'

Roberts looked across at Berlin. Berlin sensed he was about to say something. He waited.

'Yeah, mates, that's about the size of it.'

Berlin couldn't fault the lad's discretion. But there was enough information in the pause as Roberts considered his words carefully. He winked at the constable.

'Thanks, Bob. And from now on why don't we make it Charlie, after six o'clock.'

'Righto, Mr Berlin.'

Inside, Bellamy and the sergeant were having tea in his office. The sergeant had his feet up on the desk. 'Nice of you two to join us. Roberts, you get that front desk tidied up and the floors swept before you even think of pissing off home.' He stood up. 'I'm going for a slash. Berlin, the Captain here wants to have a word.'

Berlin knew that tea wouldn't be cutting it for Corrigan this late in the afternoon and that he'd definitely have a bottle stashed somewhere between the office and the lavatory.

Berlin let the sergeant pass and then leaned on the office door. He waited.

'The sergeant tells me you're very focused on this case.'

'Is that a good thing?'

The Captain smiled. 'I believe so. The sooner we get this whole affair sorted out and everything gets back to normal, the better.'

'Well, that's something we can agree on, Mr Bellamy.'

'Fine, then. I've just offered the services of my men to Sergeant Corrigan and yourself, should the need arise. We are ready and willing to help.'

'I'll keep that in mind. But I thought your blokes might have the wind up after what happened on Saturday. Or at least be finding things a tad draughty.'

'We'll be ready for them next time, believe me. My boys are itching for another go at those bastards.'

Bellamy's boys hadn't made much of a fist of their first go at the gang but Berlin decided to leave it alone. The militia might be better than nothing if it came to a fight. But how much better, he wasn't really all that anxious to find out.

THIRTY-SIX

In the dining room Berlin bumped into Lily, who was rushing back in the direction of the kitchen. She seemed flustered.

'Hello, Mr Berlin,' she said. 'Tea is roast pork, baked potatoes, steamed pumpkin and beans but I'm a bit behind, I'm afraid.' She wiped her hands on her apron. 'We've got some extra people in tonight,' she continued, 'and the girl who usually helps in the kitchen didn't show up this afternoon.'

'Take your time, Lily,' Berlin said, 'I'll have a drink while I'm waiting.'

There was laughter from across the room, where a small crowd of locals had gathered around a man with a sharp suit, well-polished shoes and Brilliantine-slicked hair. He was wearing a silk cravat with a matching pocket handkerchief and Berlin remembered the contempt the Pommy officers on his squadron had for anyone gauche enough to wear a cravat in the mess after six.

'Who's the lair?' he asked, ordering a whisky from Maisie at the bar.

'That's Brian,' she said. 'A salesman for Fly Tox, you know, the fly spray. Just got a nice new company car he tells me, a Ford V8.'

Stops in once a month, regular as clockwork.'

'So all the shopkeepers know when to lock up their teenage daughters.'

'You've got that right. Fancies himself as God's gift to women, that one.'

There was a look in her eye and a lack of malice in her voice that made Berlin think she might have opened that gift parcel sometime in the past and perhaps wouldn't mind doing it again. Brian had a pencil moustache that Berlin suspected might have had some assistance from a mascara brush. He also had a stock of jokes that kept the crowd entertained. When the laughter from one story died down he started in on the next.

Berlin spotted Rebecca at a table further across the room, smoking and reading *The Bulletin*. She was wearing a grey skirt with a matching jacket over a silky, pale blue blouse. She glanced up at him and smiled.

'You're looking a little bit better than the last time I saw you.'

Berlin nodded. 'I think I probably smell better, too. Mind if I join you? Just until someone more interesting shows up, of course.'

'Goodness gracious, Charlie, don't tell me you're in danger of developing a sense of humour.'

As he sat down there was a burst of raucous laughter from the crowd surrounding the salesman. The man grinned at his audience, finished off his beer and launched into his next story.

'So this old cove with a big nose and a leather apron, a real Ikey Mo, is standing outside Goldberg's Greengrocers on Chapel Street.'

Berlin saw Rebecca turn her head towards the group.

'Next thing you know this young bloke jumps off the tram and starts belting into him. "Why are you hitting me, why are you hitting me?" the old bloke starts whining and the young bloke says, "Cos you sank the bloody *Titanic*!"'

The crowd was smiling in anticipation and so was the salesman.

Rebecca pushed her chair back and stood up. 'Excuse me for a second will you, Charlie.' She walked across the room to the group.

The salesman continued his story in a whiny, nasal voice. '"Oy, that wasn't me, it was an iceberg what sank the *Titanic*," the old man yells —' Someone cleared their throat noisily and nudged the salesman, and then there was silence.

He turned around. Rebecca was behind him, smiling pleasantly. The salesman looked her up and down slowly, his eyes lingering on her breasts. He gave her an oily smile and Berlin felt an urge to smash the man's face in.

'Hullo, darlin', haven't seen you around here before, what might your name be?'

'It's Rebecca, Rebecca Greenbaum.'

The salesman's face froze. 'Look, girlie, I didn't mean ... I mean ...'

'Don't let me stop you.' She smiled pleasantly at the salesman. 'I think the punch line is "Iceberg, Goldberg, what's the bloody difference. You fucking Jews are all the same to me."' She spat out the words 'fucking Jews', the smile gone from her face.

'Language, please!' Maisie said from behind the bar, after an uncomfortable silence from the crowd.

Rebecca walked back to the table and sat down. The bar stayed silent until the traveller said, 'I'm shouting a round for the house. What's everyone having?'

'Mine's a gin and tonic.' Rebecca yelled her order across the room in the direction of the salesman and then winked at Berlin. 'Nothing pisses off an anti-Semite more than having to buy a drink for a Jew.'

'You're Jewish, Miss Green?' Berlin asked.

'I am indeed. Is that a problem for you, Charlie? And if you're about to tell me I don't look Jewish I should warn you I've been told that before and it really ticks me off. Jews come in all shapes and sizes.'

Berlin shook his head. 'No, I didn't mean to offend you . . . but the church in Albury . . . I assumed —'

'I wasn't there for communion or confession, Charlie, I was just keeping an eye on a friend.'

'You seemed to be familiar with it all, though.'

'I'm Jewish with a Catholic girls' school education. Sometimes it gets a bit confusing for me as well. My parents originally came from Stuttgart. I was born there.'

'You're German, too?'

She smiled. 'I'm full of surprises. Have you ever been to Stuttgart?'

Berlin shook his head. It wasn't strictly a lie. Both of his visits had been at twenty thousand feet, and all he'd seen of the city were the raging fires lit by incendiaries and fanned by the pressure waves spreading out in circles from the impact point of thousand-pound high-explosive bombs.

'My father had a commercial photography business there, in partnership with a German friend. By '34 he could see where things were going for the Jews and fortunately he still managed to get a decent price from his partner for his share of the business. We had a neighbour who'd sold farming machinery in Australia and he spoke a lot about the wide open spaces so we came here.'

'That must have been tough.'

'I was only ten, so I adjusted pretty quickly. There wasn't much work in the big cities, especially for foreigners, so my father opened a small camera shop in Ballarat. My parents weren't what you'd call observant Jews in any case, and with what was happening in Europe they decided to reinvent themselves in their new life, so Solomon and Sarah Greenbaum became Sam and Betty Green. I got to stay Rebecca but if anyone asked I was named after the one from Sunnybrook Farm. The local Catholic school was the best in the district so I was sent there.'

'I can see how that would get confusing.'

'Tell me about it. Every Friday night we had a Shabbat dinner. My mother would light the candles and my father would say a prayer over the wine and the challah.'

'What's challah?'

'It's a special kind of bread, I used to help my mother make it.'

'You really are full of surprises.'

She reached across the table and brushed her hand against his. 'You have no idea, Charlie.'

Berlin decided she was right about that.

'Then the following Monday I'd be back at school, a good little Catholic girl, sitting with my knees together and making up interesting sins to confess. Even after I left school a lot of my friends were Catholics. I really didn't think much about being Jewish until they started showing the newsreels from the camps after the war. Finding out that six million of your people were murdered simply for being Jews does make you want to stand up and be counted.' She smiled at Berlin. 'But I have to say there's nothing like going to a Catholic high school to get a great insight into Jewish jokes, if you can call them that. But if you want to hear some really good jokes, funny ones, you have to hear the ones Jews tell on themselves.'

'I went to a state school so I've got a few about Catholics. But mostly in state school they were about sex and farting.'

'Let me get my gin and tonic and then you can tell me some.'

The idea of telling Rebecca dirty jokes made Berlin slightly uncomfortable. But then he realised almost everything about this woman made him uncomfortable. And, strangely, that was something he liked.

Dinner was thick slices of pale pork drowning in rich, glossy gravy that washed over a pile of potatoes and vegetables. There was also a large wedge of crisp, golden skin on one side of the plate.

'Thanks, Lily, this is just what I needed. And I'll bet it tastes as good as it looks.'

Berlin's comment got a smile out of her. 'I've given you that extra big bit of crackling there, Mr Berlin, but if you want more just ask.' She glanced over at Rebecca.

'Will you be eating this evening, Miss Green?'

Rebecca shook her head. 'I had fish and chips in town earlier, thanks Lil.'

'Is it the pork?' Berlin asked, after Lily walked away. 'Are you a kosher person?' He pronounced it 'kosh-er'.

Rebecca shook her head. 'It's "ko-sher" and no, I'm not.'

'How was it living in Ballarat during the war? You said your old man had to go away. Was he interned?'

'He was – took it a lot better than I did. He said at least they were locking him up for being a German rather than a Jew.'

Berlin guessed at how she had taken it from the look on her face.

'Dad said he knew they'd wake up to themselves eventually, which they did.'

'He hold a grudge?'

She shook her head and Berlin decided to change the subject. 'I saw your photograph of Bellamy's militia in the paper. Not your name though.'

'I'll get there, Charlie, sooner or later. It looked okay, didn't it?'

'I suppose so. Got me some grief from my boss.'

'I'm sorry about that. I guess I owe you one.' She stood up. 'It's been a long day so if you'll excuse me I'm going upstairs to slide naked into a tub full of bubbles for a very long, very hot soak.'

Berlin watched her as she walked across the room, the image she'd left him with firmly in his head.

THIRTY-SEVEN

Just after ten there was a firm knock on Berlin's door.

'It's open.'

He wasn't expecting it to be Rebecca.

'Something wrong?'

'My room's a bit chilly.'

'That's probably why the landlord keeps his tropical orchid collection in here.'

She looked at the cheap wooden bedside table, the cracked washbasin and the sagging plywood wardrobe in the corner. 'This is grim, isn't it? Mine's not a whole lot better. How's the bed?'

'I've slept in worse places. You want a drink?' The bottle of whisky was on the side table, next to his packet of cigarettes and a box of matches.

Rebecca shook her head. 'No, apart from the odd gin and tonic I'm not a big fan of alcohol.'

She undid the snaps down the side of her skirt and stepped out of it. 'I've got other vices to make up for it though.'

'If this is about the photograph getting me into trouble . . .'

She stared at him then shook her head slowly. 'Jesus, you're a funny bastard, Berlin.'

After carefully folding the skirt she placed it over the back of the chair, putting her cardigan on top, and her blouse after that. Berlin reached for the bedside lamp, with its flyspecked bulb inside the flyspecked shade.

'You can leave it on if you like, Charlie.'

'I thought you might prefer . . .'

'When a girl finally manages to get her hands on some decent lingerie she wants to show it off. The bloke I got it from in Melbourne said it was French, pre-war. Real silk.'

She stepped out of the white half-slip. Underneath she was wearing cami knickers over her garter belt and stockings. Wriggling out of the knickers she sat on the edge of the bed, carefully removing her shoes and stockings. She had an even nicer arse than he'd imagined.

Then she reached behind and unhooked her bra. She turned around, standing naked in front of him. Her breasts were larger than he'd expected, full and round with dark-ringed nipples puckering in the cold of the room. Her pubic hair was a thick dark triangle, almost shocking against the white of her skin.

She slipped into bed next to him, and when their skin touched his whole body stiffened, except for the part that was most appropriate.

'Not exactly the sort of response I expected. Can I have a cigarette?'

Berlin took one from the packet and handed it to her. She took a long drag after he lit it.

'Sorry about . . .'

She shook her head. 'No pressure, Charlie.'

Her finger traced the line of smooth white skin running down from his shoulder. 'This the only scar you've got?'

He was silent, and she glanced up at his impassive face. 'Sorry, sometimes I talk too much.'

She stubbed out the cigarette and threw back the blankets. Berlin stared at her extraordinary body.

'But on the other hand, Charlie, I've found that sometimes a good chinwag can help to straighten things out.'

She slid down his body and her dark hair spread over his belly. Berlin gasped at the first touch of her lips.

A short time later she looked up at him and smiled. 'Told you, let me know if you want me to stop.'

He stared at her and slowly shook his head from side to side. He didn't want her to stop, not ever.

Then she was on top of him, astride him, riding him, her hair whipping across her face. Their eyes locked and he wondered what she was seeing. She was staring hard into his eyes until hers glazed and Berlin saw a flush begin between her breasts and spread up her throat to her face, and then she was gasping, gulping air in short breaths, her hands gripping his arms so hard he thought they might break. As she climaxed, eyes closed and whimpering, Berlin felt disconnected. Though he had physically been with Rebecca, their eyes and bodies locked together, their sweat pooling in the cold air of the shabby room, his mind was somewhere distant.

He looked across to the corner of the room and found himself looking into the emptiness of his own eyes. He saw the mud caked on his boots and a light dusting of snow on his woollen cap and on the shoulders of his dirty khaki greatcoat. If he had climaxed with Rebecca he was unaware of it, his body and mind having somehow lost track of each other on a country road on a freezing, sleeting morning in Poland.

Later, Rebecca watched Berlin as he slept. He looked peaceful for a few minutes and then his face started to twitch as his head jerked from side to side and he groaned. She could see his jaw muscles tighten as he ground his teeth. She stroked his head, which seemed to soothe him momentarily.

When she had first arrived in Ballarat, Rebecca's parents let her get a puppy for company. When he slept the puppy would twitch and yelp, and sometimes a tremor ran through his body and paws. Rebecca's mother would always smile and say, 'Look, Rebecca, he dreams he's chasing rabbits out in the fields.'

As Rebecca watched Berlin's face twist and contort, listening to the groans and sharp gasps, she knew whatever his dreams were they were not about chasing rabbits.

THIRTY-EIGHT

'Berlin.' The bomb-aimer's voice crackled in his headphones over the roar of the Merlins. 'Berlin dead ahead, Skipper.'

On the horizon he could see the eerie white beams of the searchlights probing the sky, hunting for the pathfinders; the flaming red of the massive, pink pansy target indicators burning on the ground; the yellow smudges of the air-bursting smoke markers staining the sky over the target.

Berlin. Fuck.

The German capital was called the Big City by the aircrew, and it was always nasty. The men in the ops briefing room groaned when the curtains were pulled back on the wall map to reveal the 'Target for Tonight' and the long lines of tape indicated flight paths converging on Berlin. There was a rumour that when the mess cooks found out the target was Berlin they drastically reduced the number of hot meals they prepared for the returning bomber crews.

Berlin. Fuck.

Pathfinder Mosquitos had followed the Oboe wireless beams, dumped their markers and fled, leaving the lone Master Bomber circling high above, over the target. The city was dead ahead, and Berlin's Lanc was closing in quickly, leading the bomber stream with the blue-white beam of the radar-controlled master searchlight relentlessly hunting him. This was the moment Berlin felt most alone, most powerless, with one master above him and one below.

Although the heavy flak from the massed anti-aircraft guns on the Kammhuber Line was miles behind them, the AA fire of the Big City's three massive flak towers was beginning to play its deadly percussive concert. *Bang! Bang! Bang!*

Berlin. Fuck.

Bang! Bang! Bang!

Berlin was sweating inside the leather jacket under his flight suit. He was going to die tonight, he just knew it.

Bang! Bang! Bang! The shells bursting closer, red-hot shards of razor-edged shrapnel peppering the Lanc's fuselage, searching for fuel tanks to ignite or oil or hydraulic lines or human veins to slash and sever, draining the life out of aircraft and crew or burning them up in a conflagration that would peak in the load of high explosives crammed in the bomb bay, blasting them all to kingdom come.

'Mr Berlin!' *Bang! Bang! Bang!* 'Mr Berlin, wake up!'

He staggered to the door, trying to remember where he was. Vern Corrigan was standing in the hallway, holding Berlin's shoes. He was wearing a frayed dressing gown that gaped open to reveal a yellowed singlet and drooping flannelette pyjama bottoms. Corrigan was staring at him as Berlin fought to clear his head. Lily should put more blue in the wash next Monday, he almost heard himself saying.

'Haven't you got any pyjamas, Berlin?'

Berlin realised he was naked and saw the landlord trying to peer over his shoulder, looking in the direction of the bed. He pulled the door half-closed.

'What the hell do you want, Corrigan? Jesus, what's the time?'

'It's just gone five. Constable Roberts is waiting for you downstairs.'

'Another robbery?'

The landlord shook his head. 'Not this time. A murder. Said to wake you straight away.'

Berlin tried to focus. Christ, a murder.

'Tell Roberts I'll be down in five minutes.'

'Look, if you'll be staying on for a bit I'm sure my wife can find you some pyjamas.'

Berlin shook his head to try to clear it. What the hell was Corrigan going on about?

'I can put the kettle on if you want a tea or a coffee but there's no milk yet.'

'Just give me my shoes.'

THIRTY-NINE

The reason there was no milk was because the milko's horse and cart were standing outside the alley where the body was. The heavily maned draught horse munched contentedly on the oats in its nose bag, shaking its head occasionally and stamping a massive foot, causing the steel ladles hanging on the lips of the almost-full milk churns to bang and rattle. Berlin noted the sweetish smell of fresh horseshit and fresh blood, and the more acrid aroma of vomit.

In the muddy alley constables Eddy and Hooper were shining torches on a shape covered with a police raincape. One torch flickered out as Berlin approached and Hooper bashed the ribbed silver case against his leg until the light was restored.

'Where's the sergeant, Constable Hooper?'

'Gone home. He's feeling a bit crook. He says you should handle this. Did Roberts warn you it's a bit bloody grim?'

Berlin knelt down by the body, careful to keep his overcoat clear of the mud. 'So what have we got here exactly, Hooper?'

Hooper lifted the cape. The girl's legs were pale and streaked with mud and something else. She was barefoot and her dark blue dress was hitched up over her knees. Hooper pulled the cape back further and Berlin sucked in his breath. 'Jesus.' Hooper lowered the cape.

'Local girl?' Berlin asked.

'Name of Jenny Lee, about sixteen. She's wearing her school uniform.'

'That's all we have?'

'Parents run a grocery store on High Street. Quiet people, no trouble, like most chinks.'

A stooped older man wearing an old-fashioned belted overcoat stood off to one side, watching. He took something from a white paper bag and put it into his mouth. Berlin saw a tremor in the hand holding the bag and he caught the smell of peppermint. 'Who's the alky, Roberts?'

'That's Doctor Morris, does the coronial work when it comes up. How'd you know he's an alky?'

'You don't need to be Sherlock Holmes to work that out. Who dragged him away from his bottle?'

'The sergeant said he wanted a cause of death certified.'

'Jesus, I'd think that would be pretty bloody obvious. You find the head yet?'

'That's how we made the identification. Trev actually found it. You know, Trev Casterton, the milko.'

'The legless charioteer?'

'That's him. Anyway, Trev was heading back to his milk cart, walking down the alley, and there was the girl's head in the middle of a puddle. It's over there.'

He pointed further up the alley to where another raincape lay on the ground, a slight bump in its centre.

'Old Trev's been pretty much spewing up his guts since he found her. Had the same effect on Sergeant Corrigan, which is why he left.'

Berlin studied the buildings on both sides of the dark alley.

'What was Casterton doing down here? I don't see any billy cans left out for milk.'

'He says he was making a delivery, and it's a shortcut, but some of us think he might have been knocking off the assistant stationmaster's wife. The alley leads round to her back door and it seems like the horse knows this is a regular stop.'

'So Trev and Jesse there were both getting their oats this morning.'

Roberts grinned. 'You could say that, I suppose.'

The doctor noisily cleared his throat. Roberts looked towards him and then quickly looked away. The doctor walked over to them. 'I'm not sure that kind of humour is appropriate here, gentlemen, given the circumstances.'

Berlin put out his hand. 'Doctor Morris, is it? I'm DC Berlin.' They shook hands and Berlin could feel the tremor he'd noticed earlier.

'Peppermint?' The doctor held out the bag.

Berlin shook his head. 'No thanks.' The mints might have disguised the whisky on the man's breath but Berlin could smell it coming out of his pores. He put the doctor at around sixty, with the rheumy eyes, reddish nose, careful concentration and ever so slightly slurred words of a competition-level drinker.

'How did they get her head off, Doc?'

'Neatly. Possibly with one blow.'

'You think they used a cleaver, Mr Berlin?' Roberts said. 'The Chinese use cleavers, so perhaps it was a family thing or a Tong killing.'

'Every butcher in this town has a cleaver, Roberts, and somehow I don't think Wodonga is a hotbed of Chinese secret societies. Perhaps it could have been a bayonet or a machete, Doctor Morris?'

The doctor shrugged. The paper bag rustled in his hand as he reached for another mint. Morris had the DTs and he had them bad.

'What about a samurai sword, then? A lot of our blokes brought them back from the islands as souvenirs.'

'That might be a possibility, DC Berlin. Samurai swords are incredibly sharp, I understand. Cec Champion's eldest boy was beheaded with one, you know.'

'I heard. You up in the islands, Doc?'

'Alas, no, I sat this one out. I was in Palestine in the first war, an army surgeon. They said I was too old in '41 and besides, I had enough to do here.'

Too old or too drunk? Berlin wondered.

He knelt down near the body, again carefully holding the bottom of his overcoat to keep it clear of the mud. He lifted a corner of the cape. 'There's blood on her legs. Could she have been assaulted or raped?'

The doctor glanced down at the body. 'It's a possibility, I suppose. I'll find out in the autopsy.'

Berlin stood up and looked around the alley. 'Not a lot of blood anywhere else, though. You'd expect a lot of blood with a decapitation, right, Doc?'

'Yes, if the victim is alive at the time.'

'Are you suggesting she was killed somewhere else, Mr Berlin?'

'Possibly, Roberts, or she was already dead when she was beheaded.'

'As I said, DC Berlin, we should perhaps wait on the autopsy. Can we move the corpse soon? My surgery is just a couple of streets over.'

Berlin shook his head. 'Sorry, but I'd like some photographs of the body in situ first. Roberts, can you head back to the hotel to rustle up Miss Green and her box brownie.' He hoped she'd be back in her own room by now. 'And make it snappy.'

Roberts returned with Rebecca in fifteen minutes. She was wearing trousers and Berlin could see that it made sense for her to dress that way. With the bending and stretching and squatting necessary to get the right angles, a skirt would have been impractical.

As she worked, Roberts and Berlin stood at the end of the alley watching the sky lighten.

'Has someone been sent to notify the girl's parents?'

'The sergeant sent First Constable Hogan.'

Berlin glanced over at Roberts. His voice was flat and he had a faraway look in his eyes. The boy had something else on his mind.

'This your first dead body, Roberts?'

'My girlfriend's old man is an undertaker over in Albury. She's shown me some dead bodies before.'

'Something else bothering you?'

'Mr Berlin, what the doctor said before, about joking around next to the body – you think it's wrong?'

Berlin offered the boy a cigarette but he shook his head.

'She's someone's daughter, Roberts, and she's dead and that's a terrible thing. But our job's not mourning her, it's finding out who killed her. She's just a case, a job we have to do. Sometimes the only way to get through it is by making the odd joke. You start taking things personally then you might as well . . .' Berlin was about to say 'blow your brains out' but he stopped. 'Pack it in and go work in a shoe shop.'

Berlin checked his watch and then flicked his cigarette butt into a puddle. The sun was just breaking the horizon and somewhere in the distance he thought he could hear the sound of motorcycles.

FORTY

Back at the hotel Berlin went up to his room while Rebecca stopped to use the telephone at the reception desk. She knocked on his door a few minutes later.

'The paper is giving me a couple of paragraphs on the news pages, with a by-line,' she said. 'Being Johnny-on-the-spot pays off.'

'Congratulations.' Berlin raised his glass of whisky in a toast.

'Bastard of a way to get the editor's attention, eh? The headline will read "Gruesome Murder in Country Town". Gruesome is right.'

'Want a drink? It's a bit early, but under the circumstances . . .'

Rebecca shook her head. She turned and walked down the hallway to the bathroom. He heard the water running in the shower and it seemed to him that it kept on running for a very long time.

Berlin washed and shaved. He wiped the mud from his shoes with the brown wrapping paper saved from his parcels, changed his shirt and then went downstairs.

Barry and Vern Corrigan were sitting at the kitchen table drinking tea but Berlin's nose told him there was more than tea in their cups. Vern looked up as Berlin walked into the kitchen.

'I'm sorry Mr Berlin, but we can't do you any breakfast this morning. Lily got real crook when Barry told her about the chink girl. She took a couple of Bex powders and now she's having a bit of a lie-down. I'll have my hands full looking after the boys and the baby so I'm afraid you'll have to try one of the cafés for something to eat.'

'Any suggestions?'

'You could try Peter's, a couple of doors up from the police station, or there's Dempster's café opposite the Terminus Hotel. They're usually open by now. It's next to that girl's . . . I mean it's next to the Lee's grocery store, where the girl lived.'

The sergeant nodded in agreement. 'Yeah, try there. But I don't know how a bloke could be hungry after seeing something like that.'

Corrigan's usually florid face was almost a natural colour, which seemed as close as he could ever get to pale. Vern patted him on the shoulder.

'Barry here's still a bit under the weather. Just look at him.'

Corrigan shrugged off his brother's hand. 'I'll be right in a while, Vern, you don't have to fuss. And I've got a bit of news for you, Berlin.'

'Is that right, Sarge.'

'I called Wangaratta about the girl, and they called Melbourne.'

Berlin knew what was coming next.

'Melbourne called me right back. Consensus is that since we have a real-life, big-city detective already on the ground here, you might as well take charge of this case, too. I'll be taking more of a supervisory role.'

Berlin saw Vern Corrigan look at his brother proudly. Was it because he knew words like 'consensus' and 'supervisory' or because he got them out without tripping over his tongue?

'I'll get started right after breakfast. Dempster's, you reckon?'

'You want a lift?' Rebecca was standing behind him in the kitchen doorway.

He'd been wondering how he'd get into town. 'Sounds good.'

'I'll warm the car up, while you get your coat and hat.'

Vern followed Berlin out into the hallway. He stood next to him, nervously shifting his weight from foot to foot as Berlin pulled on his coat. Leaning in close, he lowered his voice almost to a whisper.

'Mr Berlin, about last night and that girl, in your room I mean. This is a decent, family hotel and I've got kids and I don't want to give offence . . .'

'Then don't.' Berlin said it quietly and the two men stared at each other.

'I just mean, if you can be a bit discreet . . .'

'I guess you mean I should take a lead from you and Maisie then.'

Corrigan looked at Berlin with those hard, angry eyes until something in the other man's face made him look away. Berlin adjusted his hat. 'One more thing – that salesman bloke, Brian, was he in the hotel all night? I didn't see his car in the car park when I went out this morning.'

'I'm afraid Brian didn't avail himself of our facilities last evening, DC Berlin.'

Avail? Berlin thought. Early-morning drinking seemed to do wonders for the Corrigans' vocabularies.

'I saw him leaving with Maisie around eleven and I'm sure she'll be able to fill you in on what he got up to overnight, probably in very great detail if you want to hear it.'

Berlin decided that explained the anger in Corrigan's eyes.

'Tell Lily I hope she feels better soon.' He walked out to the car park where the Austin was idling, thin white smoke from its exhaust drifting across the loose gravel. The interior was cramped compared to the big Dodge and Berlin and Rebecca were sitting almost thigh to thigh, which he decided was not a bad thing.

Rebecca was a good driver and managed to coax some decent acceleration out of the underpowered vehicle. She put the car into top gear when they got some speed, taking her hand off the gearstick to put it on Berlin's knee.

'You certainly know how to show a girl a good time, Charlie,' she said quietly.

'I'm sorry, I hope it wasn't too awful for you.'

'You mean the sex or the dead body?'

Berlin laughed. 'You're a strange one, Rebecca.'

'I'm not the one who thought the perfect end to a perfect evening was a decapitated corpse.'

Several large trucks were parked outside Dempster's, and when Berlin saw the size of the breakfasts he understood why. They found a booth and sat opposite each other, knees touching. A young waitress brought tea unasked and took their orders.

'So, what are you starting right after breakfast, Charlie?'

'They've given me the Lee girl's murder as well as the robberies.'

Their food arrived at the same time as the junior constable.

'You had breakfast yet, Roberts?'

The boy shook his head. 'I've got full board so I usually get porridge and toast and a boiled egg. Missed out this morning since I was out early.'

'The dog get yours?'

'I suppose so. My landlady really didn't appreciate them coming to get me in the middle of the night.'

'I'll bet the Lee girl's parents didn't appreciate the early-morning knock on their door either. Order yourself something to eat, my shout.'

'Gee, thanks.'

Roberts had a long conversation with the girl behind the counter and Berlin wondered if he was ordering everything on the menu. When the lad came back Berlin could see he was trying to decide if he should sit next to Rebecca. She shifted a little closer to the wall and Roberts slid in beside her.

'Nan, the girl behind the counter there, was just asking if the rumours were true, Mr Berlin – that the motorcycle gang had moved up to murder.'

Berlin splashed tomato sauce over his charred sausages. 'News travels fast.'

'It's a very small town. She says people have been coming in since they opened talking about the Lee girl, saying the killers are returned men out to get their own back – you know, getting revenge for their mates who got killed up north. Any truth in that, you think?'

'We can't rule anything out at this stage. Right now I think we should concentrate on the girl. Can you lean on Doctor Morris for the autopsy report?'

'I'll get on to it.'

'And we also need to find out what that salesman Brian got up to last night. Apparently Maisie should be able to fill you in.'

Rebecca looked at Berlin over the top of her teacup. 'And that's not exactly headline news.'

'We don't need all the lurid details of her night with Brian, Roberts, even if she wants to supply them. Just what time he came and when he went.' Berlin glanced across at Rebecca. 'What I meant was, I want the time of his arrival and the time of his departure.'

She held up her right hand, palm outward. 'Hey, I wasn't going to say a word.'

'Good job, too.' He smiled and turned back to Roberts. 'And we also need to find out what Cec Champion was up to last night.'

Berlin and Rebecca finished their breakfasts just as Roberts' heaped plate arrived. It looked like the constable *had* ordered everything on the menu.

Rebecca whistled. 'That's some breakfast, Bob. I'll scoot out and let you get comfortable. I think you might be needing a bit of elbow room.' He stood up and she slid out of the booth.

'I'm off to get your photographs processed, Charlie. Maybe we can catch up later.'

Berlin nodded. Roberts was watching them both. Had Roberts found Rebecca in his room? Or maybe Vern had said something. He stood up when Rebecca had gone.

'I'll pay the bill and then I'm going to talk to the Lees. When you finish up here, wait for me in the car.'

'We going anywhere in particular?'

'I thought we might take a run out to Bandiana and see if Whitmore's dug up anything on Blue and his mates and then maybe head out to Bonegilla and have another chat with them. You said they've been up to some mischief with the local girls in the past.'

Roberts had a fork full of toast and egg and sausage halfway to his mouth. He stopped. 'Just us?'

'We'll be right, mate. I only want to ask a few questions.'

'Okay, if you say so.'

The constable went back to his breakfast with a lot more enthusiasm than Berlin had for his next task.

FORTY-ONE

Lee's Grocery & General Supplies was located near the big two-storey timber signal box that controlled the trains to Albury and operated the heavy railway gates. A simple corrugated-iron awning shaded the single-storey shopfront and its wooden verandah. Brightly painted tin signs for Arnott's biscuits, Kinkara tea and Persil washing powder decorated the building. The double front doors were wide open.

Inside was a jumble of mops and brooms, wooden shelving laden with tins and boxes stretching up to the ceiling, and flypaper hanging from the overhead light fittings. An Asian man stood behind the counter, next to the scales. He was wearing a grey dustcoat over a suit and tie and his face was devoid of expression.

'Can I help you?' he asked.

'Hey! No butting in.'

A young red-headed boy was waiting at the counter in front of Berlin. He was barefoot, wearing a faded plaid shirt and patched short trousers held up with braces attached by shiny chrome clips. The boy was rubbing a couple of copper coins together in his hand, looking longingly towards a glass-topped case full of firecrackers.

'Serve the kid first.' Berlin glanced down at his watch. 'And shouldn't you be in school?'

'Fair go, mister. Me mum and dad got shickered last night and Mum slept in and I didn't get no breakfast.' Berlin put the lad's age at around six or seven, going on forty. The boy turned back to the shopkeeper. 'Can I have a penny ha'peneth of broken biscuits, please? All sweet ones.'

The shopkeeper picked up a brown paper bag and lifted the lids on several square metal biscuit boxes. He began dropping pieces of broken biscuits into the bag, with the boy watching him intently over the counter.

'Make sure you chuck in some teddy bears.' He looked up at Berlin. 'I like teddy bears, especially the heads.'

Berlin smiled. 'Me too. Don't you have any shoes? It's cold today.'

'Nah, couldn't find 'em but she'll be right.'

The shopkeeper opened another biscuit box and shook his head. 'No broken teddy bears today.'

Berlin put a threepenny coin on the counter. 'There's a trey-bit, break some.'

The shopkeeper added a couple of teddy bears, weighed the bulging bag, twisted the corners and handed it over the counter. Berlin tossed the kid another coin.

'Get yourself an apple on the way to school, and move smartly. I'm a policeman and I don't want to have to lock you up.'

'Thanks for the dosh, mister. Okay if I get a sherbet bomb for play lunch with the change?'

'Just don't go buying crackers with it. Now hop it. And if I catch you wagging school again I'll spiflicate you.' The kid scuttled out of the shop and Berlin turned back to the shopkeeper, whose face was still impassive.

'I'm DC Berlin, Mr Lee. I need to talk to you about your daughter. Is this a . . .' Berlin almost said a good time, but stopped himself. 'Is this a suitable time?'

'Perhaps so. It seems a dead child is bad for business, DC Berlin. The boy was my only customer so far this morning.' He walked across the shop and closed the doors to the street. Then he walked back behind the counter to a curtained doorway.

'Please come this way.'

Berlin followed him through the doorway into the rear of the shop. There was a wok on top of a wood stove and the shelves held the same kind of bowls Berlin had eaten chow mein from in the Chinese cafés on Little Bourke Street. There was a sickly sweet smell in the air and smoke wafted from thin joss sticks burning in front of a red and gold cabinet, which held a metal bowl of fruit. On either side were framed, faded photographs of an elderly Chinese couple in traditional dress.

'My wife has been praying to our ancestors to protect our daughter. We were up all night when she failed to return home from the hotel.'

'I understand.'

'Then the policeman knocks on the door. And now my wife weeps. Will you sit down?'

He indicated the kitchen table and the two men sat down. Mr Lee raised the lid of a wicker basket and lifted a willow-patterned teapot out of the padded interior.

'Tea?'

Berlin nodded and the shopkeeper poured two cups. Berlin looked around for milk and sugar, but neither were on offer. The tiny cups had no handles so Berlin followed the shopkeeper's lead, lifting the cup and sipping. The tea was only warm and had a slightly acrid taste. He was glad it was such a small cup.

'What can you tell me about your daughter's friends, Mr Lee?'

'My daughter works here before school, in the hotel kitchen after school for pocket money, and on the weekend she studies.

Her friends are classmates she sees only at school.'

'She have anyone special? A boyfriend perhaps?'

Mr Lee shook his head. 'My daughter is an obedient child and she knows better. She obeys her parents. School, work, study.'

'Young people don't always do as they are told.'

'Gwailo children maybe, white people's children. My daughter is betrothed . . .' he paused, 'was betrothed to a young man in Melbourne, a merchant's son, from a good family.'

'When did they meet?'

'They have not met. They were to meet and marry on her eighteenth birthday.'

'She was happy with that?'

'She was happy with her parents' wishes.'

'And you, Mr Lee, do you have enemies, a dispute with anyone, anyone who might wish harm on you and your family?'

Mr Lee shook his head.

Berlin put his cup down on the table. 'I think that's all I need for now, Mr Lee. I'm sorry I had to intrude. Please give your wife my condolences.'

'Of course. Thank you for your consideration.'

He opened the doors to the street to let Berlin out, and left them open. The Dodge was waiting at the kerb and Roberts was talking to Constable Hooper. Mr Lee picked up a broom and began to slowly sweep the verandah.

'I promise we will catch the man who did this and he will hang, Mr Lee.'

The grocer looked up, his expression blank. 'My daughter is a Chinese girl, DC Berlin. Who will hang a white man for killing a Chinese girl?'

Roberts was waiting in the driver's seat when Berlin opened the passenger door and climbed in, slamming it shut behind him.

'So what did Hooper want?'

'Looks like you might have been right about hearing motorcycles earlier this morning, Mr Berlin. He came by with a message for you – the railway station in Rutherglen got knocked over by a bunch of blokes on military Harleys around five a.m.'

'Right, Roberts. We'll need all the details of the Rutherglen robbery as soon as we can get them.'

'Constable Hooper is on to that already. You want to go over there this morning? Rutherglen, I mean? I'll need to top up the petrol tank if you do.'

'Let's wait and see what the preliminary reports tell us. I really want to talk to those carpenters about the Lee girl's murder but first we should stop by Bandiana.'

FORTY-TWO

Whitmore was sitting on the steps of the Bandiana Provost's hut when the Dodge pulled up. He stubbed the butt of his cigarette out on the step then made a small hole in the dirt at his feet and buried it. Berlin thought the sergeant looked tired.

'Bit of nastiness in town last night I hear, Charlie.'

'You heard right.'

'She was a good kid.'

'You knew her?'

'I know her parents. Most people do – it's a small town, remember. Got any suspects?'

'Maybe. I just had a couple of questions you might be able to help me with, Pete. You think Kenny Champion's old man'd be capable of something like that?'

Whitmore lit another cigarette. 'Charlie, the last few years have taught me anyone is capable of anything. But if you're asking if I think Cec did it, then no. We spotted him drinking down by the water tower just after nine last night. He was too pissed to even stand up. Kenny and me ran him home in the jeep. He was tucked up in bed snoring when we left him. That was around half-past nine.'

'What about Kenny? He lost his brother to the Japs.'

'So did you, Charlie. That make you a suspect? I lost a lot of mates, too. You want to ask me what I was up to last night?'

'No. So what about the carpenters out at Bonegilla? You manage to dig up anything on them yet?'

'I've got a lot of names for you – they're all ex-military. But as far as background goes, so far I've only got info on the ringleader, the one they call Blue. His real name is Harry Kendrick. Tough bastard, really tough. Served in the Middle East. Good soldier when there was fighting but a bit of a troublemaker when things were quiet. But that happens.'

'Violent?'

'Jesus, Charlie, there was a war on, remember? Violence is what they paid us for.'

'So did they get more out of him than they paid for?'

'Too right. Bugger kept getting promoted in the field and then running amok as soon as he got leave. They reckon in the end he'd put on his sergeant's stripes with a safety pin rather than wasting time with a needle and thread. Flattened some Yank officer in Brisbane when the Sixth came back. Fight over a girl, apparently. Wound up in the Army Detention Barracks at Grovely and then he did time at Boggo Road Jail for being a troublemaker. Got snarlered just before the war ended.'

'What does snarlered mean?' Roberts asked.

'Services No Longer Required. They gave him the elbow. I'd say the rest of his mates would probably be cut from the same cloth.'

'Great.' The tone in Roberts' voice indicated he wasn't too thrilled by this news. 'We're on our way out to Bonegilla to ask them some questions about the murder. Just the two of us,' he added.

'That sounds like fun. You mind if I tag along? I'm at a loose end this morning – anything for a bit of excitement.'

'Couldn't hurt, could it, Mr Berlin?'

'Thought you didn't want to get involved in civilian business, Pete.'

'But this is just going for a bit of a drive with a mate, Charlie. I don't plan on getting involved.'

'Kenny coming too?' Roberts asked.

'Sorry, Bob, he had a bit of a big night so he's taking it easy. Let me get my hat. Dibs on the back seat.'

The sergeant settled into the leather seat of the Dodge and sighed contentedly. 'Now this is the bloody duck's nuts, eh, my good fellows? Drive on, Roberts old sausage, drive on.' He took a pack of cigarettes from his pocket. 'Anyone for a smoke?'

Berlin shook his head.

'Ya know, Charlie, every time some high mucky-muck staff officer rolled past us while we were slogging through the ooze I wondered what it would be like to be in one of these. Closest I ever managed before this was getting my boys to help roll General Blamey's car out of a ditch.'

There was a different sentry on duty at the Bonegilla camp gate when they pulled up, but he was reading the same magazine. The sentry glanced at the car.

'You blokes know where you're go— Aww, cripes!' The sentry jumped up, crumpling the magazine behind him. 'G'day, Sarge. Didn't see you there.'

'She'll be right, Tommy, didn't mean to frighten you, son. You happen to know if that carpenter Blue and his mob are around?'

'Just Blue and some other bloke. Haven't seen the rest of them today. Just follow the road here and then go left at the ablutions block.'

Roberts had the Dodge rolling forward when the guard yelled, 'You'll see that Austin down there already.'

'Stop!'

Roberts stepped on the brakes, hard. Berlin already had his door halfway open.

'What Austin?'

'Little grey job. Nice-looking sheila driving. Said she was from the newspapers. She came through about five minutes ago.'

'Get going, Roberts, and put your foot down.'

The Dodge was moving forward before Berlin got his door closed again. They took the left turn at high speed with Berlin holding on tight to the door pillar.

The Austin was parked next to the half-built hut. There was no sign of Rebecca or the two men but a couple of motorcycles were parked just in front of the car, in the shade of the building. Roberts stopped the Dodge and they jumped out. The constable slammed his door shut and got a nasty glare from Berlin. He put his hands up in apology. Offcuts of wood were strewn about the site and Berlin picked up a piece about two feet long. Roberts selected a piece that was double the length. Whitmore took it off him, handing him something shorter.

'There you go, Bob,' he said quietly. 'You don't want to go banging into the ceiling when it's some boofhead's skull you're really after.'

Inside the unfinished hut, Blue and one of the other builders had Rebecca bailed up in a corner. Blue was laughing at the six-inch hatpin she was holding. When he saw her glance past him, he turned round and grinned.

'Berlin, wasn't it? You two turn up like a couple of bad pennies. And just when the morning was starting to get interesting.'

'I reckon it's even more interesting now.' Whitmore's voice came from behind Berlin. Roberts saw Whitmore was holding the jack handle from the Dodge.

Without taking his eyes off the three men, Blue leaned down and picked up an offcut of galvanised-steel water pipe. It was about five feet long and he held it at waist height, like a rifle at the ready rather than a club. He'd boasted that he'd been good with a bayonet, Berlin recalled.

'You want yours first or last, Sarge?'

'What, me? I'm just along for the ride – this is a civilian matter. Pretend I'm not here.'

Blue was ready to parry if the policeman came at him. Sunlight through the open roof glinted on the freshly cut metal tip of the makeshift weapon. Not sharp like the point of a bayonet, but still nasty enough.

The second carpenter had picked up a hammer. Blue's face was swollen, with welts that looked like fingernail marks. The other man had a black eye.

'The girl do that to you last night?'

Blue nodded. 'Bitch. I taught her a bloody lesson though. It was fun while it lasted. This is gunna be fun, too.' He grinned and raised the steel pipe but then his body twisted awkwardly. 'Ow! Jesus, fuck!'

He spun towards Rebecca, who had jammed her hatpin into his left buttock. Berlin swung his lump of wood down hard, connecting with the man's right hand where it held the water pipe. He could hear the crunch of bone as Blue's knuckles were crushed between wood and steel. Roberts threw his club at the second man, who ducked. The throw was followed by a crash tackle that took both men out through the half-built wall of the hut.

Berlin knew Blue was still dangerous even with one hand out of action, so he swung the wood again, low this time, catching him on the left side of the knee. Blue's leg collapsed under him and he went down hard.

Berlin tossed the piece of metal pipe out the window. Roberts had the second man face-down on the ground as he fitted handcuffs. He grinned at Berlin and gave him the thumbs up.

'He was right, that was fun.'

'You want to pace yourself, Bob,' Whitmore said. 'You've got that big match on Saturday, remember.'

Berlin was breathing hard, his heart thumping. Without Rebecca's hatpin they would all have been in serious trouble.

Blue was on his back, grimacing again and cursing softly.

'Tell me about the girl.'

'Fucking tart. I paid my money and then she gets all uppity about what she will and won't do. Bugger that. The boys almost tore that dump apart before the cops showed up.'

'What the hell are you talking about?'

'Knocking shop over the border.' It was Rebecca speaking. 'They got stuck into the grog in town last night and picked up some tarts. When it got ugly around two in the morning the Albury cops showed up and piled on.'

Berlin looked down at Blue. 'That how it happened?'

'Sure, if she says so. Stumpy and the other blokes are in hospital. Couple of cops, too. Those Albury boys are a touch sensitive. Me and Thommo here got taken back to the cells for bit of a belting. Chucked us out first thing this morning without any breakfast even.'

Outside Thommo was propped up against the front wheel of the Dodge, in the shade. Roberts was examining a tear in the right shoulder of his tunic.

'Cop this, Mr Berlin, the bugger ripped my sleeve. Sergeant Corrigan isn't going to be happy.'

'Take the handcuffs off him, Roberts, they didn't kill the Lee girl.'

Roberts stood up. 'What about the robberies?'

'Not last night's – they were indisposed. And the bikes are wrong. Take a look. They're ex-military alright, but one's a British BSA and the other one's a Yank Indian.'

Roberts pulled Thommo to his feet and the man moaned. 'Your mate's dislocated my bloody shoulder.'

'Tough.' Berlin turned to Rebecca. 'And what the hell were you doing out here?'

'I went to use the darkroom at the *Border Mail* office in Albury, to develop those pictures for you. They were talking about the punch-up the night before so I thought I'd take a quick run out here to get some details and see if there was a story in it.'

'All by yourself?'

'I had my hatpin.'

'Oh, that's alright then.'

'Hey, don't you start having a go at the lady's hatpin, Charlie,' Whitmore said. 'Damned thing saved your bacon.'

FORTY-THREE

After dropping Whitmore back at Bandiana, Berlin's next stop was Cec Champion's place. They followed South Street, the road beside the railway line that the gang had used for their getaway, turning right just before they got to the creek and the trestle bridge. Dick Street was really a muddy track, but on either side of the road there were new house allotments.

Roberts stopped the car outside a dilapidated asbestos-sheet house painted grey. Berlin wondered if the paint had once been destined for a battleship. The rusted wire gate squealed loudly on its hinges when Roberts pushed it open. The two men picked their way carefully down a muddy, overgrown path littered with junk. Berlin tried to keep clear of the worst of it.

'Nice place Cec has here.'

'Used to be better, I've seen photos from before. Back when Kenny and his brother and his mum and dad all lived here. She had the garden looking real nice, Kenny's mum. Mr Champion started letting it all go to hell after she died and when Kenny's brother went missing that pretty well finished him off.'

There was a tin billy can sitting in the sun on the verandah step.

Berlin bent down and picked it up. The milko must have done this part of his rounds before finding the girl. The metal was warm and the milk inside it would probably be on the turn. He crossed the verandah, carefully avoiding several broken planks, and hammered on the door. It took a lot of hammering before Cec Champion opened the door. The fireman was barefoot, unshaven and wearing dirty striped pyjamas. He squinted at the man standing on his doorstep.

'Who the fuck are you?'

'I'm DC Berlin. I think you know Constable Roberts.'

He stared at Roberts for a moment and then looked past him down the pathway to the street. 'Hello, Bob. Kenny with you?'

'Hello, Mr Champion. No, Kenny's not with us. I'm here for work. There's been a murder.'

'Struth, a murder. Who got killed, Bob?'

'That Chinese girl, Jenny Lee. You know, her parents run the grocery down by the railway gates.'

Champion nodded his head slowly. 'That's too bad. You want to come in for a cup of tea, Bob? Who's this feller?'

'This is DC Berlin, up from Melbourne.'

'I've seen you somewhere before, haven't I?'

'That's right, you almost ran us down in the loco yards on the day of the robbery.'

'Any bastard gets hit by a train deserves it, or bloody wants it. Not as though them damn locos don't make enough noise. I think I'll put the kettle on.'

'I was in the pub last Friday night as well, Mr Champion. You remember that?'

Champion shook his head. 'Memory's getting a bit fuzzy. But you're a copper and if you say you were there then I suppose you were. That cleared things up for you?'

'You go out anywhere late last night or early this morning?'

'I think I came straight home after my shift. Might have gone for a drink first, can't remember. That sound right, Bob? Kenny's not with you?'

Berlin handed Champion the billy can. 'No, Kenny's not with us, and we won't be staying for that cup of tea. Here's your milk. Might have got a bit warm.'

'You'll tell Kenny to come see me sometime, eh, Bob? I can't find his mum's engagement ring. He might remember where I put it.'

The gate squealed again as Roberts closed it behind them. Berlin had just opened the passenger door when he heard a voice.

'What's a bloody can of oil cost, you reckon?'

He looked across the street towards a substantial brick house set back on a low rise. There were lace curtains in the windows and well-kept fruit trees in the garden. A man was leaning on the wooden picket fence watching them. He was about sixty, wearing a straw hat and overalls. Berlin crossed the muddy road, avoiding the bigger puddles.

'Sorry, I missed that.'

The man was wearing gardening gloves and had a pair of secateurs in his right hand. 'I said, what's a bloody can of oil cost?'

'I don't follow.'

'Champion's bloody gate. Squirt of oil is all it needs. Man's got no consideration for his neighbours. Starts early and comes home late all hours. Bad enough having trains down the end of the street without his bloody gate. And that place is a disgrace.'

'You heard the gate last night?'

'Course I heard it. A man's not deaf, worse luck. Two soldiers brought him home, drunk as usual. Squeak, squeak, squeak. Totally inconsiderate.'

'And after they left?'

'Bloody milkman woke me and then nothing until you two

showed up just now. You're police, right? Can't you do something about it?'

Berlin walked across the road to the car. He opened the passenger door then looked back towards the brick house. 'You got a can of oil about the house, by any chance?'

'Of course, out in the shed. Why?'

'No reason, just asking.'

FORTY-FOUR

Rebecca came to Berlin's room around ten, slipping quickly out of her clothes and into his bed. A small fire had been burning in the grate when he'd come up to the room and there were flowers in a vase and fresh sheets on the bed. Vern must have told Lily about the previous night, he guessed. And Lily obviously had a different point of view to her husband.

There was something about this evening with Rebecca that was different from last time. After they made love she slumped down beside him, gasping, sweat beading on her forehead and between her breasts. Berlin felt a strange electrical energy surrounding them both, cocooning them, not dangerous but disconcertingly protective. He thought of the blue crackling light of St Elmo's fire, the static electricity he had sometimes seen dancing on the windscreen of the Lancaster as they droned towards their target. And this time when he'd looked across the room into the empty corner there was no one there.

'That was bloody stupid, you know.'

'You're such a sweet talker, Charlie.'

'You seem to go looking for trouble.'

'You mean right now, or this morning?'

Berlin realised he wasn't sure himself. 'A bloody hatpin?'

'They taught us how to fire Owen guns in the WAAFs but I couldn't get my hands on one at short notice.'

He felt the soft fullness of her breasts on his chest and her pubic hair brushing his thigh as she reached across him for a cigarette, disturbingly casual in her nakedness. She lit the cigarette, took a drag and offered it to him. When he shook his head, she stubbed it out in the ashtray, slid back down next to him and put her chin on his chest.

'Tell me a secret, Charlie.' She was looking right into his eyes.

He put a finger to her lips and she kissed it. Why had she asked him that? His secrets were locked away down deep in a place that he didn't want to enter. 'You first.'

Berlin thought for a moment that she was angry but there was something else in her eyes. He waited.

'I lied, Charlie.'

'I'm a policeman, everybody lies to the police.'

'When I said there was no one special, I mean.'

Berlin was surprised at his disappointment. Was it the lie or was it the man, he wondered. 'Who is he?'

'An American marine, a lieutenant.'

'Where is he now?'

'Tarawa.'

'Is that in America?'

'It's an island, in the Pacific.'

'He's not coming back?'

She shook her head.

Berlin was going to say he was sorry but decided it wasn't enough. So he said nothing.

'Do you have a secret, Charlie?'

He paused. 'There was a girl, in Poland, and she . . . she was

Jewish, I think, I mean she must have been.'

Rebecca understood it was her turn to wait. Berlin was staring across the room into a corner. She turned to look too but there was only emptiness.

'I wanted to help her . . . but . . . there was nothing . . .'

After a minute of silence he shook his head. 'I'm sorry but I don't think I want to play this game any more.'

'Charlie, if I can make it better I'll do anything.'

He stared at her.

'Anything, Charlie,' she repeated, 'I'll do anything you want. Just ask me, just ask me right now. Anything.'

Charlie Berlin looked down at the incredible body of the woman sprawled on top of him in this bleak Wodonga hotel room. To his utter consternation he realised he couldn't think of a single damn thing he wanted her to do. And he knew nothing in the world was ever going to make it better.

FORTY-FIVE

Roberts and Berlin were sitting in a booth at Dempster's when Rebecca walked in. It was a little after half-past ten.

'They said at the police station you'd be here. Looks like you boys are turning this place into your office.'

Berlin moved over in the booth and she sat down next to him.

'It's got a lot going for it,' he said. 'More room and less eavesdropping than the police station, you don't have to make your own tea and they serve a mean mixed grill. What more could a bloke want from his workplace?'

'Can I order you a cup of tea, Miss Green?' Roberts offered.

'That would be nice, thanks, Bob.'

While the constable was at the counter, Rebecca studied Berlin's face.

'You're looking rested, Charlie. Must have had a good night's sleep.' She squeezed his thigh under the table and he jumped, spilling his tea. 'So where do we stand, DC Berlin?'

Berlin poured tea from the saucer back into his cup. 'If by "we" you mean the police, investigations are continuing. Details will be made public when we deem appropriate.'

'C'mon, Charlie, help a girl out.' She squeezed his thigh again.

Roberts sat down. 'Tea'll be here in a tick, Miss Green. They're a bit behind this morning.'

'Thanks, Bob. I was just asking DC Berlin here how it was all going.'

'You want to give Miss Green a rundown, Roberts?'

'Sure thing.'

'Alright, Constable Roberts. What can you tell me?'

'Not too much I'm afraid, Miss Green. As far as the Lee girl goes, Kenny's dad has a pretty solid alibi. And I checked up on Maisie and the salesman, Mr Berlin. That Ford he was driving was still parked outside her place at nine on Tuesday morning and she said he'd been in all night.'

Berlin glanced at Rebecca, his eyes narrowing.

She grinned. 'I wasn't going to say a word, Charlie, trust me. So what about the robberies?'

'We're in pretty much the same shape there too, I'm afraid. Since we know for sure it wasn't those carpenters from Bonegilla tooling around on their motorbikes on Tuesday morning we seem to be up a creek.'

'And short of a paddle?'

Berlin had noticed the broad shoulders of the man in the booth behind Roberts twisting, as if he wanted to hear more of the conversation. Now he turned halfway around.

'You people after a bunch of blokes playing silly buggers on motorcycles early yesterday morning?'

The man was wearing a rumpled white shirt with a frayed and oil-stained tweed jacket. He had a fork grasped in his right hand with half a fat pork sausage impaled on the tines. From the squint of his eyes and his grimy hands and black-rimmed fingernails, Berlin picked him as a truckie.

'You know something?'

'Dunno, mate, maybe. I was bringing a truckload of cattle down to the saleyards early and the bloody bastards nearly ran me off the road on my way in to town.' He glanced at Rebecca. 'S'cuse my French, Miss.'

'Apology accepted.'

'When and where was this?' Berlin asked.

'Round about sunrise. It was just a bit past the Bandiana army camp, down the side road near that old footy oval out there.'

'You know anything about this place, Roberts?'

'Of course. Extra sports ground the army scratched out for the camp when it was first expanded.'

The truck driver nodded. 'That's the place.'

'Construction people knocked up a couple of wooden sheds for changing rooms and such early in the war,' Roberts continued. 'Hardly ever gets used any more but we've played there a few times when our home ground is out of action.'

Berlin turned back to the truckie. 'So what can you tell me about these blokes? The ones on the bikes.'

'Not a hell of a lot, I'm afraid. Couldn't really see too much, the sun was in my eyes and they were coming right at me. Two or three bikes at least I think, with sidecars. Ran me right off the road into the bloody gravel. By the time I got my wheels back on the tarmac and the dust settled, the bastards had completely disappeared.'

'Thanks,' Berlin said, 'that's a big help. Can I buy you another cup of tea?'

'Okay, strong, with milk.'

Roberts ordered the tea at the counter and glanced at his watch when he came back to the booth.

'Do you need the car for a bit? Sergeant Corrigan wanted me to run his brother's wife and bub over to the baby health clinic at Albury Hospital. The bus doesn't run all that often and Vern can't drive, you know, because of his arm.'

'Something wrong with the kid?'

'It's just a check-up but there's polio and scarlet fever and whooping cough about, so you have to be careful.'

Rebecca had her head down, scribbling something in a notebook.

'I don't suppose you know how to get to this footy oval, do you, Rebecca?'

She looked up. 'I think I can find it. Want me to run you out there?'

'If it's not too much trouble.'

'I'm entirely at your service.' She went back to her notebook.

'I'll be right for a ride, Roberts, if you want to head off.'

Rebecca closed her notebook after the constable left. She was smiling.

'Something on your mind?'

'I've just worked out my hook for the story. I reckon my editor is going to love it. I might nip over to the post office in a minute and phone the paper.'

'Can that wait till after we go out to the football oval?'

'Of course.'

'And you're sure you don't mind taking me?'

Rebecca leaned over to Berlin and lowered her voice. 'Well, I did say I'd do anything you wanted, Charlie, and I'm happy to oblige but I think a drive in the country is showing a distinct lack of imagination.'

FORTY-SIX

Rebecca parked the Austin beside the sports oval, a scabby brown patch of ground with four white goalposts at each end. A low, single-rail fence surrounded the oval and on the far side, set back against a rocky cliff face, there was a toilet block, a scoreboard and two wooden huts.

A rain squall was passing so they waited. Wind buffeted the little car and even though it was cold, droplets of condensation began beading up on the windscreen.

'Not exactly the MCG, is it, Charlie?'

'You got that right.' The tiny country sporting ground was as far as you could get from the hallowed Melbourne Cricket Ground, where the gods of cricket and football were worshipped by the faithful on a weekly basis. 'But I wouldn't have picked you as a footy fan.'

She laughed. 'I remember when we first arrived in Melbourne. We'd only been off the ship for about fifteen minutes before people started asking my father which team he was going to support. We finally worked out football was a bit more of a religion than a sport. He eventually let me choose a team just to shut people up.'

'Who did you go for?'

'St Kilda, because I liked the colours and I thought there was something quite noble and heroic in giving a team the nickname "the Saints". Then I actually saw a match and that quickly put the idea out of my head. I must say I do like seeing a nice high mark, though. So who do you follow, Charlie?'

'Essendon.'

'The Bombers, that's appropriate.'

The rain stopped after a few minutes and the gusty wind eased to just a breeze. Berlin wound down his window and checked the sky.

'Looks like it's over for now. Let's take a squiz, shall we, Miss Green?'

Rebecca grabbed her camera from the back seat and joined him at the white rail bordering the playing field. They ducked under the rail and crossed the oval together, stopping outside the huts. They were the same type of box-like, single-storey wooden structures that made up the Bandiana camp down the road.

One hut had windows down each side and a simple verandah overlooking the oval. The building was unlocked and inside it was divided into two separate changing areas. There was a row of washbasins and shower cubicles at the back and Rebecca studied the images scratched and drawn on the tiled walls.

'Maybe the army should consider running life-drawing classes. A lot of these boys are woefully under-informed about female anatomy.'

'And doing a lot of wishful thinking about their own, from the look of it,' Berlin added.

The second hut was larger and set further back from the oval so that it butted against the cliff face. The unlocked double doors were marked EQUIPMENT STORAGE and a sloping concrete ramp led down to ground level. Berlin pushed the doors open and inside they found a lawnmower and line-marking equipment, and a pile of mops, buckets, rakes and yard brooms. In one corner was a simple kitchen with a sink, an urn, a pie warmer and some folded trestle tables.

'Wild goose chase?'

'Seems like it.'

'Nice space, though. It would make a great photo studio.'

Berlin was only half listening. 'What?'

'I said this place would make a great studio, Charlie. Just a couple of windows on the side, which would be easy to black out, and a really solid floor. Look.' She jumped up and down on the spot. 'See, solid as a rock.'

'Possibly not the most ideal location, though – not a lot of passing traffic.'

'Exactly what my old man would say. Want to head back to town now? I need to make that phone call.'

Rebecca dropped Berlin off outside the police station. He didn't feel like being cooped up in the tiny office after the cramped space of the Austin. There was a rickety bench on the verandah so he sat there, smoking and watching the passing afternoon traffic.

His leads and suspects in both cases were rapidly disappearing – and he wasn't looking forward to his next phone call to Melbourne. He lit another cigarette and his thoughts turned to Rebecca. He enjoyed her humour and she was very easy on the eye. She was pretty tough, too, and Berlin liked that. She'd done okay photographing the Lee girl's body, and that was no picnic. Of course she was crazy, no doubt about it – going out to see those carpenters with only her notebook and a hatpin. But she had used the hatpin at just the right moment, you had to give her that. And there was something else that drew him to her. Perhaps it was that for all her brashness, he knew she was hurting, too.

The blocky, two-storey Terminus Hotel across the road was

decorated with four arches that shaded and framed the entry to the public bar. Whatever elegance this architectural flourish was supposed to produce was negated for Berlin when Sergeant Corrigan and Captain Bellamy appeared through one of the arches. Corrigan saw Berlin and nudged the captain. The two men crossed the road in his direction.

Traffic on High Street was light, which was lucky since they were not the most nimble pair Berlin had ever seen. At least Bellamy had an excuse, with his cane and wooden leg. Corrigan's difficulty was very obviously alcohol-induced.

'Taking the afternoon off then, Berlin?' The sergeant was swaying ever so slightly.

'Gathering my thoughts.'

'It's been a whole bloody week! I would have thought you'd be gathering up a few suspects by now. Melbourne and Wangaratta have both been on my back again and I've got better things to do than to take the flak for your incompetence. I'm off for a slash.'

The sergeant staggered into the station. Bellamy lowered himself onto the bench next to Berlin. His cheeks were slightly flushed.

'You two been celebrating something special?'

'Just a quick counter lunch after another successful morning at the saleyards.'

'And you needed a police escort for all the cash?'

'The sergeant likes to keep an eye on things and I don't mind the company. Any luck with the motorcycle gang?'

Berlin shook his head. 'My inquiries are ongoing.'

Roberts pulled up in the Dodge and Berlin stood up and walked towards the car. 'Nice chatting with you, Bellamy, but I've got some people to meet.'

'My offer still stands, Mr Berlin. My men are at your disposal, anything we can do to help.'

'I'll keep that in mind.' Berlin slid into the passenger seat and slammed the car door.

'Your timing's perfect, Roberts. Let's get out of here.'

'Are we going anywhere in particular, Mr Berlin?'

'Anywhere but here. Just drive.'

'Back to the Diggers Rest?'

'Why not.'

They stopped outside the hotel and Roberts switched the engine off. Berlin didn't make a move to get out of the car. He checked the car park for the grey Austin, but it wasn't there.

'Bellamy and Corrigan hold hands at the saleyards on a regular basis?'

Roberts seemed a little thrown by the abruptness of the question. There was a pause before he answered.

'I suppose so.' He made the statement warily.

Berlin looked across at the constable. 'Anything else going on here I need to know about?'

Once again, Roberts paused before answering.

'There've been some stories floating about for a while, Mr Berlin. I try not to get involved.'

'What kind of stories?' Berlin was happy to wait.

Roberts weighed up his options. The Melbourne detective seemed like a straight-up-and-down character but he had to be wary of crossing his sergeant – he knew what that could lead to. But if he ever made it down to Melbourne and Berlin was still a cop and had any kind of pull, having a friend would be a good thing.

'Cattle going missing from the stockyards after the sales and winding up out at Bellamy's place. One bloke who worked the yards reckoned the abattoirs couldn't have been doing a very good job because he saw Bellamy selling off the same cow half a dozen times in the last six months.'

That explained why Bellamy and the sergeant spent so much time with their heads together. And having the local police sergeant standing next to a town councillor at the sales would send a strong message. It could also explain why the sergeant's brother always had a fridge full of beef.

Berlin offered the boy a cigarette and lit them both.

Roberts took a deep drag. 'Thanks for that, Mr Berlin, I mean Charlie.'

'No problem, Bob, I owe you one.'

The boy looked across at Berlin. Berlin winked.

Inside the Diggers Rest Berlin inquired after the health of Lily's daughter and she smiled as she told him the baby was fine and dandy. She also mentioned Miss Green was off tracking down some background on her story about the painter, so he ate dinner alone. He was surprised to realise how much he missed Rebecca's company.

FORTY-SEVEN

Hogan, the Wodonga station's senior constable, poked his head in the office door just as Berlin took off his overcoat and hung it up. 'The doctor's here to see you.'

Berlin tossed his hat on the desk and reached for a cigarette. The clock on the wall said a quarter to eleven. 'Been waiting long?'

Hogan shook his head. 'No, but you don't want to go lighting any matches around him – the alcohol fumes are so strong the whole building might blow up. And young Bob's been looking for you as well.'

Doctor Morris was at reception, holding onto the front edge of the desk for support, his eyes bloodshot and twitching. Hogan was right about the fumes.

It had been dark in the alley where they found the Chinese girl and Berlin hadn't really had a good look at Morris. Close up in daylight he seemed very old and very tired. His hat needed brushing, there was a stain on his tie and his collar was dirty and frayed. He had a white moustache, yellowed from nicotine and badly in need of a trim, and his shoes were worn and showing bare leather at the toes. God help me if I ever get to that stage, Berlin thought.

'How can I help you, Doctor Morris?'

'The Chinese girl, have you arrested anybody? For the murder.'

Berlin shook his head. 'Not yet. Not a lot to go on, I'm afraid.'

'It's not right. This is a decent town.' The doctor had a bit of trouble getting his tongue around the sibilants.

'It's a small town too, Doctor Morris, and people see things and they talk. We'll get the killer eventually.'

'The Champions – what about them?'

'What about them?'

'Are they suspects?'

'Should they be?'

'Isn't it obvious?'

'Is it?'

'They hate the Asians because of what happened to the older boy. He was decapitated same as the girl.'

'But Jenny Lee was Chinese. It was the Japanese that killed him.'

'You think the Champions would know the difference?'

'I reckon they might, but thanks for the advice. And let me know next time you need any help doing *your* job, setting a broken arm or taking out someone's appendix.'

The doctor's breathing became shallow and his hands took a firmer grip on the desk. 'Suppose . . . suppose I told you the girl was raped?'

'Suppose you did. You told Constable Roberts the autopsy results wouldn't be ready till Monday.'

Berlin could see the doctor thinking this through.

'It's a preliminary result. I thought you should know.'

The doctor had to work hard on getting 'preliminary' out without tripping over his tongue. He stretched the word carefully, not quite slurring it, speaking with the studied concentration of the experienced drunk.

'Thanks for the information, I'll look into it.'

'And arrest the Champions?'

'Let me look into it, eh?'

'Perhaps I should speak with Sergeant Corrigan.'

Berlin shook his head. 'I don't think so. The sergeant assigned the case to me. I get to say who's arrested and for what.'

The doctor pulled himself close to the front of the desk. 'Well, then, fuck you.' He seemed rather pleased that he'd managed to get the words out. Reaching awkwardly into his right coat pocket he produced a leather key case.

Behind Morris, out in the street, Berlin could see a dark green Humber Snipe, the driver's door wide open, the back end of the vehicle jutting out onto the roadway. Even by Wodonga's casual parking practices it was a fairly ordinary attempt.

'That your car, the Snipe?'

The doctor was trying to focus his eyes on his keys. His grip on the desk was the only thing keeping him vertical. 'Yes. What of it?'

'Do you really think you should be driving? How about I get someone to run you back to your surgery?'

'I have patients to see, places to go.'

'Then you should try and keep your speed down and the carnage to a minimum.'

'After forty-five years behind the wheel I don't need some whipper snapper like you telling me how to drive.'

The doctor's eyes suddenly became unfocused. He began breathing heavily through his nose and Berlin moved around the desk in time to catch the older man and break his fall. Roberts walked in the front door of the station.

'Give me a hand, Bob. We need to get him outside and into some fresh air.'

The two men manoeuvered the doctor out through the door and lowered him onto the wooden bench on the verandah.

Roberts straightened his tunic. 'Not much of the old bugger, is there? I thought he'd weigh more.'

'I'd say he's on a mostly liquid diet. Let me catch my breath and then we'll take him home.'

They loaded the doctor into the back of the Snipe and Roberts drove them the two blocks to the surgery. Morris was snoring by the time they carried him into his office and they left him in the waiting room, propped up in a chair.

'The doc have anything against the Champion family you know of?' Berlin asked as the two men walked back towards the police station.

Roberts thought for a minute. 'Mrs Champion, Kenny's mum, had TB. She passed away in a sanatorium. Cec took it real hard and that's when his drinking started. He was going around saying the doctor should have treated her for it sooner and he reckoned he was responsible for her dying. That was just before the war. Maybe you should talk to the sergeant about it? He's been here longer than me.'

'No, we'll leave the sergeant out of it for now.' They were passing a café and Berlin glanced at his watch. 'Bit early for lunch but I've worked up an appetite. This joint any good?'

'They do a pretty good hamburger.'

Berlin ordered a pork and chutney sandwich with tea and sat down in a booth. Roberts ordered a burger with the lot and a chocolate milkshake. He slid into the other side of the booth and put his helmet on the seat beside him.

'Constable Hogan said you were looking for me earlier,' said Berlin.

'That's right. I picked up this poddy dodger and he told me something that might be useful.'

'What the hell is a poddy dodger?'

'You know, a cattle thief.'

Berlin tore the cellophane off a new pack of cigarettes and offered one to Roberts, who shook his head. 'We didn't handle a lot of cattle rustling in the city, Roberts, so you might have to spell it out.'

'This bloke sneaks around at night nicking poddy calves, the baby cows that haven't been branded yet.'

Berlin lit his cigarette and took a long drag. 'I figured out the bit about the calves being baby cows, but how can he help us?'

'Well, he was fixing a puncture on his truck this morning and I stopped to give him a hand. He seemed pretty nervous about something so I took a look in the back of his truck. A lot of calves and not a brand to be seen among 'em. I marched him straight down to the station and stuck him in the lock-up. He decided we might go a bit easier on him if he helped us.'

'Helped us? How?'

'Sunday night around nine he was cruising down past the local saddling paddock in his truck with the headlights off. And he thinks he might have seen the Lee girl arguing with someone.'

'Saddling paddock?'

Roberts grinned. 'Bit of bushland down by the river. You know, somewhere private, like a lovers lane.'

'He recognise who she was arguing with?'

'No, but he says it was a soldier. He couldn't make him out clearly since the moon was well down, but he said he saw a tunic and a slouch hat for sure.'

'Ever take your girlfriend down to this "saddling paddock" for a bit of privacy?'

Roberts looked decidedly uncomfortable. 'Maybe – once or twice.'

'I'm not interested in your love life, Roberts. I just need to know if you think he's telling the truth. Could he have seen anything from the roadway in the dark?'

'I reckon he was probably fair dinkum. He put his hand up to having half a dozen stolen calves in the back of his truck at the time, which is why he had his lights off. He was just as interested in not being seen as they were.'

Berlin sat and thought about it for a minute and then he looked up at Roberts. 'Keep my seat warm, I'll be back in a tick.'

The trade at Lee's grocery store had picked up a little. Berlin waited outside while two middle-aged women in plaid skirts, cardigans and sensible shoes commiserated with Mr Lee. Mr Lee's face betrayed no emotion, and as the women left the shop with their baskets over their arms Berlin overheard one say, 'It's the Chinese way, dear, they're very stoic. I saw it in that film *The Good Earth* before the war.'

Mr Lee looked up as Berlin walked into the shop. 'There is news on my daughter's killer?'

'Not yet, and I'm sorry to disturb you, but I have to ask you again about your daughter's friends.'

'As I told you, my daughter worked here before school, in the hotel kitchen after school and studied on the weekend. Her friends she saw only at school.'

'On the night before your daughter's death, a girl was seen with a soldier down by the river. Did Jenny know any soldiers?'

'My wife and I know Sergeant Whitmore, from Bandiana. We order special items for him from Melbourne, soya sauce, chilli, noodles. And sometimes he has a meal with us. He enjoys my wife's cooking.'

'And your daughter and the sergeant were friends?'

'Friends, yes. Nothing more. Sergeant Whitmore is an honourable man.'

'When did you see him last?'

'A couple of weeks ago, perhaps. My wife roasted a duck to honour his safe return.'

'He was away?'

'In Melbourne, for a number of weeks, on army business. He said he missed my wife's cooking very much. He even lost weight being away from it.'

'And there are no other soldiers you can think of?'

'One time Sergeant Whitmore brought the young one, Champion, but that was some months ago. He didn't like the food and we did not see him again after that evening.'

'Was your daughter home that evening, the one night he came?'

'Of course. My daughter is . . .' he paused, '*was* always home in the evening.'

A few minutes later, Berlin slid back into the booth, just as Roberts' hamburger arrived. The waitress put the plate in front of the constable, along with a bottle of White Crow tomato sauce and a knife and fork tightly wrapped in a paper serviette. Berlin's sandwich and tea were already waiting for him.

'That first night you dropped me off at the hotel, Roberts . . .'

Roberts lifted the top off his burger and splashed sauce onto the charred meat. 'Last Wednesday, you mean?'

'Sergeant Whitmore and Kenny were already there and you said it was a regular visit.'

'That's right, most weeknights for a while now.'

'But I've never seen any soldiers in the Diggers Rest.'

'Well, there's lots of pubs closer to Bandiana and Bonegilla, and anyway the enlisted men and the NCOs can drink cheaper in the canteens at the camps.'

Roberts took a bite out of the hamburger. Fat oozed out of the bun and dripped down onto his plate. He chewed and swallowed. He was about to take another bite when he saw the look on Berlin's face.

'Everything okay, Mr Berlin?'

'I need you to drive out to the Bandiana camp and bring Kenny

Champion back for questioning.'

'Why? You can't really think Kenny killed that girl, Mr Berlin? The girl was Chinese, not a bloody Jap.'

'Maybe he doesn't make the distinction. And last Wednesday night I think I interrupted a barney between Kenny and the Lee girl in the kitchen at the Diggers Rest. So just bring him in, and the provost's sword. Maybe that poddy dodger can identify him.'

Roberts shook his head. 'Sergeant Corrigan's already let him go.'

'When? Why?'

'Not long after I brought him in, Captain Bellamy rang through to say the bloke was his cook's cousin and that he'd be willing to vouch for him showing up in court.'

'That was big of Bellamy. And very accommodating of the sergeant. I still want Kenny brought in.'

'I can't see Kenny doing anything like this, Mr Berlin – not Kenny. He can get rambunctious out on the footy field but he's really a bit of a quiet one otherwise.'

'I'm not sure he did it either, but I know he's involved somehow.'

FORTY-EIGHT

The Wodonga lock-up was a solid-brick building behind the police station. Surrounded by a ten-foot stone wall, the place looked downright Dickensian. Roberts led Berlin into a small exercise yard through a heavy wooden door with an iron lock. The walls of the yard were topped with glittering shards of broken glass set into a ridge of concrete.

There were two more locked doors running off the yard and Roberts opened the one on his right. The cell was about twelve feet square with a high ceiling. Light from a small, barred window near the top of the rear wall was supplemented by the feeble glow of a 25-watt bulb. On one side of the room an iron-framed bed had been bolted to the floor with a thin mattress and a couple of folded grey army blankets thrown on top. In the other corner was a black dunny can with no cover and even though the cell was freezing, several blowflies buzzed noisily over the mess inside.

Kenny Champion was sitting on the edge of the bed looking glum.

'Bob here is pretty pissed off with you.'

Constable Roberts had a bruise on his chin and a fresh rip in the sleeve of his uniform tunic.

'He shouldn't have said what he said.'

'Look, Kenny. I told him to bring you in. It was just going to be for a bit of a chat about the Lee girl, but now you could be done for assaulting a police officer – that's if Constable Roberts wants to take it further.'

'He shouldn't have said I hurt the girl. They took my belt and boot laces. When can I get them back?'

'That's just procedure. Nobody wants you hanging yourself, mate.'

'Why not? What difference would it make?'

Berlin shrugged. 'Not a lot to me. Especially if you killed her.'

'I didn't kill her. I . . .' He stopped mid-sentence.

'But you knew her?'

'Everyone knew her. She worked behind the counter in the grocery store on Saturday mornings sometimes.'

'Did you ever meet her when she wasn't behind the counter? Maybe at the Diggers', out in the kitchen or over a bowl of boiled rice, perhaps?'

'Where's Sergeant Whitmore? Does he know I'm in here?'

'Look, Kenny, all you have to do is tell us where you were between three and five o'clock on Tuesday morning.'

The kid looked at Berlin and then down at the floor. 'I was . . . I was . . . somewhere . . .'

'C'mon, Kenny. Everyone is always somewhere. I'm just asking if you were somewhere with some*one*? Doing some*thing*? Something that maybe got out of hand and you don't want to talk about?'

Kenny shook his head slowly. 'I'm not saying anything.'

'Then it's your funeral, son.'

Roberts followed Berlin back across the yard to the police station.

The young constable appeared to be worried about something.

'Mr Berlin, Kenny plays full-forward on our footy team and we've got this big match against the Yarrawonga reserves on Saturday.'

'And?'

'Kenny's our star player and if he's locked up . . .'

'He knows something about the Lee girl and I'm not letting him out of here until I find out what it is.'

'Don't you think you were a bit tough on him in there?'

'That wasn't tough, Roberts, believe me.'

After Berlin had been captured they took him by train to Frankfurt, to Dulag Luft, the infamous reception centre for Allied aircrew taken prisoner in the Reich. He was photographed, his flying kit was replaced with a shabby khaki greatcoat, and then he was locked in solitary confinement. His first interrogation was a genteel affair with a Luftwaffe senior officer, who chatted amiably over cigarettes and tea and biscuits. A few days later he was dragged from his cell and dumped in a chair in front of an SS officer. A black leather overcoat was hanging on a hook by the door of the interrogation room. Berlin reckoned it belonged to the man in the black suit sitting quietly in one corner of the room, and he also reckoned the man was probably Gestapo.

There were no tea and biscuits this time. The two Germans smoked constantly, but never once offered him a cigarette. However, they did threaten to drag him out to a courtyard to face a waiting firing squad, or downstairs to soundproofed cellars, promising that within twenty-four hours he would be begging for them to shoot him, just to end the pain.

Halfway through the three-hour session, Berlin realised that although there was a lot of shouting and threats of imminent execution and clips around the ears, the interrogators were not actually seeking any military information – they were simply intent on terrorising him. But he played along and eventually gave up a fake squadron number, aircraft type and target, knowing none of it could be checked and verified. They sent him back to his cell and he was feeling pleased with himself until he realised that at some stage in the first part of the interrogation he had wet his pants.

FORTY-NINE

Berlin opened the screen door of the police station and walked through to his office. It was a cramped space for two men and even smaller for three, especially when one of them was holding a very big sword.

Sergeant Whitmore was in uniform with his pistol in the white holster on his webbing belt. The pistol didn't worry Berlin but the sword made him uncomfortable. Whitmore had it out of the scabbard, the long, gently curved blade sparkling in the late-afternoon sunlight that streamed through the window. Roberts' eyes were locked on the blade.

'I'm going to get this back, right? When you two have finished dicking around with young Kenny.'

'Afternoon, Pete,' Berlin said. 'You want to put that sword down?'

Whitmore shook his head slowly. 'Jesus, Charlie, what's the world coming to? A bloke goes for a bit of a lie-down and wakes up to find his favourite private hauled off in the back of a police car, souvenirs pinched from his bloody wall and a barracks block half-demolished.'

'You'll get the sword back soon as we get this sorted, Pete.'

Whitmore held the sword out in front of him and looked down the edge of the blade. 'Bloody beautiful, isn't it. It's called a *katana*. This particular one is supposed to be over five hundred years old, made by a master swordsmith named Kanemoto.'

Roberts was standing well back, close to the doorway. 'It looks bloody sharp.'

Whitmore swung the blade in a gentle downward arc. 'It is bloody sharp. The Japanese have a rating called Akasaka, which means supreme sharpness. The Yanks were supposed to have an infantry training film where a bloke cuts through a machine-gun barrel with one of these.'

Roberts sneered from the safety of the doorway. 'Bullshit. All the stuff the Japs make is absolute crap. The blade would just snap off.'

Whitmore shook his head. 'No way, sunshine. These swords are handmade by master craftsmen, one at a time. It takes months. They heat special steel in a small forge and hammer it down over and over. You finish up with hundreds of layers compressed into a strong, light, flexible and very dangerous weapon.'

'Can I have a look?'

Whitmore handed the sword to Berlin. It was heavier than he expected, but well balanced. There was no question it was beautifully made, right down to the intricate woven cords covering the handle. Berlin felt an uncomfortable sense of power as he held the weapon.

He looked straight at Whitmore. 'If you could take a bloke's head off with one of these, Pete, then I guess chopping the head off a little Chinese girl would be no problem.' He studied the blade closely. 'There are marks on here that could be dried blood.'

'I don't doubt it, Charlie. These things were made to be used and I'd bet on it having been in a blue or two. I'm pretty sure those nicks along the cutting edge didn't come from slicing up a cream sponge at a Sunday school picnic.'

Berlin took one last look at the sword and handed it back to Whitmore. The soldier slid it expertly back into the scabbard and then placed the weapon carefully on Berlin's desk.

'In the old days they used to test 'em by stacking up a pile of dead bodies at an execution ground and trying to chop right though the middle. A master sword tester with a good blade could go through about five people with a single swing.'

'Bloody barbarians,' Roberts said.

'Maybe so, Bob, but they were making blades like that a couple of hundred years before a white man ever set foot in this country. They had a complex civilisation, built massive wood and stone castles and beautiful temples, dressed in the finest silks, created sophisticated artwork and made gardens out of rocks and sand, with decorative ponds filled with giant goldfish.'

'And murdered and raped their way across half of Asia. Don't leave that bit out,' Berlin said.

'I'm not. I'm just telling you I wasn't expecting to find what I did when I got to Japan. And we paid them back, we paid them back in spades. Hiroshima after the A-bomb had to be seen to be believed. And Tokyo and the other big cities. Dropping incendiaries on cities full of wood and paper buildings certainly worked a treat.'

'Taught them a lesson, didn't it?'

'Too right, Bob,' Whitmore said, 'brought it home that when it comes to war you sure as hell don't want to be on the losing side.'

Berlin thought about the German towns he saw after the Red Army had been through them, but said nothing. 'I'll be hanging on to your sword for a bit. Roberts will write you a receipt.'

'I'm here for Kenny, actually.'

'I'll hang on to him, too. He won't talk and he doesn't have an alibi for the night of the murder – at least not one he feels like sharing.'

'He's probably too embarrassed to tell you. The kid was with me all night.'

'Doing what?'

'We were playing Snakes and Ladders.'

'All night?'

'It can be a very challenging game.'

'Anyone else see you?'

'It's not exactly a spectator sport.'

'Right.'

'Look, Charlie, we had night duty and I'm giving you my word the kid was with me at the time the girl died and we were nowhere near where it happened. Isn't that enough for you, copper to copper?'

'Not when we're talking about a murder.'

'Well then bugger you, DC Berlin. Can I see him at least?'

'Roberts can take you out, but he's not going to leave you blokes alone.'

The constable was looking at his wristwatch. 'Mr Berlin, is it okay if I take off after that? It's just that we've got a training session tonight for the game on Saturday and if we don't have Kenny at full-forward we'll need to pick someone out of the juniors.'

'There you go, Charlie, you're upsetting the natural order of things. Not good in a small town.'

'Escort the sergeant through, Roberts. When he's done, you can head off for the night. Take the car if you want, I'll walk back to the hotel when I'm done here.'

When the men had left Berlin put the kettle on, and while it boiled he sat in his chair, feet up on the desk, smoking a cigarette. He studied the sword leaning in the corner and tried to imagine Whitmore in Japan. Berlin had seen the newsreel footage of

Hiroshima and watched it dispassionately. The newsreels of blitzed German cities, places he had actually seen up close on the march back from Poland, on the other hand, had made him uncomfortable, more so on the occasions when people in the audience started to cheer and clap at the devastation.

FIFTY

On his way to the Diggers Rest, Berlin walked past a locked hardware store. The smell of dry feed still hanging in the air reminded him of the pollard and bran mash his grandfather had fed to the chickens they'd kept in the backyard. As he passed an alley next to the store he heard a familiar sound – the smack of leather on leather.

Berlin walked down the alley and saw light coming from the doorway of a shed. Inside, a battered punching bag was hanging from a ceiling beam and a compact little bloke was laying into it with enthusiasm. From his build and speed Berlin judged his age to be about thirty but when he turned around Berlin saw that he was a lot older.

'Sorry, mate, hardware store's closed till tomorrow morning.'

'I was just passing. Heard you working the bag and thought I'd look in.'

The man was wearing overalls and tennis shoes and Berlin could smell sweat mixed with the aroma of stock feed, kerosene and linseed oil.

There was a sagging army cot in a corner of the shed and

photographs torn from magazines were pasted on the wall above – pictures of fighters and girls in swimsuits. There were more fighters than girls.

'You box, then?'

Berlin shook his head. 'Just a bit, as a kid. Gave it away when I got older.'

The man walked over and tilted his head to study Berlin's face. 'Time was I could look at a nose like yours and tell you the name of the bloke who broke it and whether he used his left or right.'

'You fight pro?'

'For a little bit. Won some, lost more. Just a hobby for me now.'

'Keeps you fit, though.'

The man smiled. 'That it does, and out of the pub.'

'That too. See you later, then.'

As Berlin turned to leave a poster pasted inside the shed door caught his eye. The poster was crudely printed with the words BARCLAY'S TRAVELLING BOXING EXPOSITION and some names and a photograph: a black-and-white shot of eight men in shorts posing in front of a massive tent.

'What's this about, mate?'

'Tent boxing troupe. You know the drill, half a dozen bruisers with a couple of trucks and a big marquee.'

Tent boxing troupes were a bush tradition, travelling from town to town and getting local lads to line up for a chance to climb into the ring and show off to their mates and girlfriends. It was a change from going to the pictures or a concert and the locals were more than happy to pay to watch the town smart alec get his block knocked off.

'You know any of these blokes?' Berlin asked.

'Just by reputation. Most of the other troupes have a lot of Abos in them. Good fighters in the main. Barclay's claim to fame is having all-white boxers so you don't have to get your hands dirty knocking out a darkie.'

'Or having one knock you out.'

'That'd be part of it, too. Barclay also has a reputation for not being too particular about the moral character of his fighters. I reckon a couple of them are dangerous bastards.'

Berlin would be surprised if it was just a couple. It went with the territory – if a bloke was handy with his fists and needed to clear out of the city for a bit there were worse places to hide than a travelling boxing troupe.

Berlin looked at the poster more closely and saw it listed a number of towns in northern Victoria, including Wodonga.

'They been in Wodonga yet?'

'They're in town tomorrow night and Saturday. They'll be setting up down at the racecourse.'

'You going along for a bout?'

The man shook his head. 'I've had my fill of chewing on canvas. Might be more theatre than real boxing, but a lot of these tent-show blokes are hard buggers and they can throw a proper punch when they want to.'

'Fair enough. I'll leave you to it.'

Berlin continued along High Street in the direction of the Diggers Rest. He was thinking about the poster and the locations printed on the bottom – Yackandandah, Euroa, Benalla, Wangaratta and Barnawartha. Many of these towns were where the robberies had taken place. The printing of the photograph was so bad that he could barely make out the boxers' faces, but something else caught his eye – to the left, behind the outermost boxer and partly obscured by one side of the tent, Berlin was sure he could make out the shape of a couple of motorcycles.

FIFTY-ONE

Berlin did a quick pre-flight check of the heavy Remington he had lugged into his office. There was a new ribbon installed and the paper was lined up neatly in the carriage. One sheet of white foolscap bond, carbon paper, a second sheet of white, more carbon paper and then the thin onion skin paper for his third copy.

It was Friday and Melbourne wanted his weekly report. He could do that easily enough. He typed WEEKLY REPO at the top of the page. The R and the T arms stuck together. Bastard. Disentangling the arms took only a minute. He decided to check if there was paper dust clogging up the inside of the typewriter. He might need to go out and buy some oil. He wound the paper through the carriage of the typewriter, and the gears made a zipping sound.

He put in new paper and started again. Berlin was a surprisingly good typist, but there was a definite skill to writing the weekly summary and he didn't have it. He had often watched Chater labour over his at the next desk. Chater typed with intense concentration, his tongue poking out the left side of his mouth. Chater's most used key was X. He spent a lot of time crossing things out.

Hargraves' summaries, on the other hand, were things of

beauty, despite their lack of veracity. Time spent in the early opener became 'interviewing witnesses', shaking down SP bookies for the weekly sling was listed as 'gathering evidence' and the Wednesday afternoons spent in some dingy St Kilda boarding house with his tart of the month were 'meetings with informants'.

Berlin knew his summary would be neatly typed and have reasonably accurate spelling and punctuation. But what would it say?

Robberies by motorcycle gang in Northern Victoria. Investigation – ongoing, as are the robberies. Suspects – none.

Murder of Chinese girl Jenny Lee. Investigation – ongoing. Suspects – none.

Rebecca walked into the office around a quarter to ten.

'Your timing is perfect, Miss Green. Right now I need a journalist. Someone skilled with words and a master at making things up.'

'I'm your girl. Fancy a cup of tea down at Dempster's first? You'll be paying since I've got some stuff here that might interest you.'

When they walked in, Nan smiled from behind the counter.

'G'day, DC Berlin. Your usual? Just grab a seat and I'll bring it out directly. How's everything going, Rebecca?'

'Good, Nan. Tea for me as well and I think we'll have a couple of those finger buns today. It's Charlie's treat.'

The pink-iced finger buns were thickly spread with butter and the tea was piping hot. When they'd finished the buns and poured a second cup of tea, Rebecca took her notebook out of her satchel.

'I went right through the back issues of *The Border Mail* over the past six months and all the regional papers they had on file.'

'Anything interesting?'

'Yeah, Charlie, these country newspapers are riveting. I don't know how I was able to tear myself away.'

'Hey, you offered to do it.'

'Must have been a moment of weakness, post-coital delirium perhaps.'

Berlin shook his head slightly, narrowed his eyes and indicated the waitress behind the counter with a tilt of his head.

'Oh, come on, Charlie, she can't hear us.'

Berlin wondered if anyone at the pub had been able to hear them last night. Rebecca hadn't been in for dinner and he stayed away from the grog to see if he could do it. Looking at Doctor Morris that morning had got him to thinking that perhaps he was looking at himself in a few years' time. The thought of going to sleep sober was on his mind around ten, when Rebecca had knocked gently on his door.

The sex was different, gentler, and Rebecca noticed his eyes hadn't once wandered to that empty corner. It was the first time she felt she had him all to herself.

They'd talked about the boxing troupe afterwards and then he went to sleep and she smiled when he began to snore because it was better than the gasps and moans of the other nights.

She opened her notebook and put it down next to her cup of tea. 'Okay, this Barclay character and his band of merry pugilists have been crisscrossing the state, hitting all the hot spots north of Wangaratta.'

'Do the show dates and towns match up to the robberies?'

'Some do, some don't, but even the ones that don't are only an hour or so away.'

'I might have to have a look at this Barclay's troupe tonight.'

'Mind if I come along? Sounds like an opportunity for a story and some good photographs.'

'I'm not sure it's a suitable place for a young lady.'

'As opposed to a back lane with the body of a murdered sixteen-year-old girl?'

'Good point. We'll go out after dinner.'

Berlin paid at the counter and bought some cigarettes. Nan smiled as she handed him the change. 'See you at lunchtime, DC Berlin.'

They were almost out the door when she called after them. 'That post-coital delirium is pretty good stuff, isn't it, Miss Green?'

FIFTY-TWO

Rebecca parked the Austin next to a couple of dozen other cars on the racecourse boundary. Berlin could see the outlines of some trucks and caravans in the darkness off to one side, away from the big tent.

'I'm going to go take a look and see if I can spot any motorcycles.'

'Okay, I'll see you inside.' Rebecca pulled a camera from a bag in the Austin's boot and began putting flashbulbs into her jacket pocket.

'I'm not sure a camera is going to be welcome in there.'

'C'mon, Charlie. I'll have them eating out of my hand, just you watch.'

Berlin walked through the thick grass, towards the parked trucks and vans. As he got closer he could make out the run-down condition of the vehicles and smell petrol and burnt oil. There were no motorcycles visible, but when he lifted the corner of the canvas covering one of the trucks he found them. They looked like Harleys and there were half a dozen of them.

Berlin turned at the sound of shouting and whistling from inside the tent – the night's entertainment had obviously started.

He headed towards the tent. Just outside, someone had lit a fire in an empty 44-gallon drum and half a dozen men were standing around it drinking beer from brown bottles. The empties were tossed to the side, waiting to be collected by the local bottle-o or by school kids, raising pennies for lollies or firecrackers.

Flickering firelight lit up the sagging structure, with its frayed guy ropes and patched and faded canvas skin. Paint was flaking off a banner announcing the tent was the home of MUNGO BARCLAY'S TRAVELLING BOXING ACADEMY, featuring THE COMMONWEALTH'S ONLY ALL-WHITE BOXING TROUPE. There was also a crudely painted illustration of a bare-knuckled boxer in a crouching stance who bore a faint resemblance to the 1914 Australian heavyweight champion Harold Hardwick.

A woman was standing near the entrance, counting banknotes from a leather tramways change belt around her waist. She was wearing a too-tight blazer, a pleated skirt and gumboots. An inch or so of ash was hanging off a tailor-made cigarette clamped in one corner of her mouth and, as Berlin watched, it fell away, joining a sooty grey trail running down the front of her frayed blue cardigan.

She glanced up at Berlin, flicked the butt away and smiled, revealing an incomplete set of stained, uneven teeth set off by a grey front tooth. Her reddish hair, pinned up in a bun, hadn't seen shampoo or a comb for some time.

'Hullo, handsome. Haven't seen you around before.' The look told Berlin she was available, for a price. 'First bout's already started. That'll be five —'

'I'm police.'

The woman stopped mid-sentence and sized him up again, probably trying to work out if he wanted a cut of the door take. She swung her left hand wide, indicating the entrance, and smiled again. Berlin couldn't take his eyes off that grey front tooth.

'Always happy to welcome gentlemen of the law. We run a nice clean business here so enjoy yourself, compliments of Mr Barclay.'

The tent was square, about sixty feet along each side and thirty feet high. Four central poles arranged in a ten foot square formed the ring and held up the roof. Padding had been placed over the lower six feet of the poles and a battered piece of canvas covered the dirt between them. The tent was lit by rows of bare light bulbs strung between the poles, about halfway to the roof. Noisy spectators crowded the edge of the ring and Berlin put the crowd at around a hundred, mostly men and boys, though he could see a sprinkling of wives and girlfriends.

There was the smell of stale beer, sweat and liniment. Five muscular men wearing dressing gowns over shorts, gloves and boxing boots stood in line off to one side of the tent. A sixth fighter worked the centre of the ring, toying with a barefoot local stripped down to his trousers. The boy was about twenty, with a farmer's tan, and the tent boxer was letting him land a punch or two to keep the crowd happy.

The men went into a clinch and the tent boxer slipped in a quick kidney punch, not hard but obvious. Someone in the crowed booed and yelled, 'Foul, ref! You loose your bloody glasses or something?' This would be one of the troupe geeing up the crowd in support of the local fighter to help build the excitement.

Berlin worked his way to the front and leaned on one of the poles. The woman from the entrance approached a balding, middle-aged man wearing a lairy seersucker suit with a paisley waistcoat. She whispered something in his ear and indicated Berlin. The man looked over at Berlin and smiled. He was holding a hand bell and a stopwatch and Berlin picked him as Mungo Barclay.

The boxer in the centre was looking towards Barclay, who glanced down at his watch and nodded. A soft jab to the stomach followed by a slightly firmer one-two punch to the jaw set the local contender neatly down on his backside on the canvas just as Barclay rang his bell.

There was whistling and cheering from the crowd as one of the trainers helped the boy up and quickly stripped off his gloves. The boy walked back to his friends, grinning, and was welcomed with friendly jabs, laughter, handshakes and promises of celebratory beers. The tent boxer left the ring and joined the line of waiting fighters, someone tossing a threadbare robe across his shoulders.

Mungo Barclay was in the centre of the tent now, ringing his bell to quieten the crowd before speaking.

'Gentlemen, who will be next to represent the honour of Wodonga and take on these fine specimens of Australian manhood and exponents of the pugilistic art. Champions all, and white men. A clean fight, a bit of fun, perhaps some beer money if the gods are with you – and a great way to impress the ladies. Step up and don the gloves and show your mates what you're made of.'

There was jostling and laughter in the crowd. Men were pushed forward by friends and cheerfully fought their way back into the anonymity of the mob. Berlin studied the line of boxers. They seemed fit, though all bore scars and marks, either from the ring, the war or the wharves, or perhaps from the casual violence of street gangs.

The oldest and meanest-looking fighter was about thirty. His name was Mick Reardon and Berlin knew for a fact that three of Reardon's thirty years had been spent at Melbourne's Bluestone College, Pentridge Prison. Berlin had sent him there, and when their eyes met across the tent he could see Reardon remembered him as well.

Barclay rang the bell again. 'Let's have you, gentlemen, and just for tonight you've got the chance to make the sporting pages of the papers as there is a photographer present to record your triumphs, and a beautiful photographer she is indeed.'

He pointed at Rebecca, who raised her camera over her head to cheers from the crowd, as well as several ribald comments and wolf-whistles. She does have them eating out of her hand, Berlin said to himself.

A tall, heavy-set man stepped forward. Berlin took him for a stockman.

'I'm game, but only if she'll give us a kiss after.'

'You're on.' Rebecca's answer brought more cheers and Berlin was surprised to find he felt a flash of anger and jealousy. 'If you're still awake to enjoy it,' she added. There was more applause and whistling.

The man kicked off worn elastic-sided riding boots and stripped out of a faded shirt. An older man with cauliflower ears and scarring over both eyes quickly laced him into a pair of boxing gloves. Barclay leaned towards the contender. 'Tell us your name, mate, and what you do for a crust.'

'Name's Cameron McClain. I'm a drover. Best bloody drover in this neck of the woods.'

The bloke had tickets on himself, Berlin decided, and he could guess where this bout was going.

'Ladies and gentlemen, with the blood of the proud people of Scotland running in his veins, Cameron McClain, Wodonga's own, will choose his opponent.'

McClain walked slowly down the line of fighters. Berlin knew he was looking for someone smaller than he was, but not so small as to make the bout appear one-sided. Berlin had him picked as a loudmouth and a bully and he knew which of the fighters McClain would choose. The drover finally stopped opposite a nuggetty little boxer with the bandy legs of someone who had suffered rickets in childhood. The boxer's head only came up to the drover's nose. McClain tapped him on the shoulder and Berlin wondered if the smug bastard realised exactly how muscular that shoulder was.

As the men walked into the ring, Rebecca appeared beside Berlin.

'Looks like you have a fan or two here.'

'Not getting jealous, are we, Charlie?'

Berlin grunted.

'How'd you go with the motorcycles?'

'There's half a dozen Harleys out there in the back of a truck. I'll have to come back in the daylight to get a better look at them. How's the photography going?'

'I'm not sure I'm getting any good pictures, it all happens so fast. Is this a good place to stand, you reckon?'

'It'll be happening faster in a moment or two and you might want to keep back a safe distance.'

'What do you mean?'

'I mean that in about five minutes the blood of the proud people of Scotland that's running in Cameron McClain's veins is going to be splattered all over that canvas.'

FIFTY-THREE

The fight was short and bloody, as Berlin had predicted. McClain may have been able to sit on a stock horse like he was born there, control a mob of sheep or cattle, and hold his own in a pub brawl, but out on the canvas he was awkward and uncoordinated. His longer reach meant nothing against his nimble opponent and he stumbled and flailed about ineffectually as the smaller boxer kept his distance, closing in occasionally to release a flurry of punches and then pulling back.

Rebecca took three or four photographs and Berlin noted that her flashbulbs always went off too early or too late to capture the action.

The third and final round started with McClain sweating and wheezing. Berlin could see Rebecca was getting frustrated. 'This is useless. I want to get someone landing a punch, but I always seem to miss.'

'Only one bloke out there is landing any real punches, so that should improve your odds. But you don't want to be watching their hands. Just get yourself ready and shoot when I say.'

Rebecca pushed a fresh flashbulb into its socket. 'Well, what am I looking for, then?'

'Okay, take this little bloke for instance. He telegraphs his right by dropping his left shoulder a second before he lets go.'

The crowd was getting more raucous, with a lot of the cheering for the tent boxer. McClain had made a mistake in choosing the smaller man for his opponent and the crowd was turning on him for it.

The little fighter glanced across at the ref, who nodded. Barclay was clearly orchestrating the pacing and outcome of all the bouts, and carefully building the level of excitement in the crowd with the help of his stooges. Tent boxing was a great night out and always a lot of fun for everyone, except the hapless local currently in the centre of the ring.

'Get ready, Rebecca. Our Mr McClain is about to go bye-bye.'

She lifted her camera and framed the action as the smaller boxer closed in. Berlin saw the shoulder go down, waited half a beat and shouted, 'Now!'

The fist encased in the battered glove rocketed out like a striking brown snake, and just as it connected with McClain's chin the light from Rebecca's flash flooded the scene.

Berlin guessed the punch had been pulled a little, but there was still enough power behind it to snap the drover's head back. He staggered across the ring a couple of paces and a look of confusion crossed his face briefly before his eyes glazed over and he slumped forward, landing heavily on his hands and knees.

The crowd erupted in cheers and Barclay lifted the right arm of his fighter while a couple of trainers helped the groggy drover up and walked him out of the ring.

'Evening, ladies and gents.'

Berlin turned to see Whitmore standing behind them. He was dressed in civvies – trousers, a sports jacket and a tie.

'Off duty, Pete?'

'I've been over visiting the Lees.'

'That can't have been a lot of fun.'

'Bout what you'd expect. And I hear Cec Champion is out on another world-class bender, what with his boy locked up on suspicion of murder. All in all it's been a bastard of an evening, if you'll pardon my French, Miss Green. How's it going here, Charlie?'

'Bit of a bloodbath. They're a rough mob – one of the blokes I put into Pentridge for three years.'

'I can see a couple of ex-army boys up there too, going by the tattoos – and probably not an honourable discharge between them. Which one's your bloke?'

'Mean-looking bugger on the right. In the black trunks.'

Barclay was back in the centre of the ring, calling on the crowd for another volunteer to face one of his fighters.

'You know what, Charlie?' Whitmore said, loosening his tie. 'I was thinking of stopping by the Diggers for a medicinal gin and tonic, but I reckon this might be more fun!'

Whitmore handed Berlin his jacket, shirt and tie, and stepped onto the canvas to cheers from the spectators. Barclay ran through his spiel and when Whitmore didn't bother walking down the line of fighters, Berlin knew exactly who he would point to.

Reardon smiled, shrugged off his robe and walked into the ring. The old bloke approached Whitmore with the gloves but the MP shook his head and leaned down to talk to Barclay. Barclay glanced across at Berlin. Whitmore leaned over and spoke again.

The crowd had gone quiet and there was a murmur as Barclay held up both hands. 'Ladies and gentlemen, I have had a request that the next bout be a fight to the finish, untimed and . . .' he paused, 'bare-knuckle.'

'Jesus Christ,' Rebecca said, 'does Whitmore have a death wish? Isn't bare-knuckle illegal?'

Barclay beckoned Berlin to the centre of the ring. 'I know you're a copper, and I'm not looking for any trouble here.'

Berlin looked at Whitmore. 'You sure about this, with your crook guts and all?'

Whitmore grinned. 'She'll be right, Charlie.'

'Okay, if that's the way you want it.' Berlin turned back to Barclay. 'I'm off duty tonight. It's nothing to do with me.'

There was cheering from the spectators but this time it was wary, less enthusiastic. Berlin saw a couple of the men in the crowd sending their wives and younger sons out of the tent.

'One more thing,' Barclay continued. 'Can I request . . . the young lady and the camera?'

Berlin turned and walked back to where Rebecca was standing. 'Put your camera away. And maybe you should wait out in the car.'

'Fat chance, Charlie, this isn't something you see every day.' But she put her camera down.

Back in the ring the old trainer had quickly unlaced Reardon's gloves and pulled the tape from around his fists. While Whitmore kicked off his shoes and began limbering up, Reardon left the ring and walked over to Berlin. Up close he smelled of too many days without a wash and his face had more scars and marks than when the two men had last met. 'I seen you two talking before. This cove a friend of yours?'

'You could say that,' Berlin answered.

Reardon smiled a cold smile. 'Then this is gunna be a bloody pleasure, Berlin, you prick.'

FIFTY-FOUR

Barclay rang the bell to start the bout and then put it down next to one of the tent poles. This fight would last as long as it lasted, till one of the men was too bloodied or broken to get back to his feet. The crowd was surprisingly subdued and the trainers were unlacing the gloves of the waiting boxers. This fight would be the final bout for the evening and possibly the final bout for a long time for one or both of the participants.

Berlin figured Reardon wouldn't get a lot of fights in the tent because only the very brave or very stupid would be willing to go toe-to-toe with him. The man was dangerous, and a smart operator like Barclay would understand that it was in his interest to limit the damage to his reputation and to his customers' bodies by carefully hand-picking Reardon's opponents. Most of his matches would be against hard men who knew exactly what they were in for, or local thugs and bullies whom the townspeople would appreciate getting a good belting.

While tent boxing was primarily family entertainment, news of the occasional bloody, bone-crushing stoush would spread rapidly via the bush telegraph, adding a bit of gloss to the reputation of a troupe and meaning bigger crowds at the next town.

If Reardon had any training or talent for ring boxing it wasn't on show now. He circled Whitmore slowly, arms by his side, smiling, occasionally wetting his lips with his tongue. Whitmore kept his eyes locked on him as he slowly opened and closed his fists. Finally, Reardon seemed to have decided he had the measure of his opponent and brought his fists up, tucking his elbows into his side. He smiled once more and then let fly.

To Rebecca the fight was a blur – a flurry of fists and a series of grunts and gasps and the sharp smack of knuckles on bone or muscle. Berlin saw Whitmore block or deflect several early punches and land one of his own on Reardon's chin when he left himself open. Reardon stepped back, pausing momentarily to reassess Whitmore, and then charged in again, arms flailing. Whitmore wrapped his arms round the other man's torso in a clinch and Berlin heard him say, 'Shall we dance?'

'Dance with this, cunt,' Reardon grunted, and brought his fist down hard, delivering a blow to Whitmore's left kidney. Whitmore gasped in pain and staggered back, leaving himself open to a quick left-right punch to the lower abdomen. The crowd was on its feet, booing and shouting 'Foul!' and 'Below the belt!' Barclay opened his hands to them in a 'what can I do' gesture.

Both men were sweating now, and breathing hard. Reardon was at the edge of the canvas, bouncing on his toes, showing off. Whitmore was bent double, breathing in gasps, but he straightened up as Reardon closed in again. Whitmore blocked a second one-two combination and then pulled his opponent into another clinch. Reardon smiled and then stopped smiling when Whitmore gave him a classic Glasgow kiss, smashing his forehead hard into the other man's brow.

The crowd roared as Reardon staggered backwards, blood

streaming from a gash above his right eye. He straightened up, shaking his head from side to side. Blood and sweat flew off his forehead and Berlin heard a low animal growl in the man's throat before he hurled himself across the ring at Whitmore.

Any pretence that this was a boxing match was now gone. Whitmore wasn't a dirty fighter, but he gave back what he got. A rabbit punch or blow to the groin was answered in kind and the crowds' shouting had an increasingly nasty edge to it. Berlin saw the fighters from the boxing troupe were almost on the canvas with the two fighters, screaming abuse at Whitmore and encouragement to Reardon. He wished he'd been firmer about getting Rebecca to leave. 'This looks like it could get ugly.'

Rebecca was staring at the two men as they traded punches, wincing with every blow that landed. 'Uglier than this, Charlie? You have got to be kidding.'

The end came quickly, set up by Reardon, who was almost blinded by blood from the cut to his forehead. He tried to get his thumbs into Whitmore's eyes and Whitmore brought his arms up, breaking Reardon's grip and opening him up to a hard right to the midriff. The air was blasted out of Reardon on impact and Whitmore brought his knee up into the other man's chin as he doubled over from the punch. There was a crunching sound of broken bone and Reardon went down hard.

Berlin had the small Browning pistol out of his pocket and pointed at the fighters who were closing in on Whitmore. 'I'm back on duty now you bastards, so leave it alone. Sergeant Whitmore here is in my custody.'

The tent was eerily silent again as Berlin and Rebecca helped the soldier out to her car. They put him in the passenger seat and Berlin tilted the driver's seat forward to get into the rear. He slid across the seat to sit behind the soldier and hold him up.

The road out of the racecourse was badly rutted and Whitmore winced at every bump. Rebecca concentrated on making the ride as smooth as possible.

'You think he needs to go to the hospital, Charlie?' she asked.

Whitmore shook his head. 'I'll be right, don't you worry about me. There's a decent sick bay at the camp. Nothing's broken.'

'I think you might need an X-ray, mate, just to be on the safe side.'

They hit another bump and Rebecca gasped in unison with Whitmore.

'Sorry about that, Pete. And Charlie's right, you need to get properly checked out.'

'Okay, but only because it's you asking.'

They were on the main road now, and the ride was smoother.

'Can you take him to the hospital, Rebecca, and drop me at the police station on the way?'

'Of course, Charlie.'

'Thanks. I want to check up on Kenny and make some phone calls. I can walk back to the hotel.'

When Berlin arrived at the police station, it was empty and unlocked. After he watched the Austin drive off, he rummaged around and found the keys to the cells. Kenny was half-asleep, sitting on the bed, hunched up and wrapped in a blanket.

'You okay there, Kenny? They get you something for tea?'

The boy ignored him.

Back in his office Berlin picked up the phone. When he was finally connected to the Melbourne number, he recognised the voice of the nurse who answered. She couldn't place him until he gave his old ward and bed numbers, and then she remembered and asked how he was doing. She seemed surprised that he was back with the police so soon.

It took her ten minutes to find the doctor and while Berlin waited he could hear screaming in the background. The doctor offered to hunt down the file while Berlin held on but he said he'd call back in the morning. Ten minutes of the screaming was already more than he could take.

FIFTY-FIVE

The night air was crisp when Berlin set off on foot for the Diggers Rest. As he reached the edge of town the street lighting faded quickly behind him and the road ahead was dark with only a faint glimmer of the hotel in the distance.

Berlin counted the paces as he had on his monotonous circuits inside the warning wire of the POW camp, and through mile after mile of the slush and mud of Polish country roads. His head was down, his hands were deep in the pockets of his overcoat and he was wishing he had a scarf when he heard the sound of the motorcycle.

It was somewhere behind him, not far, but when he glanced back there was nothing. He rounded a bend in the road and the town's streetlights disappeared behind a low hill. There was just blackness and the sound of an engine almost idling, just a little blip of power now and again to keep it moving slowly, at walking pace, his pace.

Berlin considered making a break for the paddocks on his left but decided against it. A motorcycle would have no trouble keeping up and had the advantage of a headlight – an advantage that was suddenly apparent as two lights flared in front of him, almost blinding him. He put up a hand and squinted into the glare through his fingers, but it didn't help. What did help was the motorcycle behind him flicking on its headlight.

Behind each of the lights in front of him he could just make out the shape of a bike with a sidecar, a single rider on each machine. The little Browning automatic was in his overcoat pocket, but if these were the men he was after he knew they would have Tommy guns. Berlin waited silently, trapped in the triple beams like a lone bomber coned by searchlights. What else could he do? The bike that had been following him switched off its engine. The headlight, now powered by the bike's battery alone, dimmed slightly.

Berlin heard springs creak as someone dismounted and then the crunch of gravel under boots. A figure stood silhouetted between him and the light, and he could see overalls, a balaclava and brown leather motorcycle gauntlets. He moved his right hand towards his pocket and heard a rasping metallic sound from behind – the bolt of a submachine gun being cocked. He raised his hands, fingers outstretched.

'Okay. I'm not going to do anything stupid.'

'Glad to hear it.' It was the man standing in front of him speaking, but Berlin didn't recognise the voice.

He lowered his hands slowly to his sides. 'This meeting just a lucky accident, or is there something you boys want?'

'Lot of nasty rumours going round town.'

'That's right,' Berlin said. 'Lot of nasty business happening in town, which is probably why. I don't suppose you blokes are here to give yourselves up?'

'We'll admit to the robberies, but the Chinese girl, that was nothing to do with us.'

'In that case you're all under arrest for armed robbery.'

The silhouetted figure chuckled. 'You're a pretty funny bugger, aren't you? You should be in the movies.'

Berlin had slowly moved to the left, sizing up the other man and looking for an opening, a way to bring the man down. These blokes had used blanks before, but what were the odds that their weapons were loaded with blanks right now? There was only one way to find out.

The fight was short and brutal. Berlin's fist connected with the other man's jaw and he blocked the first return punch. He quickly realised the other bloke was more of a street fighter, and a lefty to boot, but Berlin was fast and powerful. He landed a couple more punches before a sharp jab to the solar plexus got through and he went down, winded, his hat coming off and rolling away into the darkness. He gasped for breath, wondering if the bastard had made him tear his new coat.

A hand in a gauntlet was offered. 'Nice try, pal. You almost had me worried for a moment there.'

Berlin took the hand with his left, and as he hauled himself to his feet he followed the momentum through with a right fist to the other man's groin. There was a sudden exhalation, a yelp of pain and a gasped, 'Fuck me sideways!' The man fell to his knees, shoulders bent, both hands jammed between his legs.

Berlin carefully checked his coat then glanced down at his opponent, now doubled over and breathing rapidly. 'You'll understand if I don't offer to help you up.'

Berlin was sweating from the brief exertion. His opponent staggered back to his feet and slowly limped over to his motorcycle. The man sat on the sidecar for a moment, bent over.

'Bit of a low blow, mate.' The words came out in a wheeze of pain.

Berlin was looking around for his hat. 'No bugger said anything about Marquis of Queensbury rules.'

He waited to see what would happen next, not expecting to hear laughter from the figure on the motorbike behind him.'

'I like your style, Berlin. Let's hit the friggin' road, gents.'

Berlin found his hat and picked it up. 'You blokes are still under arrest, you know.'

There was more laughter and the sound of engines kick-starting, and then they were gone in a swirling storm of dust and gravel.

Berlin put on his hat and checked his pockets. He still had the Browning, but a fat lot of good that would have done him against Tommy guns. When he had his breath back and his knees had stopped shaking, he started off for the Diggers Rest again.

FIFTY-SIX

The dining room was almost empty. Berlin ordered a whisky at the bar. He would have stayed there but Maisie wasn't her usual bubbly self so he took his drink and sat down at a table. A moment later Cec Champion slammed his empty beer glass on the table in front of Berlin. From the way Champion was swaying it was obvious it wasn't the first glass he'd emptied during the evening.

'You are a prize prick, Berlin.'

'So people tell me. You want another beer?'

Champion thought for a moment before answering. 'Okay, why not?'

Berlin caught Maisie's eye and pointed to Champion's empty glass. She nodded.

Champion slumped down in the chair opposite Berlin. 'You put my boy in jail. He didn't kill the girl.'

'Probably not,' Berlin said, but Champion didn't seem to hear him.

Maisie put a full glass of beer on the table and took away the empty. Champion stared at the glass. 'You want me to confess to it, don't you?'

Berlin shrugged. 'You can if you want to, why not? You've got an alibi, but it's one more thing off my plate if you do.'

The two men drank.

'What's it like being a fireman?'

Champion stared at him, confused. 'It's good, I suppose.'

'Hard work, shovelling all that coal?'

'Shovelling coal is the easy part, all that takes is muscle. The job's more than that.'

'Really?'

'Jesus, man, you're a copper. What would you know about it.'

'So tell me.'

'A bloody loco is just a hundred or so tons of black iron and pistons and driving wheels, and a firebox and a boiler full of cold water, until we come along. You light yourself a nice little fire and then feed it, make it bigger, tend to it, spread it until the coals are burning hot and even, because it's a problem if you get a spot in the firebox that's too hot or too cool. You need to keep the water level up proper or you can bust the boiler and a steam burn from a busted boiler will take the flesh off a bloke right down to the bone. I've seen it.'

He took another drink. 'And then a bugger needs to know the tracks, the bends and the inclines, to know what's coming so you can build extra steam for when it's needed by the engine driver. Then at night you bank her down and leave the coals just right so next morning you can bring her back to steam in double quick time. Being a fireman is not just shovelling bloody coal, believe me, not by a long chalk.'

Berlin nodded. 'Sounds like it.'

'And all our locomotives are bloody stuffed anyway. They got neglected for want of money back in the Depression and then with the war they got worked twice as bloody hard as they should have been and they made us burn lousy coal you wouldn't even put in your mother-in-law's fireplace. The only reason most of those locos can still pull a load is that buggers like me are coaxing one more ride out of 'em.'

'I was a pilot. I got us there and I got us back. But there was a flight engineer coaxing what was needed out of the engines the whole time. And they were shooting at him the same as they were shooting at me.'

Champion was looking at his beer glass. 'They didn't shoot my boy,' he said quietly, 'they cut off the poor little bugger's head. Why would they do that? Shooting I can understand, it was a war, but not that.' He looked up at Berlin defiantly. 'That's why I cut off the Lee girl's head.'

Berlin shook his head. 'No you didn't, Cec, and we both know it. You could never make another family go through what you have, so don't waste my time.'

'Kenny didn't do it neither so why don't you let him go?'

'Kenny knows something about the girl, Cec, and he's not doing himself a lot of good by keeping his mouth shut. I'm hanging on to him until he tells me what I want to know.'

Champion stood up. 'You're a cold, cold bastard, Berlin, you bloody know that?' He put his empty glass down and moved off unsteadily towards the doorway.

Fifteen minutes later, Rebecca joined Berlin at his table. 'They're keeping Whitmore overnight for observation.'

'Much damage?'

'He was coughing up a fair bit of blood but the doctor reckons nothing's broken. Has to be a miracle, considering that fight. He's a lucky bloke. Did you eat yet?'

'I was waiting for you.'

The kitchen was closed, but there was bread, cold ham, potato salad and beetroot set out under damp tea towels on the bar. Rebecca filled a couple of plates while Berlin ordered drinks.

He glanced up when the light fitting hanging above the barmaid's head began to swing gently.

Maisie saw Berlin staring at the ceiling. 'Probably just Vern prowling about upstairs. He's in one of his moods again. I don't envy Lily, being married to him.'

Berlin kept staring.

'I wouldn't be too worried, this old place might creak and sway a bit but Vern reckons she's got rock-solid foundations and good beams. I'm sure it's not going to fall down around our ears just yet.'

Berlin watched the light fitting slowly settle and he looked at the spot on the ceiling that Whitmore had said would be torn to bits by a burst from a Tommy gun.

He turned to Rebecca, who was standing next to him holding two plates heaped with food. 'You have a torch in your car, by any chance?'

'Of course. I'm a seasoned reporter, Charlie, and a former Girl Guide.'

'Then grab your coat. We're going back out to the football oval at Bandiana.'

'What about dinner?'

'Dinner can wait.'

FIFTY-SEVEN

In the dark, the sports ground seemed even more forlorn than on the wet afternoon of their earlier visit. Berlin had Rebecca park the Austin with its headlights shining directly on the storage shed. He took the torch and walked across to the hut that housed the changing rooms and showers and squatted down, shining the light under the building.

'See that?'

Rebecca squatted beside him. 'What am I looking at?'

'This hut is pretty much your standard army design. Easy enough for any half-decent team of carpenters to knock up quickly out of local materials. You whack in some stumps, lay your cross-bearers, joists and floorboards and then you put up the walls and stick on a tin roof. Solid enough, but there's usually a bit of give in the floor.'

They walked back to the larger maintenance shed that butted up against the cliff. Berlin shone the torch around the base of the structure.

'Now this one looks the same, but it's built on a concrete base. You commented on how solid the floor was the other day but I didn't realise what that meant.' He swung the torch beam up to a heavy power line strung overhead. 'And there's a hell of a lot of juice coming into this building just to run a pie warmer, an urn and a few 60-watt bulbs. So you've got all that power going in, those big double doors and the concrete ramp at the front.'

'Maybe they need to store other machinery here sometimes.'

'Take a look at how thick this concrete is. You could drive a bloody Sherman tank into that place.'

Inside the dark, unlocked shed there was a strong smell of exhaust fumes and the beam of Berlin's torch picked up a gleam on the concrete floor. Kneeling down, he dabbed a fingertip into a small, dark puddle and then rubbed his finger and thumb together. The slippery feel and a quick sniff told him it was motor oil.

Rebecca found a light switch and Berlin turned off the torch. He began inspecting the rear wall where the back of the shed met the rock face. The wall was bare apart from some girlie calendars and covers torn from *Man* magazine. He ran his fingers up a vertical section of the wall next to a wooden beam. After searching for a couple of minutes Berlin found what he was looking for – an indentation. 'Gotcha.'

Rebecca heard a click and then Berlin pulled back a vertical half-section of the wall, which was hinged on one side. It swung easily into the room. As did the other half. Behind the wall the concrete floor of the hut continued on into a black space. Berlin used the torch to search the darkness inside the entrance until he found a wooden-handled, heavy-duty electrical switch. Pulling down on the switch produced a slight arcing sound, and then lights snapped on.

The tunnel was carved out of solid rock and widened as it got further away from the entrance until it was about thirty feet across and ten feet high. Light bulbs in green metal army fittings hung from the roof at six-foot intervals. Large wooden crates were stacked as high as the ceiling along one wall. Stencilled lettering on some of the crates indicated they held ammunition and bully beef. Against the other wall there were drums of fuel and water and metal workbenches with tools. And three Harley-Davidson motorcycles with sidecars. Berlin put his hand on the engine of each of the motorcycles. They were still warm.

Several empty 44-gallon fuel drums with the tops cut off were lined up near a workbench. Berlin looked inside one and whistled.

Rebecca peered into the drum and whistled too. There was a jumble of coloured bank notes, the browns and greens and blues of ten-bob and one- and five- and ten-pound notes filling the container almost to the top.

'There must be thousands of quid in here, Charlie.'

'Could be tens of thousands, but if you're thinking no one is going to miss a fiver or two I'd get that idea out of your head quick smart.'

A pair of coveralls were hanging over the lip of another drum and when Berlin lifted them up a black woollen balaclava fell to the floor. He picked it up and tossed it back into the drum, along with the coveralls.

'Nice work, Charlie. Looks like you've found the Bandiana Boys' hideout.'

'Who?'

'The Bandiana Boys. That's the name I came up with for the gang. My editor liked it and we're going to be using it in the stories.'

'Makes them sound a bit too glamorous for my liking, but I suppose it sells papers.'

'That's the name of the game. How far back do you think this tunnel goes?'

Berlin was wondering that himself. 'Buggered if I know. Could be miles, but I'm not going to go exploring. They might show up and I've had enough of these blokes for one night.'

'What do you mean?'

'I'll tell you about it later. Right now we're going to close this place up like we were never here and head back into town. In the morning I'll organise some surveillance but we'll need more men and a lot more firepower if we're going to take this gang on.'

In the Austin, driving back to the hotel, Rebecca asked, 'What do you think the place was built for, Charlie?'

'What?' Berlin's mind was elsewhere.

'The hideout, what do you think it was built for?'

'My guess is that in the panic after Pearl Harbor someone decided a concealed workshop and storage area would be the go. It's far enough away from the main camp and innocuous-looking enough to be hardly worth wasting a bomb on. And then when the Nips didn't invade and the war moved up into the islands and away towards Japan they forgot about it.'

'C'mon, how could you forget about something like this?'

'Easy as pie. There was a war on, remember. I'll bet the engineers who built this did it secretly and then they would have been shipped out to where the fighting was and a lot would have been killed. Maybe some wound up billeted in Darwin or Perth or bloody Port Moresby. It's just one more thing they'd built along with all the bridges and wharves and warehouses, and then the war ends and all they want to do is get back to their old lives. Why would they care about a tunnel they once dug or a hut with a false back wall they knocked up at a football field out the back of woop woop?'

They ate dinner back at the hotel and Berlin told her about the run-in with the gang. After dinner they went up to her room, and when he undressed Rebecca gasped at the bruising on his stomach and arms. She wanted to ask Lily for Goanna Oil but he said he was fine and besides, he didn't want to smell like a goanna.

She laughed and they made love gently, Rebecca wary of hurting him. Afterwards she fell asleep on top of him. Berlin held her and listened to her breathing. He wondered if he could bear to love her and just how much he would hurt her before it was over.

FIFTY-EIGHT

The pub kitchen was empty when Berlin went downstairs. He used a tea towel to lift the lids on a couple of large black cast-iron pots on top of the slow-combustion range. One pot held porridge and the other a delicious-looking stew of lamb chops, potatoes and carrots.

Through the back door of the kitchen there was the sound of an axe splitting wood. He stepped over a scrawny kelpie sleeping on the porch and wandered out into the backyard. It was still quite crisp and it looked like the sky was having an each-way bet on rain before sunset. In a doorless outside washhouse he could see fire flickering under a steaming copper boiler. A hand-cranked wringer was mounted on the side of a concrete wash trough. Sheets and towels and children's socks and underwear were pegged on several rope clotheslines held up by forked wooden poles wedged into the muddy soil.

There were several fruit trees and a well-tended vegetable garden set along one side of the paling fence that surrounded the back yard. He could see pumpkins among the ground cover, and beans and peas spiralled up the chicken wire nailed to the fence posts.

More chicken wire surrounded a run where half a dozen chooks pecked busily away at the dirt. A rusty flat-bed Ford with frayed, deflated tyres and flaking duco stood in a corner of the yard. The truck looked like it hadn't run since well before the war.

A wicker pram was parked near an enormous pile of firewood. Lily, wearing an apron over her shapeless dress, was wielding an axe. She swung it awkwardly down onto a reddish lump of wood resting on a thick upright stump. The axe bounced off the wood, which shot sideways off the stump and landed at Berlin's feet. He picked up the gnarled lump and tossed it back on the pile.

'Those mallee roots burn well, but they're a real bugger to chop, aren't they?'

Lily nodded and put another root on the tree stump. 'My brother's got a soldier settler block in the Mallee, over near Sea Lake. He runs a ute load over to me every few weeks. I usually put them in the stove last thing to give me a good, slow overnight fire and coals for the morning.'

'What's your brother farming?'

'Wheat, he hopes, but right now, Mallee roots. They cleared the scrub but the roots still have to come out. Smash up your machinery if you try to work the soil first but they're the devil to move.'

Berlin took off his jacket and hung it over one of the clothesline posts. 'Let me have a go.'

'Vern wouldn't like me letting a guest do any work.'

Berlin held out his hand for the axe. 'We won't tell him then, eh?'

The axe had a black butt handle worn smooth by use. A slight pressure of his thumb on the edge of the blade told him it was sharp enough. A blunt axe is a dangerous thing, he remembered his granddad telling him.

Lily sat down on the laundry steps and pulled a box of Capstan cork tips from her apron pocket. She lit the cigarette with a match and sat smoking and rocking the pram with one hand, watching him.

'My brother usually chops a few day's worth before he leaves, and sometimes I'll pay one of the local high-school kids a couple of bob to do me a pile. Vern is no use at it, obviously, and my boys are still too young to do it – little blighters would take off an arm or a leg for sure.'

Berlin hefted the axe and felt the balance. 'I used to chop firewood for my grandad after school. Started chopping wood when I was six – the axe was taller than I was.' He stood with his feet apart and, as he swung the axe, he felt a pain in his ribs from the night before. He ignored it and brought the blade down. The axe head jammed in the heart of the root.

'How'd your mum feel about that?' Lily asked.

A second heavy swing with the axe head and root locked together jolted the stump and shattered the dense red wood.

'Mum and dad died when I was four and my brother six. Our grandparents raised us.'

'I'm sorry.'

Berlin grunted as another root split in two. 'Boating accident. Grandad was a policeman, they barely ever got a day off back then so me and my brother did as much as we could to help out.'

'Your brother a policeman too?'

'Apprentice carpenter. Died in the war. Missing at least – no chance he's coming back after all this time. Our gran died before the war started so she missed that part, which was good, I guess. Grandpa got run down by a car in the brownouts. Poor bugger should have been long retired, really.'

He picked up another lump of Mallee root. 'There isn't anything you might want me to have a word with Vern about, is there, Lily?'

Lily touched the bruise on her cheek, trying to cover it, and shook her head.

'Okay, if you're sure, but I don't mind.'

She shook her head again. 'No, I'm good, Mr Berlin.' She took a drag on her cigarette. 'Vern isn't such a bad bloke, you know. He was a different man before he lost his hand. He was going to be a big hero and come back to me with a medal and the poor feller didn't even get to finish training. He can go a bit off the rails from time to time but he's a good father to the kids, I guarantee you that.'

Berlin swung the axe again. He had a rhythm going now and he was starting to enjoy it. Swing, split, replace, swing, split.

'Sorry about breakfast the last few days. I didn't feel up to it, with the girl, you know. What can I get you this morning?'

'Don't worry about it. I'll grab something later in town.'

'Okay. If you're certain.'

The pile of split wood was growing at Berlin's feet. 'Stew looks good,' he said.

'That's for tea. We get the football crowd in after the game and they need something hearty.'

'Must be tough being shorthanded,' he said, 'without the girl to help, I mean.'

Lily glanced over towards the pub and lowered her voice.

'Jenny was a good kid. Young, but a hard worker. Pretty, too. But being young and pretty can get you into all sorts of trouble. I know that from experience, though you wouldn't think it to look at me now.'

Berlin let her comment pass. 'Did she have any special friends?'

Lily glanced towards the pub again. 'There was a young soldier fellow, that's all I know, from Bandiana. She thought she was in love.'

Berlin swung his axe down hard again. 'Kenny Champion is a young soldier fellow from out at Bandiana, isn't he?'

She looked away. 'They met when he went to her parents' place for dinner once. Kenny didn't kill that girl, Mr Berlin, he loved her. He's a good kid and God knows he needed a little bit of joy in his life.'

'But something went wrong?'

'I tried to warn her, tell her what precautions to take, but kids are kids, poor little bugger. She was devastated – said she had disgraced her parents and they'd disown her. She was desperate.'

'How would someone go about getting themselves out of that kind of situation in this town?' He swung the axe again, giving her time to make up her mind about answering.

'They'd talk to Doctor Morris. I gave her the twenty quid she was short out of my holiday money tin.'

'Kenny know she was planning that?'

'Kenny was happy, he thought they were going to run off together to Sydney and get hitched and have the baby. You know, Mr Berlin, I really don't know why you men think it's us woman who are hopeless romantics.'

Berlin split another root and Lily stood up and crushed her cigarette butt underfoot. 'That's plenty, you can stop now, thank you – that's more than enough for me to be going on with.'

Berlin swung the axe overhead one last time and buried it deep into the stump. Near the woodpile there was a small billycart made out of a fruit box, some two-by-fours and pram wheels, and Lily began tossing lumps of firewood into it.

'I'll make sure you get an extra big helping of stew later.'

'I'm really looking forward to that, Lily,' Berlin said, slipping his suit jacket back on. 'You going to add peas?'

'Of course. I'm about to pick them, once I get this wood inside. I might make dumplings too, and maybe a cream sponge for later.' She threw one more piece of wood into the billycart and glanced up at him.

'Rebecca . . . Miss Green is nice.'

Berlin nodded.

'You won't hurt her, will you, Mr Berlin? I don't think she's really as tough as she pretends to be.'

'I never set out to hurt anybody, Lily.' It just seems to be what happens, he said to himself.

'And you won't mention any of this to Vern, will you?'

Berlin smiled. 'About me chopping those Mallee roots, you mean?'

'Yes, about you chopping the Mallee roots.'

'No one else needs to know, Lily. It'll be our secret.'

FIFTY-NINE

Rebecca had still been asleep when Berlin went out to the yard. He took her a cup of tea from the kitchen after his talk with Lily but the bed was empty. When Berlin looked out the upstairs window her Austin was gone. There were a couple of art magazines out on the bedside table and he thumbed through one, stopping at a colour reproduction of a painting credited to Russell Drysdale.

The picture was all brownish tones, and it showed a young soldier sitting with his canvas kitbag, waiting somewhere – perhaps a wintry railway station – with ankles crossed and hands thrust deep into his khaki greatcoat pockets. Berlin had never taken much interest in art and was surprised when he felt a knotting in his stomach and a deep sense of recognition and empathy wash over him just from looking at the image.

Berlin thought about his brother when he looked at the soldier's face, framed between the brim of the slouch hat and his upturned coat collar. The face expressed loss, loneliness, a fear of the unknown, and just plain aching bone weariness, the eyes locked in a stare off into some other world – a stare that Berlin himself had seen at railway stations in Australia and Canada and

England, and on that bitter road leading westward out of Poland.

When he walked out the hotel's side door the Dodge was waiting. Roberts, leaning on the rear mudguard, was smoking and idly kicking at the gravel in the car park. He was dressed for football in baggy shorts, a long-sleeved maroon and white jumper, and long socks.

'Morning, Roberts. That's no way to treat a decent pair of boots.'

The lad rubbed the toe of his boot on his sock. 'Sorry, Mr Berlin. I just wanted to see if you needed me for anything. I usually get the morning off if I'm playing.'

'What time's your match start?'

'Under eighteens generally play at eleven and the reserves come on after that. But we're stuffed anyway. With Kenny in the lock-up we don't stand a chance against those bloody Pigeons.'

So that's why he was really here, Berlin thought to himself, to see what I'm going to do about Kenny. 'Pigeons?'

'The Yarrawonga Pigeons. Kenny might have had to play in the first-grade match anyway, since he's the best in the reserves. Spud's their full-forward and he came up with a groin strain.'

'At training on Thursday?'

'No, he was okay at training. I only heard about it this morning. We really need Kenny, Mr Berlin.'

'I'm sure you do. You get a big turnout for these games?'

'Depends who we're playing and what's on at the Saturday matinee at the flicks. Fair few regulars, plus some of the army blokes. Sergeant Whitmore usually does the timekeeping when we play at home.'

'I might see if I can get there.'

'I can still score you a jumper and a spare pair of boots if you want a run. We usually only just manage to field eighteen men so no one would complain. You're getting to be sort of a local anyway and . . .' Roberts trailed off.

'And I'm the reason you're down a full-forward?'

'I suppose.'

'Thanks for the offer but I've got more than enough aches and pains to deal with at the moment. What have you got planned for tonight?'

'I'm taking Alice to the Globe in Albury for drinks, and then dancing later at the Ritz ballroom.'

'Sorry, but you may have to put that off. You and I might be spending tonight keeping an eye on an empty shed.'

'We'll be doing a stakeout?' The young constable was grinning.

'Keeping it under surveillance, if the sergeant asks. And when you tell your girlfriend I'd try not to sound too excited about it.'

Berlin looked at his watch. It was a little after nine.

Roberts dropped his cigarette butt and leaned forward to press it into the ground with his toe. Something glinted where he disturbed the gravel. Bending down, he moved it aside with his finger. 'Two bob, eh? Looks like it's my lucky day after all.'

He straightened up and looked at Berlin, who was staring at the coin. 'Something wrong, Mr Berlin?'

'Change of plans, Roberts. That blacktracker who was at the loco sheds the other day, you know where we can find him?'

'Sure, he's got a woodcutting gang down near the river. It's not far, about five miles out of town. You want to go out there now?'

Berlin was already opening the passenger door of the Dodge.

Rain clouds were beginning to gather in the west when Roberts pulled the car over and pointed to a dirt track branching off the main road. 'About half a mile in, they reckon. Bit of a hike. I can probably run you down there easy enough.'

'I'll walk. You wait for me here.'

The track leading in to the woodcutter's camp was rutted from the wheels of the horse-drawn jinkers used to haul the timber to the mill. Berlin studied the track as it disappeared off into the forest. Gravel, what a bastard. Gravel would chip and cut at the soles of his shoes and if it was half a mile in and half a mile out then that was the same as a couple of months on paved streets.

It was cool under the canopy of trees but after fifteen minutes Berlin was sweating. On both sides of the track the undergrowth was lush, filled with flowering plants and ferns with rich green leaves, and he could hear the occasional small animal scattering in panic as he trudged past. There was the smell of wood smoke in the air and after another few minutes he found the camp.

Six men were sitting on logs around a small fire. A circle of stones bordered the fire and a blackened tin billycan rested amongst the flames. The men were smoking hand-rolled cigarettes and some of them were casually working the edges of their axes on whetstones. Several of the men looked up at Berlin's approach and then quickly lowered their gaze.

'I'm looking for Jacky.'

Someone grunted in amusement.

'We all Jacky here, Boss,' one of the men said quietly.

Another of the men stared at Berlin for a moment, spat on his whetstone and went back to sharpening his axe. Berlin casually put his hand into his overcoat pocket to confirm that the automatic was still there.

He had never really had much contact with Aboriginals before and he was intrigued by the facial structure and skin colour of the men. A couple were light-skinned, almost white, while the man who had spoken had skin with a rich blue-black hue under a coating of wood ash from the fire. The men's clothes were tattered and ripped, the shirts collarless and their waistcoats flecked with small tears, from the clutching branches of the trees they worked with. Two of the men wore battered, laceless old boots while the others were barefoot, with feet as calloused as their hands.

'Neville.' The voice came from somewhere behind him. Berlin

turned. The blacktracker from the loco sheds was approaching, doing up his fly buttons.

'Just draining the lizard.' He held out a hand. 'The name's Neville, Neville Morgan.'

Berlin shook his hand. 'Sorry, back in town the other morning, at the loco sheds, they called you Jacky.'

'Around here they call all us blackfellas Jacky. You must be a city boy.'

'My name's Berlin, but you can call me Charlie.'

'I'm sure I can, Mr Berlin, I'm sure I can. You're the Melbourne copper, right?'

'Right. And you're the blackfella tree feller.'

Neville laughed. 'Yep.'

Berlin took the pack of State Express from his overcoat and offered Neville a cigarette. The man shook his head.

'No, thanks.' He pulled a pack of Drum and some Tally-Ho papers from his waistcoat pocket. 'I'll just roll myself a durrie while we chat.'

'You don't talk like you did in town.'

Neville deftly worked the tobacco in his palm with his thumb before filling and rolling the cigarette paper. 'I had me a good education, mission school, but I found out smart little black boys sometimes make you white people uncomfortable.'

'Fair enough. I just got the feeling there was something you weren't saying back at the loco sheds.'

Neville licked and sealed the paper, tossing the pack of tobacco to one of the men sitting on the logs before pulling a burning twig from the fire. Berlin could smell the sweet odour of eucalyptus as he lit both their cigarettes.

'That Corrigan bloke couldn't find his arse with both hands. No point in telling him anything.'

'So what did you see?'

Neville looked at the ground and took a long drag on his cigarette before he spoke. 'Boots.'

'Boots?'

Neville nodded and glanced down towards his feet.

Berlin looked at the man's leather boots. They were neatly laced and still showed some evidence of polish.

'These are army boots, military surplus. I never even wore shoes till I was eighteen. Had feet like bloody leather. Have to wear boots all the time now. Totally stuffed my feet up in the Guinea, on the track.'

'Kokoda?'

Neville took another drag on his cigarette and nodded.

'Jesus, what were you doing up there?'

Neville laughed. 'I was in the army, a corporal. Fighting to save your white women from the rapacious clutches of the heathen Shintos. That surprise you?'

'I suppose it does.'

'Like I said, I never wore boots before the army, and now I have to wear 'em all the time. Boots ruined my feet, made 'em soft.'

'So tell me about the boots at the loco sheds.'

'They were army boots.'

'There's a lot of surplus military footwear floating about. And a lot of demobbed blokes still have the ones they wore in the service.'

Neville unlaced his right boot and pulled it off. He wasn't wearing any socks. Turning it over, he showed the sole to Berlin. 'See how that's worn down?'

Berlin shrugged. 'So you need to get them re-soled, so what?'

'You're looking but you're not seeing. Doing that got a lot of blokes killed in the jungle.'

'So tell me. What am I not seeing?'

'Look closer. My boots are worn down from walking dirt tracks and crossing riverbeds and clambering all over trees. That wears the leather a certain way, irregular like.' He slipped the boot back on and tied the laces. 'The boot tracks in that loco yard, at least the ones those dopey coppers hadn't trampled all over, were worn down differently.'

'Differently? How?'

Neville smiled, stood up and suddenly snapped to attention. 'Corporal Morgan reporting as ordered, sah!' he shouted, saluting smartly. 'Corporal Morgan, you black bastard, stand haaat ease.'

He stamped his left foot wide, clasped his hands behind his back and stuck out his chin, eyes front.

Berlin remembered his early air-force drills at the camp at Somers, and later at the training schools on Canada's Prince Edward Island and on the bleak, windswept prairies of Calgary. He'd hated the constant marching backwards and forwards and the saluting practice and the sergeants who screamed abuse at the cadets in their charge.

'Square-bashing on asphalt or concrete wears the leather differently, Mr Berlin. You can see it if you know what to look for. The blokes who did that robbery spend a lot of time marching up and down a parade ground, I reckon.'

'And what about that silver coin you picked up? It wasn't a two-bob piece, was it?'

The woodcutter took a final puff of his cigarette before pinching the end out between his thumb and forefinger. He leaned forward, scratched a shallow hole in the dirt, dropped the butt in and covered it. Reaching into his pocket, he pulled out a silver disk and handed it to Berlin. It was heavy, with a square hole cut out of the centre and Oriental symbols embossed around the edges on both sides.

'Some sort of Shinto coin,' Neville said, 'that's what the funny writing is. I dunno what it means. We used to find 'em in Jap camps and on bodies after – you know. Some blokes kept them for souvenirs. You can have it, if you think it means anything.'

Berlin slipped the coin into his coat pocket. Behind Neville one of the woodcutters was swinging the billycan around at arm's length to settle the tea leaves.

'Looks like tea's up, Mr Berlin. You fancy a cuppa? We've only got sugar, no milk.'

'Tea sounds good.'

The two men sat on a log and drank the tea in silence. Berlin could hear the soft burble of a stream somewhere, the sound of birds and the gentle creaking of timber in the treetops. The sweet tea in Berlin's enamel mug tasted of smoke and eucalyptus.

'How was coming home?'

Neville grunted. 'You fight alongside a bloke and he's your best fucking friend and then you get back and you can't have a beer with him, even though you've been wearing the same uniform and dodging the same bullets. You get chucked out of a pub and no one stands up for you, not one fucking bloke, not one fucking mate. One day it's "Good work, Corp, you held the yellow bastards, I'm putting you in for medal," and then all of a sudden it's over and they don't want to know you. You're back to being just another lazy shiftless darkie.'

'You ever regret enlisting?'

Neville looked Berlin in the eye. 'Course not. This was my country a long, long time before you white bastards got here.' He sipped his tea. 'What about you?'

'Me?'

The woodcutter nodded. 'Changes a fella, doesn't it? You come back and you don't fit in somehow.'

'That about sums it up.'

Neville looked down at the black skin on the back of his callused hand. 'Not that I ever really did.'

Berlin sipped his tea, watching the smoke from the fire wafting in the slight breeze and listening to the water gurgling in the creek. Somewhere a kookaburra laughed and Berlin smiled. His body still ached from the run-in with the gang and from chopping the firewood but right now it was an ache he could live with.

Neville tossed the last of his tea onto the hot stones surrounding the fire. The tea sizzled and formed a quick cloud of steam. He stood up and stretched. 'Time to get back to work, eh, Mr Berlin? No rest for the wicked.'

Berlin tossed his tea onto the hot stones. 'You got that bloody right.'

SIXTY

Kenny Champion looked up as Berlin entered the cell. His eyes were red and Berlin felt a pang of sympathy. Poor little bugger.

'How's it going, Kenny?'

The boy didn't answer, he just pulled the grey blanket tight around his shoulders.

'They give you some breakfast?'

'What do you care?'

'You'll probably need to eat something if you're going to play today.'

Berlin was holding the boy's slouch hat, and his belt and laces were in it.

'How can I play if I'm locked up? What's going on?'

'Just tell me the truth and you walk out of here right now.'

The boy looked at him with hard eyes. Berlin didn't feel like waiting the stare out.

'Okay, for starters, Kenny, I know you didn't hurt the girl.'

The boy stayed silent.

'Jesus, mate, you don't bloody make it easy, do you? Okay, here's what I know, and correct me if I'm wrong. You met the girl at dinner at the Lees with Sergeant Whitmore. Since then you two have been playing slap and tickle at the Diggers Rest, with Lily looking the other way.'

'It wasn't like that! Me and Jenny, we were in love, you bastard.'

Berlin realised he had forgotten what it was like to be eighteen and in love. God, how many centuries ago had that been? 'Sorry mate, bad choice of words. You two were in love and you got yourselves into a bit of bother.'

'We were going to run away to Sydney and get married. I had my mum's ring and I'd been saving up.' He had started to cry.

You poor little shit, Berlin thought. The girl was only sixteen yet she knew there was really only one way out.

'The bastard priest in Albury said he couldn't marry us. He made me confess we'd been, you know ... doing it, and he reckoned we were both sinners and were going to hell. And then someone killed her.'

'And I know it wasn't you, Kenny. Just tell me where you were the night of Jenny's ... the night Jenny died.'

Kenny wiped his eyes on his sleeve and sat up straight. 'I'm not saying and you can leave me locked up forever for all I care.'

'Kenny, I'm sorry about Jenny, really. And I'm going to get the person who did it.' Berlin tossed the boy's hat onto the cot. 'Here, get dressed and bugger off.'

The boy stared up at him. 'You mean it?'

'Just get moving before I change my mind.' Kenny stood up, dropped the blanket on the bed and reached for his hat.

'Don't know if you feel like playing today, but Bob's waiting outside and I reckon he and the rest of the team would appreciate it. Might help get your mind off things, too.'

Berlin sent them off in the Dodge and used the phone at the front desk to call the local exchange. The operator connected him to the Melbourne number he'd called the night before and the information he had asked for was waiting. He listened and made notes as the details were read out to him. It was a short call and thankfully there was no screaming in the background this time. Daylight had always helped to chase away the demons in that place, he remembered.

SIXTY-ONE

There was no sign of the doctor's Snipe at the surgery and no answer to Berlin's repeated knocking on the front door. A woman working in her garden across the street waved to get his attention.

'He's gone off to the football. He's the team doctor.'

'Been gone long?'

'An hour, I suppose.'

'Is there a bus that goes to the football oval?'

'I think you just missed it. You could try the ladies down at the railway station. They send pies and cakes over to sell at half-time – I'm sure someone will give you a lift.'

The reserves match third-quarter break was under way when Berlin arrived at the ground. There were thirty-six players on the field, plus the umpires and perhaps triple that number of spectators outside the fence. The team from Yarrawonga and some supporters and officials had travelled down crammed into the back of an old Bedford removalist's van. About a dozen cars were parked around the outer edges of the ground, including the grey Austin.

He spotted Rebecca leaning on the boundary fence, wearing a black beret and a long woollen coat over her trousers.

'I missed you this morning.' He thought he might feel embarrassed saying it but he didn't.

'That's very nice to hear, Charlie.'

The wail of a siren announced the start of the final quarter. Berlin saw that the siren came from a military police jeep parked on the other side of the oval and he could make out Sergeant Whitmore behind the wheel.

'You picked a winner yet?' he asked. The scoreboard showed the teams were about even.

Rebecca shook her head. 'But your Constable Roberts is very handy, as it happens, and it doesn't seem like Kenny has suffered from being locked up and accused of chopping off his girlfriend's head.'

'How'd you know about that?' Berlin asked. 'Kenny and the girl keeping company?'

'I've been asking around, Charlie, that's what reporters do. You know she was going to get an abortion?'

Berlin nodded. 'Shame she had to go to a butcher.'

'Can you prove it?'

'Not yet. I can't imagine that anyone in this town is going to come forward and point the finger.'

There was a sudden roar from the crowd and angry shouts aimed at the umpire from the Yarrawonga supporters.

'My, my,' said Rebecca, 'Kenny *is* getting a little bit physical out there today. I reckon we might have to call for the doctor before this is over.'

Berlin scanned the crowd. 'Have you seen him?'

'Parked under that gum tree. Looks like he's staying inside, out of the cold and close to his bottle.'

Berlin could see the doctor sitting behind the wheel of the Snipe.

Rebecca's prediction of on-field injury came true just before full time. Kenny ran up the back of a Yarrawonga winger while chasing a soaring punt kick from Roberts and came down hard on the arm of an opposing player. Berlin winced at the cracking sound that carried clearly across the oval. Champion ignored the player writhing on the ground and snapped a punt right between the centre goalposts to score six points and put Wodonga in front.

There was a pause while the winger was helped off the ground and over towards the Snipe. Berlin watched the doctor climb awkwardly out of the big saloon car. The examination he gave the player was perfunctory at best.

'Probably having a bit of trouble remembering if the knee bone's connected to the thigh bone or the elbow,' Rebecca said.

'I reckon it was probably Champion's knee bone connecting to the young bloke's wrist that did the damage.'

The doctor waved over a waiting ute, which drove across the grass and stopped near the Snipe. The injured player climbed into the passenger seat and a couple of his mates clambered into the back. As the ute drove out of the sports ground it bounced heavily over several deep ruts and they could almost hear the gasps of pain from inside the cab.

The players were back in action and the Pigeons were fired up and looking for revenge.

'You have any plans for after the game?' Rebecca asked. '*The Postman Always Rings Twice* is on at the Regent in Albury. According to the trailer Garfield and Turner are supposed to steam up the screen. Or there's dancing at the hall down by the water tower in town.'

'I'll be keeping an eye on that shed at Bandiana with Roberts.'

'You think they'll be on the road tonight?'

'Who knows, but if they are, I plan on being there. But right now I'm going to wander over and have a word with the doctor.'

Morris was leaning on the front mudguard of his car and Berlin could smell whisky from about ten feet away.

'Broken arm?'

'Probably. I sent him off to the hospital in Albury for an X-ray and a cast.'

'Young Kenny Champion seems to be in a bit of a mood out there.'

'I thought you had him locked up. Change your mind? Do you think it was his father?'

Berlin shook his head. 'Right now I know who didn't kill Jenny Lee, and I've got a fair idea who did. I'm just putting the pieces together and, as us coppers like to say, we're getting very close to making an arrest.'

But Berlin knew he was a long way from making an arrest because he had no real evidence yet. If Morris was the local abortionist it would only be with the full knowledge and acquiescence of the cops, and no woman would ever be willing to give evidence that he had performed an abortion on them or someone they knew. It was the same in the city, so why should it be any different here? Everyone just closed their eyes and turned their backs and pretended it never happened.

'No offence intended, Doc, but I'm planning on having the girl's body released from the mortuary and getting a second autopsy done over in Albury.'

'You don't trust my judgement?'

'I don't trust anybody's judgement but my own. That's what comes with being a copper.'

A siren blast from Whitmore's jeep announced full-time for the reserves match.

'I'll be in touch, Doctor Morris. Enjoy your afternoon.'

Morris climbed back into his car as the reserve players left the field to scattered applause. The spectators climbed back into their cars to wait for the first-grade game to begin. The wind was picking up a little and dark grey clouds were building in the east. Berlin pulled on his gloves, tightened his scarf and crossed the oval towards Whitmore's jeep.

SIXTY-TWO

Despite the cold, Whitmore had the canvas top of the jeep folded back and the hinged windscreen lying forward on the bonnet. He was in the driver's seat, wearing a heavy khaki greatcoat over his uniform with a knitted woollen beanie, also khaki, pulled down around his ears. The left side of the sergeant's face was bruised, his right eyebrow was swollen and there was a single stitch sewn into a blackened lower lip.

'I'd say that I'd like to see what the other bloke looked like, Pete, but I already did.'

'Hullo, Charlie. Hop in.' He indicated the passenger seat and Berlin climbed in. 'Had you picked as a sporting man from the beginning – the broken nose is always a giveaway.'

'First time was boxing and then it was football. I guess I'm a slow learner.'

'And then you became a cop so I'd say there's no guessing about it. You catch our young Kenny out on the paddock?'

'I saw some blokes going down and teeth flying so I figured that Kenny might be involved somewhere.'

'He had a pretty good game, all things considered. What do

you reckon, think he might have a chance of playing with the big boys?'

'He's got good form and he's not afraid to go in boots and all. If he can sort things out with his old man and stay away from bad influences he probably could have a shot with a Melbourne team.'

'You talking bad influences as in a woman?'

'I know he didn't kill the Lee girl, Pete, that's why he's out playing.'

'You know who did?'

'I think so.'

'Her parents would appreciate you getting that sorted. I told them you would.'

'How'd you get friendly with them?'

'I developed a taste for Asian food while I was up north, and in Japan. It's good tucker. I started to order a bit of stuff up from Chinatown in Melbourne through their shop and one day Mrs Lee got curious and invited me out the back for dinner. She almost fell off her chair when she saw I could use chopsticks and that I actually liked Chinese tea. You want some hot coffee, by the way?'

'Thanks, that'd be good.'

'Help yourself, there's a thermos and a couple of tin mugs in the back.'

Berlin twisted awkwardly and found the thermos and a mug. 'You having one?'

Whitmore shook his head.

Berlin pulled the cork from the thermos. 'Guts still crook?'

'Yep. Last night's entertainment didn't help a whole lot, either.'

'I'll bloody bet.' Berlin held the hot enamel mug with both hands to warm them and sipped the coffee. 'Why did you think that was a good idea?'

'Bit of a blue keeps the old blood pumping, Charlie. Lets a man know he's still alive. It's the ladies who do it for some blokes, but for me it's a little bit of biff, a little bit of knuckle action that gets the adrenalin flowing.'

'Do you reckon it might be the same for the Bandiana Boys?'

'Who?'

'That's what Rebecca's christened the gang doing those robberies.'

'It's very catchy, but why Bandiana? Why not Barnawartha, say?'

'We had a report of some blokes on bikes pulling a disappearing act near the Bandiana oval on Tuesday morning. And Bandiana seems to be central to what's been going on around here, geographically speaking. Take a good look at a map of all the robberies and you'll see they've all been within easy driving distance of Wodonga and never more than a three- or four-hour round trip.'

'That so?'

'And never over the river, never in New South Wales.'

'You don't cross bridges if you can help it, Charlie. Bridges are choke points. If someone's on the run the last thing they want to have to do is cross a bridge. Too easy to bail someone up. A couple of phone calls and you can quickly block all the crossing points.'

'They taught us that in Europe, too, in case we got shot down.'

The first-grade teams were on the ground now, the Wodonga Bulldogs in their brown and white jumpers and the visiting Pigeons in blue and white. They were bigger and more solid men than the reserves. Whitmore glanced at his watch, leaned down to the dash and flipped a switch, starting the siren mounted on the jeep's front mudguard wailing. As the sound faded, the umpire standing centre field blew his whistle and bounced the ball hard. The ruckmen went up after it and then the Wodonga rover had the ball and it was on.

Berlin watched the game with an eye sharpened by his

grandfather's observations and opinions. There was little skill in most of the play and it was rough and tumble from the start. When it began to drizzle halfway through the second quarter it became a muddy free-for-all, but no one seemed to mind. Whitmore put the roof up on the jeep but left the windscreen down and at half-time, after he hit the siren, he had a sudden coughing fit. Berlin saw blood in his handkerchief.

'You being a New South Welshman, Pete, I'm surprised you follow Australian Rules.'

Whitmore casually folded his handkerchief, hiding the red stain. 'I grew up with Rugby League but I don't mind this game. And Spud plays sometimes so you have to support your mates.'

'Spud's not out there today, is he?'

'Spud did something silly last night and got himself injured. Self-inflicted wound I'd classify it as, and by rights he should be on a charge.'

Whitmore had another coughing spasm and there was more blood on the handkerchief.

'That sounds nasty.'

'Just some wog that's going around.' Whitmore folded the handkerchief carefully and smiled. 'I'll shake it soon enough.'

'You want to start looking after yourself, Pete. Get some early nights, maybe. Stay inside, out of the night air. You know what they say, it's not the cough that will carry you off, it's the coffin they carry you off in.'

'You're a bit of a smart bugger, aren't you, Charlie?'

'That's what people keep telling me lately. Down in Melbourne they reckon I'm the bottom of the barrel, Pete.'

'Bugger 'em, Charlie, don't sell yourself short. The cream always rises, just give it time. That's in milk, of course. The police and the military are more like septic tanks I'm afraid – what rises to the top is another matter entirely.'

'Spoken like a career NCO.' Berlin raised his enamel mug in a toast.

'Backbone of the service, Charlie, your NCOs, your sergeants.' He paused for a moment. 'And your sergeant pilots ... and detective constables. Unconstrained by polite education and good breeding and manners we are free to pursue the task at hand.' He glanced at his watch and leaned forward towards the siren switch. 'And the task at hand right now is getting this game back under way.'

The two men sat silently for the second half of the match. It was beginning to get dark as the last quarter played out, but the rain held off. Yarrawonga took advantage of Spud Murphy's absence and brought the game right up to Wodonga, who were only four points ahead with just minutes to play. A fumble by one of the Bulldogs players gave the ball to the Pigeons, who began moving it quickly upfield, towards the goalposts and a shot at the six points they would need for victory.

'This is looking a bit grim, Charlie,' Whitmore said, and then he checked his watch and leaned forward and flicked the siren on. Out on the field a mystified umpire checked his own watch and then shrugged and called the game for Wodonga.

Whitmore grinned at Berlin and winked. 'No bugger said anything about Marquis of Queensbury rules, Charlie old son.'

'You're right there, Pete, no bugger did.'

SIXTY-THREE

Cold beer and hot pies were available after the game but it was getting dark and very chilly. There were unhappy mutterings about the timekeeping from a number of Pigeons players and supporters and the projected after-match party didn't look like it would happen. Berlin went looking for Roberts. He'd been hoping to get a ride with Rebecca but after the siren sounded the Austin was gone. There was no sign of the doctor or his dark green Humber Snipe, either.

Berlin spotted Rebecca's Austin parked outside the surgery, next to the Snipe, and told Roberts to pull over. He left Roberts in the car and walked to the surgery's front door. The brass plaque mounted beside the door was lit by an overhead electric lamp, with SURGERY etched in the red glass shade. Strange how red lights are the signs for whores and doctors, Berlin thought to himself. Then he heard the gunshot.

Roberts was already halfway out of the car when Berlin yelled, 'Get round the back and don't go doing anything stupid.'

The front door was unlocked and he let himself into a darkened corridor, holding the little Browning in his right hand. The place had the carbolic acid and chloroform smells he associated with doctors. And something else, something he associated with death. Berlin badly wanted not to take another step but he knew he had to.

Further down the corridor, light came out of an open door with a sign reading WAITING ROOM. Another door, half ajar, was marked DOCTOR in faded gold lettering. Berlin pushed the door open slowly with his foot, holding the pistol out in front of him. There was an examination bed in one corner, draped in white sheets with a movable, metal-framed screen beside it. A washbasin was fitted into another corner, near a glass-fronted cabinet full of surgical instruments. The only light in the room was coming from a brass banker's lamp on the desk. The smell of death was much stronger in this room and now his instinct was to turn and run as fast and as far away from it as he could.

The doctor's desk had a Morocco leather top protected by a sheet of glass. There was a pen and inkwell desk set in the middle and to one side a black telephone and pile of medical texts. A metal tray held a bottle of Scotch and a Bakelite ice bucket with the name WHITE HORSE WHISKY embossed in red under the symbol of a prancing horse. There were two cut-glass tumblers on the desk. The one in front of Rebecca was half-full and the one in front of the doctor was on its side, the whisky gathered in a small golden puddle.

Rebecca was sitting in a chair facing the desk, with her back to the door. She didn't move when Berlin came into the room. On the other side of the desk the upper part of the doctor's body was in shadow. He was leaning back in a chair with leather-padded armrests. The shotgun had stayed balanced between his legs, upright, with his left hand hanging limply, the index finger still inside the trigger guard. The smell of burnt gunpowder lingered in the air and Berlin's mind flashed to that morning on the Polish–German border when the Jewess had chosen her time to go and the SS officer with the missing finger and the pistol, for the first and possibly last time in his life, had done exactly what a Jew wanted of him.

Rebecca picked up the whisky glass. She was shaking and it took both hands to get it up to her mouth. 'He started drinking after his wife died, well drinking seriously anyway. His patients started drifting away and eventually there were only the post-mortems and abortions left. He helped the police out with one and they left him alone to do the other. Poor bugger said the only people he got to see in the end were the dead and the desperate.'

'He say what happened with the Lee girl?'

'He botched the abortion, pissed as a cricket, and she bled to death on the bed over there.'

Berlin could see where someone had almost scrubbed all the lacquer off the floorboards. Morris had probably used bleach to try to remove all the blood.

'He panicked afterwards and dumped the body in the alley.'

Berlin poured her more whisky. 'And he cut off her head, figuring the local cops would probably blame Kenny or his old man.'

'That's about the size of it, Charlie. Since he'd be doing the autopsy no one needed to know about the abortion. And with her being Chinese he figured the police around here wouldn't investigate too thoroughly.'

'Sounds like you two had quite a chat.'

'Not really, I just sat here and listened. He wanted to tell someone and I was the one who walked in the door.'

'What made you come here?'

'You needed proof that he was doing abortions. I was going to get it for you.'

'You think he was planning on doing this tonight?'

'He said you were on to him, Charlie, that it was only a matter of time.'

'That's true, but I'd have had trouble proving it.'

'There's a confession in an envelope under the glass on the desk. He had the shotgun ready next to his chair – Jesus that gun made a lot of noise, my ears are still ringing.' As she stood up she saw the flecks of blood and brain matter on her clothes. 'I think I might have to vomit now, Charlie.'

She said it quite calmly and Berlin led her gently to the basin in the corner. He held her hair clear as she bent over the basin and her hands grasped the brass taps tightly. While she groaned and her shoulders heaved he wondered if the smell of blood and vomit and gunpowder and death was going to follow him all his life.

SIXTY-FOUR

Lily looked up from her sewing when Berlin helped Rebecca into the hotel kitchen. Rebecca had Berlin's coat draped over her shoulders and she was shivering.

'Sit her down here.' Lily pulled a chair out from the table and put her arm around Rebecca's shoulder. 'You poor love, you look dreadful. Shall I put the kettle on then, or do you fancy a brandy?'

'Tea would be nice,' Rebecca said.

Lily gently took Berlin's coat from Rebecca's shoulders and tossed it over the back of a chair. She gasped as she saw the blood on Rebecca's blouse. 'What on earth happened?'

Berlin shook his head. 'I'll tell you about it later, Lil. Right now she needs to get out of those clothes.'

'I'll take good care of her. She'll be right, don't you worry. Nice cup of tea and then a long hot bath is what she needs.'

Berlin found Roberts at the bar in the dining room having a lemon squash. Corrigan was behind the bar and there was no sign of Maisie. The landlord put a glass in front of Berlin and poured a triple without asking.

'The boy here says Doc Morris blew his brains out in front of

Miss Green. That true?'

Berlin nodded.

'Jesus Christ.'

Berlin took a solid swallow of the whisky and when he put the glass down Corrigan topped it up. 'The Lee girl died during an abortion and Doctor Morris chopped her head off in a panic. He figured it would get the police looking elsewhere. He left a written confession on his desk and then shot himself.'

Berlin took another drink. Roberts looked pale. 'Poor Miss Green, witnessing something like that. Can't see how you'd ever get a thing like that out of your head.'

'Phone the station will you, Bob, and report it as a suicide. Might as well tell them not to bother contacting the coroner because I think he already knows.'

The constable was back in less than a minute. 'They need us back at the station right away, Mr Berlin. There's trouble.'

'I'll get my coat.'

In the kitchen Rebecca looked up from a steaming mug of tea. She had a blanket around her shoulders and there was some colour back in her cheeks.

'Tea must be helping, you look a lot better.' Berlin slipped on his overcoat. 'I have to pop down to the station for a while.'

'Did I hear Bob say there was trouble?'

'Most likely it's nothing. I shouldn't be long.'

'Is it the Bandiana Boys?'

'Maybe, I'm not sure.'

Her eyes searched the kitchen. 'Hang on a sec, Charlie, where's my satchel?'

'Don't fret, love,' said Lily. 'Bob put it over by the door there. Let me get it for you.'

Rebecca opened the satchel and rummaged inside. She pulled out a handkerchief with its corners tied together, handing it to Berlin.

'You might need these.'

Berlin unwrapped the handkerchief and smiled at her. 'Thanks.' He dropped the eight cartridges into his left pocket.

'Aren't you going to load your gun?'

Berlin took the pistol from his right pocket and pulled out the magazine. Rebecca could see the shiny brass of shell casings and the dull grey of the lead bullets. 'Oh,' she said.

He slid the magazine back into the butt of the pistol. 'I reloaded it with ammo from the station.'

'When did you notice?'

'Sunday night after church, down by the river, when I sobered up. The gun seemed a fair bit lighter.'

'I guess I should have realised that.'

He dropped the pistol back into his coat pocket. 'I guess so.' He put his hand on her head and gently stroked her hair. 'But it's the thought that counts.'

'Does it count, Charlie, really?'

He smiled and bent down and kissed her on the forehead.

'Yes, Rebecca,' he said, 'it really does.'

SIXTY-FIVE

Berlin was surprised to find the street in front of the police station filled with vehicles. There were Fords and Humbers, flat-bed farm trucks, and utes with kelpies and heelers in the back. There was even a horse-drawn nightsoil wagon, the double row of hinged doors along each side hiding the freshly tar-coated empty pans and the full pans with their noxious loads held firmly under clamped lids. Roberts nosed the Dodge into the kerb next to Bellamy's blue Chevrolet.

Twenty or so men were milling about outside, smoking and not talking in the way that country people do. Berlin recognised some of them from the militia's ill-fated manoeuvres by the bridge the previous Saturday. There was something different this time – each of the men was armed with a very new-looking Lee Enfield No. 4 service rifle.

Inside the police station Bellamy and the sergeant were looking at a map pinned to the wall. It showed Wodonga and its outskirts. The sergeant turned to Berlin. 'Just in time, DC Berlin. We've had a tip-off that the bastards are planning a raid tonight. I'm issuing side arms to police personnel.'

'You think we'll need them with Bellamy's night-cart commandos outside?'

'This is my station, Berlin, so it's my call and I reckon we need to have as much firepower as we can when we take on these blokes. And since Captain Bellamy has military experience I'm putting him in command.'

'I've got a better idea. This is my case, so I'm in charge.'

Bellamy stared at the sergeant, who took a step forward. 'Didn't you hear what I just said, Berlin?'

The sergeant's belly was getting uncomfortably close. 'Tell you what, boys, why don't we vote on it? Hands up all those in favour of me being in charge. And your vote doesn't count if you're currently involved in a criminal conspiracy to steal cattle and defraud the local saleyards.'

Berlin raised his right hand. Bellamy and the sergeant exchanged glances. The sergeant's red face had turned white.

Berlin waited for a minute before he spoke. 'No one else? Then I think that makes it unanimous. Now tell me about this informant, Bellamy.'

'There was an anonymous phone call to my home about an hour ago. The message was that the Bandiana Boys would be on the roads tonight and to wait at the police station for the exact location where we could intercept them.'

'And that's what they called the gang, the Bandiana Boys?'

'Cook took the message. That's what she wrote down. Fortuitously we were having another drill this evening so we were able to get here double time.'

'And you think those bolt-action Lee Enfields out the front will be a match for submachine guns firing .45-calibre ammo?'

'They won't be having it all their own way, DC Berlin. I was actually demonstrating this to the men when the call came through.' Bellamy picked up a heavy brown oilcloth bundle from the desktop, unrolled it and took out a submachine gun.

'Jesus Christ, Bellamy, where the hell did you get a Sten gun? And is that bloody thing even legal?'

Bellamy picked up a metal magazine from the oilcloth and clipped it into the side of the weapon. 'These bastards aren't the only ones with some firepower now.'

'Listen, Bellamy, don't cock it or bump it. And keep the muzzle pointed down. Those bloody things go off if you look at them sideways.'

The Sten submachine gun was crude and cheap to make, but the low tolerances used in manufacturing and assembly meant it could be as dangerous to the user as to the intended target.

Bellamy had just removed the magazine and put the weapon back on the desk when there was noise outside. First a murmur of voices, then shouting and dogs barking, then the throaty roar of a motorcycle revving high and braking hard.

'What the fuck . . . ?' The sergeant was drowned out by the hammering of heavy automatic gunfire. Bellamy and the sergeant made a dive for the floor. Berlin sprinted for the doorway, with Roberts close behind.

Outside the police station Bellamy's militia, like their commanding officer, were flat on the ground. Berlin saw an olive drab motorcycle with a single rider and an empty sidecar race away from the police station. Two more motorcycle–sidecar combinations were waiting up the road, under a streetlight. Only four men, Berlin noted. It looked like the boys were down one player tonight. The two waiting motorcycles turned and sped off while the third stopped. The balaclava-clad rider turned back towards the station, gunning the engine as if taunting them.

Berlin looked around. Men were scrambling to their feet, some pulling at the bolts of .303s, others fumbling, trying to remember where their safety catches were.

'Anyone hurt?'

The men were patting themselves down, looking for signs of injuries.

'Smells like some bugger shit themselves,' someone said. Several of the men laughed nervously.

'It's the bloody honey wagon,' another voice yelled.

The nightsoil truck looked like it had taken the full magazine from the Tommy gun. A number of the hinged wooden doors hiding the pans were splintered and broken and thick brown stinking sludge was oozing down the side of the vehicle.

'Roberts, let's go!'

The constable joined Berlin, who was sprinting towards the Dodge. As Roberts put the staff car through a three-point turn, Berlin took the Browning from his pocket. The constable was crashing gears and grunting as he pulled on the heavy steering wheel. He finally straightened the car and as he did, the waiting motorcyclist gunned his engine and headed off into the darkness.

SIXTY-SIX

The vehicles carrying the police sergeant and Bellamy's men caught up with the Dodge just out of town. They were tailgating and honking and the glare of their headlights lit up the interior of Robert's car, making it difficult to see. When they rounded the bend and saw what was ahead there was only one option.

'Jesus Christ, Roberts. Brake!'

Roberts jammed his foot to the floor and the car slowed, skidded and then the rear wheels spun as he accelerated into the skid, showering the following cars with gravel from the verge. Berlin had his hands out against the dash as the vehicle shuddered and finally stopped. Behind them was the noise of skidding, a car horn and shouting and then the crunch of metal on metal and the sound of breaking glass.

The motorcycle was parked across the white line, side-on to the pursuing convoy. In the distance Berlin could see the tail-lights of the rest of the gang as they made their escape. The man on the parked motorcycle changed the magazine on his Tommy gun. He pulled the cocking slide back on the weapon and fired a long burst into the air. Roberts and Berlin ducked just below the level of the dash and peered out through the windscreen.

'Where's my rifle?' someone yelled from the cars behind them. There was the sound of car doors opening and movement and then the man on the motorcycle pushed the Tommy gun muzzle-first into the sidecar and leaned in after it. When he straightened up he was holding something in his hand. He tossed the object towards the police convoy and it left a thin trail of smoke in its wake.

'Grenade!' Berlin grabbed Roberts by the neck and pushed him under the dash as he yelled out the warning. A bright flash lit up the interior of the car and there was a deafening bang. As the ringing in Berlin's ears faded, he heard the high-pitched revs of the motorcycle tearing away.

Then Bellamy was at Berlin's passenger window.

'Anyone hurt out there, Bellamy?'

'It was only a thunder-flash, a training simulator. Just a very big bang and a lot of bright light.'

'Bought him some time, though. C'mon, get after him, Roberts, for God's sake.'

The Dodge's engine caught on the third try and then they were back in pursuit. Berlin looked through the rear window and he could see a police car with a crumpled mudguard just behind them.

As they came up on the football ground a few moments later, Berlin saw that the lights were on in the equipment shed and muddy motorcycle tracks ran up the ramp and in through the wide-open double doors.

'That way! Go right, through the gate.'

Roberts turned the steering wheel hard and they bounced through the low drainage ditch and past the gateposts with the other vehicles following.

'What's going on, Mr Berlin? Why did they lead us here?'

'Buggered if I know but this place is their hideout. There's a tunnel into the cliff at the back of the hut. Pull up about fifty feet out, and keep your headlights on the doorway.'

Roberts did as he was told. The lights from the Dodge threw a giant shadow of the hut up onto the cliff face.

Berlin was already outside, crouching behind the heavy door of the Dodge with the Browning in his hand. 'Out through my door, and keep your head down.'

Roberts wriggled out and flopped on the wet ground beside him. 'You think this might be an ambush?'

'I'm not sure what it is but I reckon we'll find out before too long.'

Berlin was waving to the other vehicles in the convoy as they arrived, trying to direct them to form a cordon, but it was impossible. Bellamy and his men were excited by the thought of revenge and the cars and utes stopped in a jumble, with several of the occupants climbing out and standing in full view of the hut.

'Get the fuck under cover!' Berlin shouted. 'They've got Tommy guns, you idiots.'

The fat police sergeant, wheezing and holding a double-barrelled shotgun, stared at Berlin, who was frantically waving him in the direction of one of the cars. He glanced at the hut, at Berlin, at the car, at Berlin again and finally got the message. He stumbled towards a militia utility, tripped on a tree root and fell between two cars, the shotgun flying out of his hands and landing in the dirt.

It took almost five minutes before everyone was in position. Bellamy moved confidently among his men, pulling some behind proper shelter, pushing others into positions where they could cover the sides of the building and reminding a couple where their rifle safety catches were. Berlin didn't care much for the man's politics, but right now he was acting like a soldier and that was exactly what they needed.

When he was satisfied, Bellamy, keeping low, hobbled between the cars until he was beside Berlin. Sitting on the rear bumper of the Dodge with his wooden leg stretched out, he unwrapped the oilskin parcel.

'Do you have a plan, DC Berlin?'

'You're the soldier, Captain Bellamy. Do you have any suggestions?'

Bellamy pushed a magazine into the Sten. 'As far as weapons go they have the upper hand. In an enclosed space like that hut submachine guns have the advantage over bolt-action rifles. We could wait them out, I suppose.'

'I don't think so. There's a tunnel into the cliff face behind the building. They've been using it as a hideout and it's stocked with ammo and food and water.'

'We could send some men across to the camp and try to borrow a tank or an armoured car. Or a bazooka.'

'I'm guessing the paperwork on that would take about six months.'

'Hey, Charlie, you feel like coming in for a bit of a chat?' The voice came through the open doors of the hut.

Roberts glanced over at Berlin. 'That sounds like . . .'

Berlin nodded.

'That might be possible,' he yelled, 'but how do I know you won't shoot me?'

There was laughter from inside the building. 'I don't think it's me you have to worry about, sport. I'd make sure your mug posse there all have their fingers well away from their triggers before you get between them and this hut. Just a suggestion.'

Berlin stood up. 'I'm going inside. No one does any shooting until I give the order. Is that understood?'

There was some grumbling from the group and then Bellamy spoke.

'Safety catches on and muzzles in the air until DC Berlin is safely inside, that's an order!'

'You sure this is sensible, Mr Berlin?' Roberts asked quietly.
'Wouldn't be the first silly thing I've done in my life, Bob.'
'Maybe not. But you wouldn't want it to be the last.'

SIXTY-SEVEN

'Not thinking of doing anything heroic with that peashooter you've got in your pocket, are you, sport?'

Berlin raised his hands and shook his head.

Whitmore was sitting on the wooden table, legs dangling, the Tommy gun cradled loosely in his arms. Behind him the hidden doors to the tunnel were wide open and Berlin could see a single parked motorcycle.

'Handy little hideout you have here. How'd you find it?'

'Army engineer bloke up in the islands, bit of a demolitions expert. Came along on a patrol to help us blow up this concealed Japanese bunker complex we'd captured. Said the Jap place was a total joke and went on about how he and his company had built a series of secret command posts up and down the east coast back home. They did it in case there was an invasion and we were forced to make a fighting withdrawal south. He said there was one outside Wodonga and when I got posted here I went looking.'

'Bit better than those forts you built up round Bathurst as a kid, I'll bet.'

'Too right, Charlie. But then of course when a bloke's got the perfect hideout he really needs someone to be hiding out from. It just started as a bit of a lark one night when we were bored. I have to tell you, sitting around on your arse drinking tea or rounding up drunks and stopping mechanics nicking off with screwdrivers and drums of lubricating oil – or even pinching the odd Bailey Bridge – isn't all that exciting. We planned it so no one would get hurt.'

'That's why you had blanks in the Tommy gun, right?'

'That was a nice catch on your part, Charlie. I'm not sure how all the other coppers missed it.'

'That was also a nice move on your part, Pete, drawing us off like that so that your boys could get away.'

'It's how we did it up north if things got hot – split up and some lucky bugger tries to lead the enemy in the wrong direction.'

'Didn't really matter, I'd already found your hideout and the money. I was about to organise a little welcome-home party out here tonight when you showed up at the police station.'

'I figured you were on to us, Charlie. What tipped you?'

'You did, but it took me a while to realise it. You asked if Rebecca gave me the photograph of the gang at the loco sheds, remember? The only people who knew she'd taken it were her and me and the robbers.'

'I should learn to keep my trap shut.'

'We'll get the rest of them, you know.'

Whitmore shook his head. 'I don't think so. The bikes and guns and the rest of the clobber are all at the bottom of a billabong somewhere by now. You'll never find 'em. The station at Rutherglen was our last raid. And now it's over.'

'Final instalment in your own little pension plan?'

'C'mon, mate, it was never about the money. The dough's in a petrol drum back there and all accounted for. Fun sorta went out of it somehow after Spud clocked that paymaster. Don't know what happened there and, like I said, no one was supposed to get hurt. He's on the mend, they tell me.'

'That's what I hear. Cheered up a bit by your donation to his holiday fund. Oh, and I think you went looking for this in the wrong spot.' Berlin reached into his pocket. His fingers closed round the empty Benzedrine inhaler he had almost forgotten about and then found the disk. He took it slowly from his pocket and tossed it across to the soldier. 'I got it this morning, blacktracker bloke found it outside the loco sheds pay office. You must have lost it in the scuffle with the paymaster.'

Whitmore rubbed the disk slowly between his thumb and fingers. 'It was a gift from Hiroko. She found it in the ruins of her house. It's my good luck charm. Thanks.'

'I'll need to hold onto it, as evidence.'

'What do you need evidence for? I told you, the Bandiana Boys are gone for good.'

'It's not that easy, Pete.'

'It's as easy or as hard as a bloke wants to make it.' He tossed the disk back to Berlin. 'And you don't have a lot of evidence, just a Japanese coin and the word of some blackfella.'

'I've got you.'

Whitmore smiled. 'Not for long, sport. Can't say there would have been a lot of value in me pinching money for a pension plan, in any case.'

'Because of the cancer?'

'You don't miss much, do you, Charlie? How'd you know?'

'When a bloke acts like he's got nothing to lose you have to figure sometimes maybe he doesn't. Mr Lee said you were in Melbourne recently so I spoke to someone I know at the repat hospital and they dug out your file. Your treatment dates were the same as the Bandiana Boys' little holiday.'

'Funny that.'

'They figure out where it came from? The radiation from the A-bomb, maybe? They say that can cause cancer.'

'Might have been that – who knows? There were some pretty crook people in Hiroshima when I was there, with a lot of Yank military doctors photographing and prodding and poking them. Some were dying quick and some slow.' He paused. 'It was the kids that were hardest to take.'

'The repat doc said six months to a year.'

'Yeah, he told me that six months back so you'd need to make it a pretty quick trial, eh?'

'I'm sorry.'

'What have you got to be sorry about, Charlie? Life's a gamble, I learned that pretty early, on that railway track in Queensland.'

'You could make things more comfortable for yourself if you gave evidence about the others.'

'Do you really think that would make me comfortable, old son?'

'I guess not.'

'Anyway, Charlie, I don't know who they were. We were all wearing masks, remember. Just a bunch of complete strangers looking for a bit of excitement in a bloody boring world.'

'War's over, Pete, for now this bloody boring world is all we've got.'

'You telling me you don't miss the thrills, living life right on the edge?'

Berlin shook his head. 'Not one cracker.'

'Takes all kinds, I suppose.'

'What about the kid? Kenny. What's his story?'

'Commandos and the independents take care of their own, and the families. When we found out about his brother we started looking out for him.'

'Keeping him out of trouble, you mean? By taking him out on armed robberies?'

'Didn't happen. Kenny doesn't know anything. Right now you'd find he's home with his old man if you were to check.'

'That's a pretty good alibi, Pete, and I might choose to buy that story, but I'm not sure I could sell it.'

'Kenny's a good kid, Charlie, he doesn't need any more grief. Lost his brother in horrendous circumstances, his dad goes a bit doolally and who can blame him, and then the silly little bugger goes and falls for a girl the old bloke is never going to accept.'

'That was the reason for your regular visits to the Diggers Rest, right? So he and Jenny could get together without their parents catching on?'

'They were just a couple of kids in love. Who was it going to hurt?'

'Well, at least Kenny's in the clear for the murder. Doctor Morris botched an abortion on the girl and tried to cover it up by implicating the Champions – he wrote a confession before topping himself.'

'Jenny was up the duff? Kenny never mentioned that. He's a quiet one. Keeps things bottled up inside, and that's not good for a bloke.'

'He figured they could run off to Sydney together and get married.'

'Jesus. Kids, eh?'

'Everything okay in there, DC Berlin?' It was Bellamy, shouting from behind the Dodge.

'Might be time to make a move, Pete.'

'Seems like it, Charlie. Maybe you should go in front – I have a feeling those bozos might be a little trigger-happy.'

'Fine with me.' He put out his hand and Whitmore gave him the Tommy gun.

'It's only loaded with blanks now, you know.'

'Just the same . . .'

Whitmore was right about the bloody thing being heavy. The wooden pistol grips on the weapon were worn smooth and the hundred-round ammo drum was scratched and dented.

Berlin walked out onto the verandah. 'Hold your fire! We're coming out.' Whitmore's boots scraped on the concrete behind him.

'The kid had nothing to do with anything, you'll tell them that, right, Charlie? It was all down to me. Me and my anonymous friends.'

'Like I said, I'm not sure how much I can sell them on that score.'

'Do your best, eh? We went to a lot of trouble to make sure nobody got hurt, remember, and maybe it'll help that it's a dying man's confession. See you round, Charlie.'

Whitmore's shoulder slammed hard into Berlin's back, and as his body spun from the impact he felt the Tommy gun being jerked out of his hand. He was flying backwards, falling, rolling and he heard the bolt go back on the Tommy gun. Face-down in the dirt, he yelled, 'Don't shoot, you bastards, he's firing blanks!' Then he heard the Tommy gun open up behind him, and from in front blasts of rifle fire and the stutter of Bellamy's Sten gun.

There was the *zip, zip, zip* of bullets passing overhead and the sound of splintering wood and the dull smack of lead striking flesh. Berlin rolled over just in time to see Whitmore punched backwards into the hut, the door and the windows disintegrating into shards and splinters around him.

SIXTY-EIGHT

Berlin found the Tommy gun on the floor just inside the hut. A heavy blood trail led away from the weapon and into the cavernous space behind the false wall. He took out his Browning and followed the trail into the tunnel.

Whitmore was slumped against the rock about thirty feet in. He was sitting upright, legs outstretched, with a heavy Colt automatic pistol cradled in his arms. He had been hit at least five or six times, from what Berlin could see, and he was losing a lot of blood.

Whitmore smiled weakly. 'I'd say the bastards couldn't hit the broad side of a barn, except it looks like that's exactly where most of their bullets went.'

'You wanna drop the gun, Pete?' Berlin asked.

Whitmore shook his head slowly. 'I don't think so.'

'It's over.'

Whitmore smiled and coughed. 'It's never over till you say it's over, Charlie. You should know that.'

Berlin's pistol was by his side and he raised it when the other man's hand twitched. One of the bullets had hit Whitmore in the right elbow and he grimaced in pain as he attempted to lift his weapon. He was trying to raise the muzzle up towards his chest.

'Couldn't give an old digger a bit of a hand, could you?'

Berlin shook his head. 'I don't think so.'

Whitmore grunted in pain. 'C'mon, mate. You said it, now I'm saying it. It's over.'

'Not this way.'

'What other way is there? And don't tell me you never thought about it.'

Whitmore coughed again, a thin trickle of blood leaking from the corner of his mouth.

I chose my time. Remember me, Berlin said to himself.

He dropped his pistol into his pocket and walked forward. The floor around the soldier was slippery with blood.

'You wanna be careful with that nice overcoat there, Charlie.' Whitmore's voice was a croak, and he grimaced with pain as he spoke.

Kneeling beside him, Berlin gently took Whitmore's gun hand and raised the pistol up till the muzzle was under the soldier's chin.

'Thanks, mate,' the sergeant said through gritted teeth.

'You sure about this, Pete?'

Whitmore nodded. His eyes were beginning to glaze over and as his finger fluttered on the trigger he gasped in pain.

'Bugger,' he said softly.

Berlin could see small spurts of blood pulsing from the shattered right elbow. Whitmore looked into Berlin's eyes and smiled.

Berlin slipped his finger inside the trigger guard, on top of Whitmore's.

I am your witness.

Berlin had never fired a big gun like the Colt. He was surprised at how much effort it took to pull the trigger.

ACKNOWLEDGEMENTS

Though my characters and the Diggers Rest Hotel are fictional, Wodonga, Albury and Bandiana are of course real locations and any success I have had in recreating them in time is due in large part to the assistance I received from Uta Wiltshire and Jean Whitla OAM at the Wodonga Historical Society and Major Graeme Docksey OAM, Pat Shanahan and Bob Matejcic at the Army Museum Bandiana (a fantastic museum which is well worth a visit). I am most grateful for the time and access they gave me. Any mistakes, historical or geographical, are all my own work.

Thanks also to Ben Ball, Miriam Cannell and Julia Carlomagno at Penguin, and to John Canty for his cover design. Very, very special thanks to my always supportive and encouraging agent Selwa Anthony for her tireless work, and to the wonderful Estelle Adamek for her insight.

Many thanks and much love go to Wilma Schinella, who combines steely resolve with a sharp eye for detail, untiring energy and enthusiasm, a compassionate understanding of the fragility and strengths of people – both real and imaginary – and a wicked sense of humour.

ALSO IN THE CHARLIE BERLIN SERIES

BLACKWATTLE CREEK

'A flawless novel that offers everything one could
wish for in crime fiction.'
Ned Kelly Award judges' comments

When a recently widowed friend asks a favour, ex-bomber pilot and former POW Detective Charlie Berlin is dropped into something much bigger than he bargained for. What starts with body parts disappearing from funeral parlours leads to Blackwattle Creek, once an asylum for the criminally insane and now home to even darker evils. If Berlin thought government machinations during World War II were devious, those of the Cold War leave them for dead.

'A well-written, compelling crime novel that delves into some
very dark places . . . A very impressive novel, and Berlin,
a complex, intriguing character.'
Canberra Times

'Intelligent, historically well informed and moves
at a cracking pace. A great read on many levels.'
Good Reading

'With his intricate plotting, his sharp eye for detail, skilful
characterisation and brilliantly believable dialogue, there
is not much this marvellous writer can't do.'
Sunday Tasmanian

read more
my penguin e-newsletter

Subscribe to receive *read more*, your monthly e-newsletter from Penguin Australia. As a *read more* subscriber you'll receive sneak peeks of new books, be kept up to date with what's hot, have the opportunity to meet your favourite authors, download reading guides for your book club, receive special offers, be in the running to win exclusive subscriber-only prizes, plus much more.

Visit penguin.com.au/readmore to subscribe